'Men!' sh   **patiently. 'You're all the same.'**

'Now, there you're almost certainly mistaken,' he lazily informed her, making no attempt to disguise his wolfishly thorough appraisal of her well-displayed charms. 'We're all different, but we *think* alike when presented with nigh irresistible temptation such as you pose any red-blooded male by going about dressed like *that*. At the moment I'm too busy fantasising about the feel of your magnificent body writhing under me as you desperately beg me to take you to paradise to waste much of my energy on rational thought, my darling.'

'I'm not your darling, and I'm prepared to bet you don't know the first thing about what would truly transport a woman to paradise,' Louisa snapped back.

'Aren't you willing to add me to your stable of lucrative lovers, then, my darling doxy?' he suddenly asked, as if he had every right to insult her.

'Firstly, I'm very particular whom I allow to even call me darling, Captain .... and secondly, even .... 'dn't take a man like ....

AUTHOR NOTE

Welcome to A MOST UNLADYLIKE ADVENTURE. While you might recognise one or two of the characters here from my other books, this one is a self-contained adventure and I've had a ball while telling Louisa Alstone's story. Louisa is passionate, unconventional and loyal, and survived a childhood that would drive most well-bred females of her time to despair. Then there's her flawed, embittered and utterly irresistible hero…

As soon as dark and brooding Captain Hugh stepped onto the page in a previous book, REBELLIOUS RAKE, INNOCENT GOVERNESS, I knew there had to be an intriguing adventure behind his wooing and winning of the Earl of Carnwood's little sister, and, now I've been lucky enough to have the chance to tell it. I hope you enjoy reading A MOST UNLADYLIKE ADVENTURE as much as I have loved writing it.

Somehow I had to revisit the Alstones one last time to tell Louisa and her piratical Captain's story, and the action of this novel takes place several years before my other Alstone books—A LESS THAN PERFECT LADY, REBELLIOUS RAKE, INNOCENT GOVERNESS and ONE LAST SEASON—begin. This book should have been at the start of it all, but I'm a less than perfect author who got beguiled along the way, so I really hope you enjoy Hugh and Louisa's love story and forgive me for leaving them until last!

A MOST UNLADYLIKE ADVENTURE

Elizabeth Beacon

MILLS & BOON

All Rights Reserved including the right of reproduction in whole or
in part in any form. This edition is published by arrangement with
Harlequin Enterprises II BV/S.à.r.l. The text of this publication or
any part thereof may not be reproduced or transmitted in any form
or by any means, electronic or mechanical, including photocopying,
recording, storage in an information retrieval system, or otherwise,
without the written permission of the publisher.

This book is sold subject to the condition that it shall not, by way of
trade or otherwise, be lent, resold, hired out or otherwise circulated
without the prior consent of the publisher in any form of binding or
cover other than that in which it is published and without a similar
condition including this condition being imposed on the subsequent
purchaser.

® and TM are trademarks owned and used by the trademark owner
and/or its licensee. Trademarks marked with ® are registered with the
United Kingdom Patent Office and/or the Office for Harmonisation in
the Internal Market and in other countries.

First published in Great Britain 2012
by Mills & Boon, an imprint of Harlequin (UK) Limited.
Harlequin (UK) Limited, Eton House, 18-24 Paradise Road,
Richmond, Surrey TW9 1SR

© Elizabeth Beacon 2012

ISBN: 978 0 263 89230 7

Harlequin (UK) policy is to use papers that are natural, renewable
and recyclable products and made from wood grown in sustainable
forests. The logging and manufacturing process conform to the
legal environmental regulations of the country of origin.

Printed and bound in Spain
by Blackprint CPI, Barcelona

Elizabeth Beacon lives in the beautiful English West Country, and is finally putting her insatiable curiosity about the past to good use. Over the years Elizabeth has worked in her family's horticultural business, became a mature student, qualified as an English teacher, worked as a secretary and briefly tried to be a civil servant. She is now happily ensconced behind her computer, when not trying to exhaust her bouncy rescue dog with as many walks as the inexhaustible Lurcher can finagle. Elizabeth can't bring herself to call researching the wonderfully diverse, scandalous Regency period and creating charismatic heroes and feisty heroines *work*, and she is waiting for someone to find out how much fun she is having and tell her to stop it.

Previous novels by the same author:

AN INNOCENT COURTESAN
HOUSEMAID HEIRESS
A LESS THAN PERFECT LADY
THE RAKE OF HOLLOWHURST CASTLE
REBELLIOUS RAKE, INNOCENT GOVERNESS
CAPTAIN LANGTHORNE'S PROPOSAL

I would like to dedicate this book to
Margaret J, Amanda G, Katie, Melanie and most of all
to Nicola—all selfless and dedicated supporters of the
Romantic Novelists' Association, UK, and particularly
of the wonderful New Writers' Scheme, which has
given so many of us the self-discipline and hope to
keep on trying. Without you I would definitely not be
doing this now—so thank you for everything!

Chapter One

Wondering if she could still climb like a cat, Louisa Alstone swung her feet out of the window and eased into the spring night; considering the thought of marrying Charlton Hawberry was unendurable, she supposed she'd find out soon enough. His purloined breeches shifted about her lithely feminine legs as she flexed muscles she hadn't used properly in six years and did her best not to look down. She'd certainly changed since the last time she had chased through the London streets, or scampered across rooftops above them, but she fervently hoped she hadn't forgotten all her street-urchin skills.

She should be far too much of a lady to consider such a desperate escape now, but silently prayed her agility hadn't deserted her as she tried not to shake like a leaf in a high wind. Her brother, Christopher, or Kit Stone as he went by in business, was off with his best friend and business partner Ben Shaw, too busy having adventures on the high seas, so there was really no point waiting around for them to rescue her. Since she'd rather die than wed a man who would happily force her up the aisle after she had refused to marry him, she let go of the window mouldings and edged out along the parapet.

This would work; she refused to think of the swift death awaiting her if she fumbled. She boosted herself across the next window and blessed the builder of these narrow town houses for insisting every shutter fitted so neatly no hint of her passing outside would shadow the closely barred wood. She still breathed a little more easily when no one stirred within and felt for her next shallow grip on Charlton Hawberry's house.

If she managed this, then where was there to go next? No point asking Uncle William and Aunt Prudence for help when they were calluding with Charlton. Uncle William would sell his soul to the devil for a good enough price and Kit's growing wealth hadn't endeared him or his sisters to their uncle, especially since her brother made sure their uncle got as little of it as possible, which left only her sister and brother-in-law to turn to. Maria and Brandon Heathcote would be deeply shocked at Charlton's appalling behaviour and give her sanctuary, but how could she bring scandal down on their comfortable Kentish rectory when neither of them deserved such notoriety? Then there was Maria's ridiculous soft-heartedness to contend with and Louisa grimaced at the thought of her sister feeling sorry for lying, cheating, facilely good-looking Charlton Hawberry.

You must learn to be less extreme in your opinions, my dearest, Maria had written in reply to Louisa's last letter, in which she announced she'd rather die than marry the wretched man after his third proposal in as many weeks. *And why not consider Mr Hawberry's proposals a little more seriously?* she had continued. *For all you persist in believing you will never marry, he sounds well enough looking and genuinely devoted to you. Being wed is so much better than dwindling into spinsterhood, my love, and I really think you should try to find yourself an agreeable hus-*

*band, rather than regretting becoming an old
maid when it is too late to remedy.*

Louisa no more believed in that love of
Charlton's than she did in her own ridiculous persona of lovely, impossibly fussy Miss
Alstone, Ice Diamond of the *ton*, rumoured
to have rejected more suitors than most
débutantes imagined in their wildest dreams.
Louisa knew her resistance to marriage would
make her a curiosity to the bored gentlemen of
the *ton*, so she'd made herself treat them coldly
from the outset. Now her carefully cultivated
aloofness was in ruins and, if she escaped
Charlton, she'd be besieged by suitors and
would-be seducers. In truth, neither Maria nor
amiable, optimistic Brandon had it in them to
stand up to Charlton for long and Uncle William and Aunt Prudence wouldn't even try, so
her reputation was already gone—a lost cause
she couldn't bring herself to mourn deeply.
Perhaps it would persuade Kit to let her keep
his house and help in his business, she decided, an old hope lightening her heart as she
edged along the ledge, teeth gritted against the
compulsion to look down into three-storeys'
worth of shadowy space.

'I'd sooner starve,' she'd told Uncle William
truthfully when Charlton brought him into the

unappealingly luxurious bedchamber she was imprisoned in to show how compromised she was only an hour ago.

'As you please. I won't have a notorious woman under my roof, so you can go back to the streets we took you from as far as your aunt and I are concerned,' Uncle William had replied with a Judas shrug and added, 'If you don't want to wed Hawberry, you shouldn't have run off with him in the first place.'

'He abducted me from that wretched masked ball Aunt Prudence insisted on attending and you know very well I hate the man. Won't you send me to Chelsea to await my brother's return, even if you won't help me in any other way?'

'I'm done with you, madam. I wish I'd never taken you into my home when your return for my foolishness was to ruin your cousin's chance of making a good match by stealing all her suitors.'

'I couldn't do that if I tried. I've no idea where Sophia gets her looks or her sweet nature since it's clearly not from you. A normal brother would have helped us when Mama died out of compassion for your orphan nieces and love for your only sister, but *you* had to be paid a king's ransom to house us once Kit was at sea mending all our fortunes,' she told him bitterly as she saw the weasel look in his eyes and realised he'd known about this horrid scheme all along. 'Don't worry, Uncle William, I wouldn't spend five minutes under your roof now if the only alternative was the workhouse.'

Which seemed unlikely since her dowry was substantial, thanks to Kit's efforts; if she could escape Charlton she'd live on that if Kit wouldn't let her share his new bachelor home in Chelsea. A share of her fortune would fill Uncle William's coffers very nicely, of course, but while her uncle and aunt had clearly plotted against her, could her cousin Sophia have known what was afoot? Louisa shook her head very warily and decided to trust one of two certainties in this shifting world that she suddenly seemed to have stumbled into. Cousin Sophia was far too amiable and feather-headed to be party to such a plan. She wondered how Uncle William came to have a sister like her lion-hearted, stubborn mother, and such a sweet widgeon for a daughter. Deciding the mysteries of heredity were unaccountable, she crept on along the façade of the hired town house, still trying to block the killing drop to the flagged pavement three storeys below from her thoughts.

Louisa didn't intend to marry; now the man she didn't want to marry most of all was threatening her very soul, she wished she'd never agreed to give the marriage mart another try to appease her brother and sister. Her heart hammered against her breastbone as she took an unwary glance into the street below and fancied Death was creeping along the ledge behind her, his cold breath on her neck and bony fingers clutching a ghostly scythe. Since she'd rather die than wed Charlton, she crept on, keeping her thoughts busy with what came next.

Could she evade her uncle and Charlton until her brother came home to dismiss their antics as the farce they ought to be? Her brother's house would be the first place anyone would look for her and his minions lacked the authority or power to repel her enemies. Not quite true; one of Kit's employees had both and she recalled her encounter with Kit's most notorious captain as she ghosted past the empty rooms on this part of the third floor inch by heart-racing inch. Captain Hugh Darke had made a vivid impression on her, but he was one step from being a pirate and the rudest man she'd ever met, so little wonder if the image of him had lingered on her senses and her memory long after the man had left her alone in Kit's office.

Considering she'd spent mere seconds in Captain Darke's darkly brooding, offensively arrogant company, his abrupt insolence and the satirical glint in his silver-blue eyes shouldn't haunt her as they did. She fumbled her handhold on the neatly jointed stone at the very thought of explaining this latest misadventure to sternly indifferent Hugh Darke and had to swallow a very unladylike curse while she scrambled for another and terror threatened to ruin her escape in a very final way.

'Confoundedly inconvenient, ill-mannered, cocksure braggart of a man,' she muttered very softly to herself as she inched round the corner of the Portland Stone–faced building and finally reached the drainpipe to cling onto until the rapid beat of her heart slowed while she thought out her next move.

Better with solid-feeling metal under her clutching hands, she decided to go upwards, since she'd got this far and risked being seen on the way down. Better to wait for solid ground under her feet after she had reached the last of this terrace of genteel houses, where there was less chance of being discovered clambering down from the rooftops of a stranger's house, than if she swarmed down this one like some large and very fearful fly. The idea of meeting Charlton's bullies again made her shudder with horror and she forced herself to forget their jeering comments and greedy eyes as she crept across the rooftops of Charlton's unsuspecting neighbours.

She reached the quiet and blissfully sleeping house on the end of the row and wasted a few precious moments debating whether to risk the roofs of the humbler mews that ran alongside the high town houses and reluctantly decided against it. Night had made courts and alleyways, relatively safe in daylight, into the haunts of the desperate and dangerous, but there were too many leaps into the unknown to spring across uncharted voids and risk the slightest miscalculation bringing her crashing down to earth.

Slipping very cautiously to the ground at last, Louisa blessed Charlton's love of the macabre for the ridiculous suit of black she'd found in a chest he'd thought safely locked. She grinned at the idea of him clumsily creeping about in the dark in some half-hearted imitation of Francis Dashwood's infamous

Hell-Fire Club of the last century and refused to even consider what Charlton got up to in his other life. His dark clothes had helped her escape and made her hard to see in the dark, so she blessed his secret vices for once and crept on through the chilling night.

Kit's house was the only place that offered her immediate sanctuary and access to the store of money he'd once shown her, in case she was ever in dire need of it and he was away from home. How prophetic of him, she decided, and at least she would be safe until dawn. Apparently six years of dull respectability had taught her to fear her native streets, so she launched into the fuggy darkness with her heart beating like a war drum and prayed she'd find her way in the dark before she aroused the interest of the night-hawks.

Captain Hugh Darke woke very reluctantly from the nice little drunken stupor that he'd worked hard to achieve all the previous evening and peered at the ceiling above his head with only the faint, town-bred moonlight to help him work out whose it was and, more importantly, why some malicious elf was jumping about on his mysterious host's roof and waking him from the best sleep he'd had in weeks.

'And now I've got the devil of a head as well,' he muttered, much aggrieved at such a lack of consideration by whoever owned the bed he was currently occupying.

An insomniac clog dancer, perhaps? Or an iron master with a rush order his unfortunate founders must work all night to fulfil? Although that didn't work; even he knew no iron founder would carry out his sulphurous trade anywhere but on the ground floor and there'd be smoke, lots of smoke, and flaring furnaces belching out infernal heat, and, if anything, it was rather cool in here. In a moment of reluctant fairness, he forced himself to admit it was a very quiet racket, furtive even; he wondered uneasily what bad company he'd got himself into this time. He shrugged, decided he wasn't that good company himself and concluded there was no point trying to sleep through it, reminding himself he'd faced down far worse threats than an incompetent burglar before now.

Not being content to cower under the bedclothes and wait for this now almost-silent menace to pass him by—if only he'd bothered to get under them in the first place, of course—he decided to find whoever it was and silence them so he could get back to sleep. If he went about it briskly enough, perhaps he could avoid succumbing to the best cure for his various ills that he'd ever come across—a hair of the dog who'd bitten him—and spare himself an even worse hangover come morning. He'd long ago given up pretending everything about his life he didn't like would go away if he ignored it, so he swung his feet to the floor; even as his head left the pillow it thumped violently in protest, as if the elf had gotten bored with dancing on the ceiling and come into his room to beat out a dance on the inside of his reeling skull instead.

'Confounded din,' he mumbled and, liking the sound of his own voice in the suddenly eerily quiet house, he roared out a challenge in his best hear-it-over-a-hurricane-at-sea bark. 'I *said* you're making a confounded din!' he bellowed as he stamped through the doorway into a stairwell that looked vaguely familiar.

'Not half as much of a one as you are,' a woman's voice snapped back as if he were the intruder and she had a perfect right to steal about in the dark.

Her voice was as low and throaty as it was distinctive, so Hugh wondered if she was more afraid of drawing attention to her peculiar nocturnal activities than she was willing to admit. Yet the very sound of her husky tones roused fantasies he'd been trying to forget for days. Her voice reminded him of honey and mid-summer, and the response of his fool body to her presence made him groan out loud, before he reminded himself the witch was Kit Stone's woman and would never be his.

He cursed the day he'd first laid eyes on the expensive-looking houri in his friend's fine new offices dressed in an excellent imitation of a lady's restrained finery, with an outrageous bonnet whose curling feathers had been dyed to try to match the apparently matchless dark eyes she had stared so boldly at him with. Such a speculative, unladylike deep-blue gaze it had been as well, wide and curious and fathomless as the Mediterranean, and he'd felt his body respond like a warhorse to the drum without permission from his furious brain. It had seemed more urgent that Kit never discover his notorious captain lusted after his mistress than handing over the report of his latest voyage his employer had demanded as soon as he'd docked in person, so Hugh had left the expensive high-stepper alone in Kit's office with a gauchely mumbled excuse and a loud sigh of relief.

She'd responded to his gaucherie with a few cool words and a dismissive glance that made him feel like an overgrown schoolboy, instead of a seasoned captain of eight and twenty with an adventurous naval career behind him and one in front as master of a fine ship of the merchant marine. Since he was done with reckless adventures, he did his best to avoid the enemy nowadays, as well as his old naval brothers-in-arms, who thought it quite legitimate to hunt down ships like his in order to steal his crew of experienced mariners and press them into the navy. It was a second chance that Hugh valued, so somehow he'd kept his eager hands off his employer's whore and returned to his ship and the relative peace of his cabin to await Kit Stone's summons to discuss this last voyage and plan the next one.

Now Kit had gone off on some mysterious mission known only to himself; and the other half of Stone & Shaw was probably in the Caribbean by now, while Hugh Darke was drunk, in charge of Kit Stone's house and business and fantasising over his doxy. There'd be hell to pay if Kit heard so much as a whisper of them being here in the middle of

the night together, him stale drunk and her…
What exactly was the high-and-mighty little
light-skirt doing here when her lover was ab-
sent, and in the stilly watches of the night to
make bad worse as well?

'Did you hear me?' she demanded from far
too close for comfort.

He swayed a little, then corrected himself
impatiently as he wished the annoying witch
would stop nagging and let him think. 'How
the devil could I avoid it, woman? You're yelling in my ear like a fishwife.'

'I'm not yelling, you are,' she informed him
haughtily, 'and where's my b…?' She seemed
to hesitate for a long moment.

Which, even still half-drunk as he was,
Hugh thought very unlike the headlong siren
who'd so tempted him with her ultramarine
come-hither gaze that day in the city. Confound the witchy creature, but he'd had to
drink out of the island to get a decent night's
sleep all these weeks later because she had
haunted his dreams with the most heated and
unattainably alluring fantasies any female had
ever troubled him with in an eventful life. He
couldn't have her, had told himself time and
time again that he didn't really want her and it
was just a normal lust-driven urge that drove

him to dream about her, given he was a normal lusty male and she was very definitely a desirable and perhaps equally lusty female, given her profession. Then he'd gone on to reassure himself that she was nothing like the almost mythically sensuous creature he was fantasising her to be.

In reality, the rackety female was probably coarse and calculating under all that lovely outer glamour and fine packaging. Far too often he'd reassured himself she was just a Cyprian, told himself he'd only have to know her to learn to despise her for selling all that boldness and beauty to the highest bidder. Somehow, now she was so close to him again and he was so lightly in control of his senses after all that cognac, the sensible voice of reason was in danger of being drowned out by the hard, primitive demand of his body for hers, as the very sound of her husky feminine tones rendered him powerfully, uncomfortably erect the instant they loomed out of the night and wrapped her toils round him. He fervently hoped her night eyes and well-developed instincts weren't honed enough to tell her what a parlous state he was in and he bit down on a string of invectives that might have shocked even such an experienced night-stalker as her.

'Where's my bad, bold Kit?' she finally managed, secretly horrified at what her very correct and stern brother would have to say about her various deceits, if he ever found out about them, of course.

'No idea, he's his own man and goes his own way,' he told her absently, wondering why she wasn't much-better informed about Kit's whereabouts than he was, considering her supposedly special status in his life.

If she were his woman, he wouldn't let her out of his sight long enough to even look elsewhere, let alone allow her to roam about in a dark and virtually deserted house in the middle of the night, tormenting a poor devil like him who didn't much care whether he lived or died at the best of times. Yet with her here, the scent and elusive shadows of a playful moon and its lightly concealing clouds playing with her face and form, and the night cool and silent all around them, suddenly the threat of Kit's wrath wasn't the deterrent it ought to be. When they had first met, his youthful employer had sobered Hugh up from a far worse carouse than this one before recklessly trusting him with the command of one of his best ships when nobody else would risk a rowboat to his sole charge, for how could a captain control his ship when he couldn't control himself, or even care that he'd fallen from master of nearly all he surveyed headlong into the gutter?

Until this dratted woman sparked all these unwanted urges and one or two wickedly tempting fantasies that made him recall his other life and all the bitter betrayals it had contained, he'd been doing so splendidly at sobriety as well. He'd almost been in danger of becoming a useful member of society, until something occurred to remind him how useless he actually was; but, he decided with a cynical twist of his lips that might have passed for a smile in a dim light, it would have been a fine joke on society if he'd only managed to bring it off.

'Drat him for not telling me, then,' the major cause of his latest downfall muttered at his gruff disclaimer and there wasn't light enough to see if she looked as defeated and desperate as she sounded, before she seemed to recall another option and asked in a brighter voice, 'Has Ben gone too?'

'I dare say Captain Shaw will be in the West Indies or even Virginia by now. So at least *he*'s out there earning us all some money, whilst I'm stuck on shore sailing nothing bet-

ter than a desk and your Kit's off on some wild
goose chase all of his own that I would have
expected you to know about far better than I
do.'

'Aye, Ben's proving himself the best of us
all as usual,' she said, affection very evident
in her husky voice, and Hugh frowned fleetingly at hearing her so neatly avoid his implication she wasn't as close to her protector as
she hoped she was.

Then he forgot his doubts about that position himself as he pondered the possibility of
her maintaining intimate relations with Kit's
business partner as well as Kit himself. He
silently cursed the blond giant for apparently
taking shares in his best friend's doxy, especially when Kit could have shared her with
him instead.

'So why are *you* still here? You could easily
have gone to sea in Ben's stead, and I doubt
very much anyone would have missed you,'
she informed him irritably.

Which was perfectly correct, he allowed
fairly, even if it was brutally frank and deliberately tactless. Once upon a time, when
he'd gone by another name and still possessed
a relatively innocent soul, a number of good
people had cared what became of him and

some had even claimed to miss him sadly whilst he was away at sea. The few who were left to recall the blithe young idiot he'd once been probably welcomed the disappearance of the cynical sot he'd become from their lives with unalloyed relief, when he finally had the good manners to remove himself from polite society and the place he'd once thought of as home.

He reminded himself sourly that the past was dead and gone and he'd resolved to live for the day when he became Hugh Darke, a man who congratulated himself on caring for nobody, just as nobody cared for him, except somewhere along the way he'd come to value the good opinion of his rescuers. Still, at least he'd been able to tell himself that he'd never again be the gullible, arrogant young fool he'd been back then, before his world fell apart and everything he'd thought solid and safe melted away like mist.

Memory of the wanton havoc a careless and selfish woman could create in the life of a so-called gentleman should make him turn away from this one and barricade himself into his borrowed chamber until she gave up on him and went back into the night as swiftly and silently as she'd come. Unfortunately, she fascinated him far too much, even when he was sober and responsible; now he was three-parts' castaway, he was much too forgetful that whatever sort of woman she was, she certainly wasn't his, for all his driven wanting of her.

'I've been ordered to stay ashore and run things here while they're both busy playing on the high seas, or wherever Kit Stone happens to be hiding himself just now,' he admitted gruffly at last.

His ruffled feelings about his part of their current mission were too apparent in his aggrieved tone and he hated to hear that faint whine of discontent in his own voice. From what he could see of his unexpected visitor's face through the shadowed gloom, she looked quite tempted to push him down the stairs and have done with him for good. A part of himself he'd almost managed to smother in drink and duty would almost be glad if she could put a period to his worthless existence as well, but he shook off the deep sense of melancholy he suspected had a lot to do with returning sobriety and wondered how soon he could drown it in brandy again. The sooner he got rid of the confounded woman and got back to this useless excuse for a life the better, he decided bitterly, then frowned fiercely at the intruder, which made it a crying shame she probably couldn't see in the dark how very little he wanted her here.

Chapter Two

'So you're playing at being in charge of Kit and Ben's business ashore, whenever you manage to stay sober enough to care if it sinks or swims for the odd half-hour you can spare it, whilst they're both busy risking their lives to make your fortune for you?' the intrusive female asked Hugh, condemnation heavy in otherwise dulcet tones.

How irresistible her voice might be if she ever found anything to like about him, he mused foolishly. As it was, her question echoed about his head like knife blades and he wondered if she'd been sent to torture him with her nagging questions and the haunting scent of her, the ridiculous sensuality of her very presence in the same room with him when it was too dark for him to see the outline of her superb body. A vital, unignorable here-and-now allure that somehow reminded him with every breath that she was a very human woman and not a haughty goddess after all. A woman well used to satisfying a man's every fantasy on her back—as long as that man had enough gold in his pockets to pay for the privilege. And, thanks to Kit Stone and Ben Shaw, he had more than enough gelt to buy a lovely woman for their mutual pleasure nowadays, and keep her in comfort while he did so. How unfortunate that the one he wanted at the moment belonged to a friend he already owed so much to that he must leave her as untouched as a vestal virgin.

'I mind my own business—would I could say the same for you, madam,' he informed her sharply, in the hope she couldn't read his bitter frustration at her unavailability or discern his ridiculous state in this gloom.

'Kit and Ben *are* my business,' she informed him impatiently and confirmed every conclusion he'd already reached about her, which really shouldn't disappoint him as bitterly as it did somehow, especially considering he already expected the worst of her and most of her gender.

'Not at the moment they're not, since there's a few hundred leagues of ocean between you and their moneybags, so you'll just have to ply your trade elsewhere until they return,' he drawled as insultingly as he could manage.

'That's it! Out you; go on, you get out of this house right now, you verminous toad!' she ordered as if she had every right to evict him from the house Kit had told him to treat as his own while he was away.

'Firstly, you'll cease your screeching, my girl,' he ordered as he grasped her arms in a steely hold, in case she started scratching and biting in retaliation for being thwarted as was the habit of her type—bred in the gutter and inclined to revert to it at the slightest provocation he decided unfairly, considering he'd long ago concluded nobody could help where they were born, mansion or hovel, and that he preferred hovel dwellers over their better-off neighbours nine times out of ten.

'Damn you, I'll screech as long and as loud as I choose to,' she snapped back and he shook her in the hope it would rob her of breath. Her noise and her closeness and the elusive, womanly scent of her as she fought his grip with a determination he secretly admired was making his head pound again.

'Secondly, you'll get out of my room,' he went on doggedly.

'We're not in a room; even if we were, it wouldn't be yours.'

'Irrelevant,' he dismissed and felt something strange under the controlling grip he couldn't bring himself to make a punishing one, despite his disillusionment with her sex and the urgent need he felt to be rid of her before disaster struck, something besides warm, soft, tempting woman. 'And what the devil are you doing running wild about the place dressed in a man's shirt and breeches and not just asking for trouble but begging for it, you idiot woman?' he demanded harshly, quite put off his list of demands by that shocking discovery.

At least he wished fervently he really did find her unconventional attire shocking, instead of far too sensually appealing for comfort or safety as his exploring hand on her neat *derrière* made her squirm even more determinedly against him and curse him with an impressive, if far from ladylike, fluency while she was doing so.

'How I choose to dress is none of your business and never will be,' she informed him sharply at last, but if she could still blush he was almost sure she was doing so from the sudden increase in body heat under his exploring fingers.

'No, it's clearly Kit Stone's or Ben Shaw's business, and therefore mine in their absence,' he asserted, senses sharpening despite the brandy, as he felt a terrible threat to his jealously guarded aloofness in that demand for more information and carried on all the same. 'Come on,' he urged recklessly, making her obedience irrelevant by tugging her after him all the way downstairs and into the kitchen, where at least a fire was still burning faintly, even if the manservant Kit employed was snoring in the porter's chair in the hall, more drunk than Hugh had managed to become so far despite all his efforts before this confounded woman came along and spoilt his chance of a decent night's stupor.

Now, he supposed bitterly, he'd have to endure his usual nightmare-haunted sleep replaying a past he'd so much rather forget, if he was to be allowed any rest this night at all, which currently seemed doubtful with Kit Stone's woman actually here in the flesh rather than in spirit for once and making sure he had no chance of resting, even when he wasn't dreaming about her writhing under him, moaning out her desire and then her lusty pleasure as he satisfied every single one.

Setting a taper to the dying fire, Hugh lit a candle, decided he didn't believe his eyes and lit a whole branch of them. He wasn't often rendered speechless nowadays, but he couldn't think of a single word to say as his eyes roved over this extraordinary night visitor with numb astonishment. Numb because all the blood and feeling he still had left in him rushed straight to his loins and stopped there to torture him with the mere sight of such blatant allure. It should definitely be a crime for any woman to go about dressed like that, he decided bitterly. A felony carrying with it some sort of severe but not deadly punishment that would put her off taunting poor devils like him with her goddess's body and those endless, neatly feminine legs. An amateurish attempt at binding her breasts had only made them seem all the more worthy of a sensual exploration and as for that sweetly rounded *derrière* of hers... If she didn't realise what a temptation it posed to any red-blooded male who set eyes on her, then she ought to be locked up for her own safety until he'd taught her to know better.

'What the devil are you doing strutting the

streets at night dressed like a female resur-
rectionist or an undertaker's apprentice?' he
finally managed, faintly surprised, until they
came out of his mouth, that he'd got that many
words left in him.

'It's nothing to do with you what I choose to
do, or where I decide to go while I'm doing it,'
she told him and wrenched her arm out of his
slackened grip at last so she could fold it bel-
ligerently across her body, trying her best to
look as if she'd every right to go about dressed
in black breeches and a dark shirt with a black
cravat knotted about her slender neck. Her
crow's-wing dark locks suddenly cascaded
down her back, like the wickedest promise
he'd seen in a long time, when she shook her
head defiantly at him and her neat black-velvet
cap finally gave up trying to contain so much
dusky luxuriance.

'You just made it a lot to do with me,
Witch,' he informed her hoarsely and let his
eyes rove as they pleased over the very feminine body he'd reluctantly fantasised over
since the black day he'd found her waiting in
Kit's office, looking as if she had every right
to be there and he was the intruder.

'Men!' she condemned impatiently, as if his
sudden fascination with her long slender legs

and those neatly rounded, womanly curves, so blatantly on show, was entirely his fault and nothing to do with her unconventional garb or extraordinary behaviour at all. 'You're all the same.'

'Now there you're almost certainly mistaken,' he lazily informed her, making no attempt to disguise his wolfishly thorough appraisal of her well-displayed charms, for if she aspired to meet some impossibly gallant chevalier who'd be so overwhelmed by her sensual beauty that he'd offer her anything she demanded of him during her peculiar night wanderings, she should never have embarked on a career of selling herself to the highest bidder in the first place. 'We're all different, but we *think* alike when presented with nigh-irresistible temptation, such as you pose any red-blooded male by going about dressed like that.'

'On the contrary, it seems to me that you don't think at all,' she muttered darkly and frowned at him as if she had the right to find his blatantly sexual scrutiny of her outrageously displayed body ill-mannered at best and deeply insulting at worst.

Hugh wondered how she expected any red-blooded male to actually *think* while she was standing there displaying her assets so generously that he'd soon only function on pure, or impure, instinct alone if she wasn't very careful.

'You could be right,' he told her with a wickedly unrepentant grin as he forgot his headache and began to enjoy himself by living down to her expectations. 'At the moment I'm too busy fantasising about the feel of your magnificent body writhing under me as you desperately beg me to take you to paradise to waste much of my energy on rational thought, my darling.'

'I'm not your darling and I'm prepared to bet you don't know the first thing about what would truly transport a woman to paradise,' Louisa snapped back, wishing she felt as cool as she sounded as she stood in front of this outrageous, drunken and dissipated man in her shirt sleeves with everything going wrong with her wonderful plan of escape, even now she'd finally got away from Charlton.

She'd shed her jacket and been forced to leave it behind when it had been caught on a spike put there by an inconsiderate neighbour of Kit's to prevent the stealthy and desperate using their roof for nefarious purposes such as hers. Doing her best not to remember how terrified she'd been then, swinging between safety and a forty-foot drop to her death by one hand as she had wrestled the inextricably trapped coat undone so that she could finally wriggle out of it and haul herself to safety, she shivered in the unreliable light of those untrimmed candle wicks this sot had lit to inspect her by.

Until her brother or Ben came back to put the world right for her, she might still be discovered and marched up the aisle so fast the vicar wouldn't have time to ask what she'd been up to that she deserved this and why she was protesting every step of the way. She reassured herself that could only happen if she was caught and resolved to stay in this scandalous disguise for the rest of her life if she had to, rather than endure such a fate. So she did her best to glare defiance at the wretched man while she convinced herself even his company was preferable to roaming the streets now she was grown up and vulnerable, open to the use and abuse such a reckless female might attract from rogues like this one, if she wandered about even more freely dressed in what was left of Charlton's fantasy disguise.

'Aren't you willing to add me to your stable of lucrative lovers then, my darling doxy?' he suddenly asked as if he had every right to insult her.

He'd only set eyes on her twice in his life, for goodness' sake, and she doubted he even remembered their first encounter now, given the reek of brandy on his breath whenever he came near her. Not knowing her at all, he somehow thought he had every right to eye her like a starving dog slavering over a juicy bone—surely he couldn't know a visceral, wayward part of her was inclined to look at him the same way and only made the rest more furious.

'Firstly, I'm very particular whom I allow to even call me darling, Captain Darke, and secondly, I certainly wouldn't take a man like you to my bed, even if I wasn't,' she informed him haughtily, kicking herself for letting him know she'd been fascinated enough to find out what his name was after that first sight of him in Kit's office.

'You put such a high price on your charms, then?' he asked as if he was surprised.

She had to bless his consumption of brandy for fogging his wits that he hadn't even noticed her *faux pas*, even if it fuddled him into mistaking her for Kit's mistress rather than his sister. After all, she didn't want him to think of her as his employer's close kin, did she? No, of course she didn't. If he knew who she really was, he might ruin everything by handing her back to her temporary guardians, so it was far better if he thought her no better than she should be and let her stop here for the night.

'A very high one indeed,' she assured him with a toss of her head, which she hoped told him it was beyond anything he could pay, if he had anything left of his share of the last cargo after buying enough brandy to inebriate even him.

'How's a man supposed to know if a woman's price is worth the paying when he's not even been permitted to check the quality of the goods? Strikes me you're asking a man to buy a pig in a poke, my dear.'

Good heavens! The appalling man really thought she was a streetwalker, casually selling her body for a bed and food in her belly as well as the clothes on her back. More of a roof-walker, her sense of the ridiculous reminded her, and the past years of suffocating respectability threatened to fall away under the liberty of his wild conclusions about Miss Alstone, spinster of impeccable birth, if not exactly unimpeachable upbringing. Maybe Aunt Prudence was right and she'd never be the proper lady she should have been since birth, if only said birth hadn't taken place in a rundown lodging-house, so perilously close to the rookeries of St Giles it was almost a part of them.

She'd never know now how differently she might have felt about the world if she'd come into it at lofty Wychwood Court, a vast Tudor mansion in the county of Derbyshire that was the Alstones' ancestral home. A house she'd never been invited to visit and doubtless never would be now, since her Alstone cousins seemed intent on ignoring any relations low enough to run the streets for most of their childhood and then lower the family name still more by taking to trade in order to make up their lamentable lack of the proverbial penny to bless themselves with. Reminded how little she'd enjoyed a life of cramping propriety, she made herself meet this monster of depravity's sceptical gaze and match his cynical scrutiny with one she hoped he'd find just as difficult to meet.

'The customer always has the choice not to buy,' she said boldly, as if she fended off such outrageous provocation every day of the week and reminded herself that, if not for Kit and Ben, she'd probably be exactly what this poor apology for a gentleman thought her right now. 'And I can take my pick of those who want to do so whenever I like.'

'The most readily caught fish doesn't always taste sweetest.'

'But if you throw them back, I've found the little ones often live to grow up and learn a lot more, which makes catching them again into much better sport.'

'I'll have to be the one that got away, then, for hooking me would prove a challenge even to the most cunning enchantress, let alone an amateur angler like yourself, Miss... Confound it, whatever is your name, woman?'

'Miss Confoundit? Now why didn't I think of that?'

'I'll just make one up to call you by then, shall I?'

'No, it's...' Louisa racked her brains for something suitably exotic, something an aspiring Cyprian might use to intrigue ardent gentlemen with plenty of gold in their pockets, if not rude and probably impoverished sea captains. 'Eloise La Rochelle,' she invented on the spur of the moment and decided she rather liked it.

Nobody would dare drive Eloise La Rochelle to such desperation that she'd risk climbing out of a second-floor window to escape her uncle's machinations and her importunate suitor, she decided whimsically. Indeed, Eloise would doubtless have far less respectable gentlemen than even this one climbing up the creepers to her scented balcony in their droves of a night-time to beg for her nigh-on legendary favours instead.

Would she accept any of them? she wondered, as she slipped deeper into the dangerous fantasy of being a very different female from the one she was in reality, or make them climb back into the night? Charlton could go back the way he came as fast as gravity could take him and she hoped it would teach him a salutary lesson, but Hugh Darke? Daring, dashing Eloise La Rochelle might just let him stay for a while, because he amused and intrigued her, of course, and to enchant him into parting with the dark secrets that lurked in those ironic grey-blue eyes of his, until he finally laid even his cynical heart at her feet. Then he could take his brooding gaze and his warrior's body down the stairs when he left, to scandalise and intrigue passing dowager duchesses with his disreputable looks and piratical charm and make them long to be as young, bold, stunningly beautiful and irresistibly seductive as the notorious Eloise La Rochelle of such scandalous fame even they couldn't pretend never to have heard of her.

No, she revised her story, he wouldn't be *able* to leave. He'd demand, then beg, then sell his soul to stay with her, if he still had one. Infamous Eloise La Rochelle would spoil him for every other female he ever met and in return he'd satisfy her as extravagantly as she would him, or be banished to decline and fall alone as a punishment for his sensual failure.

'And I'm the Queen of Sheba,' he responded sceptically to her exotic *nom de plume*, bringing her back to here and now with an unpleasant jolt, as she struggled with the uneasy certainty that he wouldn't fail to pleasure her in such an encounter, even if she was a little foggy about what such sensual satisfaction would involve.

A very uncomfortable present it was as well, where he didn't look at all enchanted by her assumed name or shockingly displayed charms and probably wouldn't beg aught but peace from the likes of her, so he could broach another bottle and swinishly lose himself in drink once more.

'I suggest you act a little more regally from now on, then,' she told him crossly, turning her back on that ridiculous fantasy of him falling at her feet, tortured by passion and his searing, insatiable need for her as she searched the Spartan-looking kitchen for something to eat instead.

'Make yourself at home, why don't you?' he muttered ungraciously.

'Certainly I shall and you can build up the fire whilst I do so,' she demanded, wishing she could find something more appealing than a hunk of hard and cracked cheese and some pickled onions along with, of all things, a naval officer's dress sword, in Kit's larder.

'Coste sends out for food whenever we're hungry,' Hugh told her as if that explained everything and, since they were both men, it probably did.

'On the rare occasions either of you forsake the brandy bottle long enough to bother to eat at all, I suppose?' she asked sweetly.

'Whatever our domestic arrangements may or may not be, we certainly didn't invite you here in the middle of the night to see if they were up to scratch,' he mumbled gruffly as he bent to stoke the fire.

'Which is just as well, considering you clearly don't have any,' she informed him disgustedly as she chewed valiantly on the hunk of cheese and wondered if even she was hungry enough to indulge in a pickled onion or two to force it down with, as she could see no sign of anything else remotely edible or drinkable.

'We don't need them,' he informed her defensively, looking endearingly sheepish even as he did so. 'Neither of us wanted a female nagging and criticising and poking her nose in everywhere it wasn't wanted when we can manage very well for ourselves.'

'No, you can't. I can assure you that you and Coste really, really can't manage anything more refined than a sty, Captain Darke,' she told him fervently, as she finally gave up on finding anything else remotely edible in the dusty larder and purloined his branch of almost-gutted candles to make a more thorough tour round the dusty, dirty, unused room and the once-pristine scullery on the other side of the kitchen that turned out to be piled with every glass, tankard and mug Kit's house possessed. All were dirty and looked as if they'd been so for too long. 'And wherever have Mrs Calhoun and Midge gone off to?' she asked at last.

'Kit's housekeeper wouldn't stay once he'd been gone awhile, nor let Midge stop here without her. She said we lived like swine and she'd no mind to go on mucking out a pigsty every morning, so you two obviously have a lot in common.'

'How very sensible of her, but wherever did they go?' she asked and when he didn't reply, she walked back into the kitchen to find him watching her as if he wished she'd conveniently disappear as well.

Oddly hurt by his clear preference for her room over her company, she frowned and tapped an impatient foot as if waiting for his answer, when she suspected both women would be at Brandon and Maria's rectory in Kent, awaiting the return of their master before they deigned to come back.

'She just said Kit would know where to find her when he wanted his house made civilised again,' he drawled unrepentantly.

'How insightful of her,' she said with a scornful glance round the room.

'I'll borrow a few deckhands to clean up next time we unload a ship.'

'In the meantime you intend to go on treating my br...brave Kit's house worse than a stable? At least a well-run stable is mucked out every day, but this place has obviously been going to rack and ruin ever since he left.'

Was Captain Darke actually blushing? Louisa wondered. Her half-guttered candles were flickering annoyingly and refused to illuminate him properly, but she was surprised he'd even heard it could be done, let alone learnt how to do it himself.

'He said I was to treat the place as my own,' he excused himself gruffly.

'And you truly think so little of yourself, Captain?'

'Yes, Miss Eloise so-called Rochelle, I do, and this is all I want or need of any place I lay my head nowadays,' he rasped harshly, as if she'd stepped on to forbidden ground by even asking that question.

'Why?' she asked, biting back a ladylike apology for intruding on his private thoughts and opinions.

'Because… Devil fly away with it all, woman, what right have you to break in here and interrogate me like some long-nosed inquisitor? While we're on the subject of the devil, where's Coste hidden the rest of the brandy, so I can get back to my previous occupation when you leave us or at least stop your infernal nagging?'

'Inside himself from the look of it,' she answered impatiently and watched him with an implacable look Kit called her I'll-find-out-if-it-kills-us-both stare.

'Selfish bastard,' he grated in a much-tried voice and tried to look as if he didn't know he was being inspected by his unwanted night visitor and found wanting.

'You probably have enough left in your system to inebriate a goat.'

'I never saw a drunken goat, but what an interesting life you must have lived to have done so, Miss Le Havre.'

'Yes, I have,' she informed him truthfully, or at least she had until she'd been hauled off to learn respectability at the age of thirteen, much against her will. 'And it's not Miss Le Havre, but Miss La Rochelle, if you're capable of remembering your own name, of course, let alone mine, which I sincerely doubt just at the moment.'

'I know that too well, but I dare say you could tell a tale or two about that life, could you not?'

'I could, but I won't.'

'Yet you expect me to tell you my entire life story, whilst you reveal nothing of your own? You're an implacably demanding, as well as an insensitive and intrusive, female footpad, are you not, Miss Rockyshore?'

'You really have no idea, Captain Darke.'

'So, *is* that how you keep your lovers under your slender little thumb?' he drawled in his velvet-rubbed-the-wrong-way voice. 'By dragging their darkest secrets out of them when they're drunk, then holding them over the unfortunate idiots?'

'Nothing about me is so very little, sir, I'm above average height for a woman,' she parried coolly, ignoring the urge to counter the rest of his accusations as beneath her notice.

Trust him to take her words as an open invitation to let his silver-blue eyes rove over her boldly. He was good at defending his privacy, she mused, as he let his gaze track over her until those eyes had all but stripped her bare. Then the renegade let that blatant stare of his rest explicitly on the secret centre of her and she had to fight not to press her legs together and visibly, physically clamp down on the fiery demand suddenly all too alive and wildly curious for more under his outrageous scrutiny. Kit and Ben hadn't fought battle after battle to preserve her honour in their youth so she could be secretly tempted to throw it away on a ne'er-do-well like this.

Yet that fully-formed temptation stopped her thundering scold and sharp exit in its tracks. If she let him take her virginity, then she'd lose all her value on the marriage mart the instant he did so. Not even a Charlton Hawberry would take another man's leavings, so deeply ingrained as it was in a gentleman's psyche that he must marry a virgin, or at the very least a virtuous widow—she would certainly be neither after a night in the ungallant captain's bed. It might be a desperate idea, almost as reckless as climbing out of a second-floor window at midnight, but she wasn't in a position to discard any possibility just now.

'So I see,' he said with a pantomime leer she almost applauded, but there was something deeper and darker than simple lust in his eyes as well. It suddenly occurred to her that the real Captain Darke, whoever he might be under all this dark and dangerous front he faced the world behind, could break her heart if she had one. Luckily she didn't and stared boldly back at him.

'That could change,' she warned, 'if you don't stop staring at me.'

'Me, Miss Rockisle?' he said, and his silvery-blue eyes were beginning to lose the haze of brandy and world-weariness that had clouded them until now. She dare not look lower to find out if his body was as blatantly aroused as his cocky smile and intent gaze argued it must be.

'Yes, you—we were discussing your total lack of ambition and self-respect rather than my height and frame, if you remember?' she said coldly.

'You can talk as much as you like, my lovely, if you have the breath left for it after I've finished with you,' he mocked as he sauntered confidently towards her.

'I know when a man is determined to shut me up at any price,' she blustered.

Suddenly it was very quiet in the house, echoingly empty but for the unconscious Coste, who she would have to swear to keep her identity from Hugh Darke, and two almost-adversaries, each determined to give no quarter. Louisa was too much a child of the streets to yield an inch in the eternal battle to make every choice her own, however wrongheaded and contrary it might be, and stood her ground while she wondered what that next choice would be.

'And I know just as surely when a woman wants me as much as I do her, my dear,' he said and stepped closer, silvery-blue eyes full of sensual challenge.

'I'm not your dear,' she argued and tried to tell herself it didn't matter.

'And if you're not, what do you care? In a profession where "affection" is traded for expensive jewellery, fine gowns and a rich man's protection, you can't afford emotions, can you?'

Chapter Three

Temper had always been her undoing, Louisa decided as she lost it spectacularly and did her best to punch him in the gut. The wretched, ungentlemanly Captain Darke countered her onslaught by engulfing her in such a tight hold there wasn't even a tissue of air to shield them from each other and it sparked a heat set burning weeks ago, when they had first laid eyes on each other and wondered 'what if?'. It was like a force of nature, fuelled by some terrible need she hadn't known could come so urgent it might tear into her very soul in order to make them indivisible.

She moaned at the shock of wanting more so desperately and should have been shaken instead of fascinated by the novel hardness of his rampant male member nudging explicitly, demandingly against her very core. Logic, scruples, reality—they could all wait. She needed to indulge, to learn, to luxuriate. His mouth took hers in an open-mouthed kiss that stole her breath and sent her straight into sensual arousal no real lady would feel for a lover, at least until he'd chipped away at her scruples and guarded heart for weeks, or maybe even months.

Louisa's heart kicked with a shameless thrill at being so easily seduced, so starkly introduced to rampant sexual hunger, to the merciless drive of one achingly aroused body for another. She was all too ready to lose herself in the heat and novelty, and didn't that prove her uncle and aunt had been right all along and she'd never make a proper lady?

Unable to resist the urge to explore him with every sense as he amply demonstrated his skills as a lover of passionate women, she lazily let the tips of her fingers take a census of his features. His chin felt as firm as if he chewed nails for a pastime, when not seducing very unlikely maidens, and it was intriguingly shadowed with fine, dark whiskers.

'I'd have barbered myself if I'd known you were coming,' he told her wryly in a brief moment of respite, then ran his index finger over her tingling lips as if they fascinated him as much as his did her, before kissing her again as if he couldn't help himself test their softness and their welcome.

The small part of her brain not occupied with kissing him back went on with her sensual exploration of his intriguing features. He'd broken his nose once upon a time, as she felt a slight twist in his regally aquiline nose, and she decided it made his wickedly handsome face more human. His mouth was all sensuality just now; his firm lips on her softer ones were a balm, the impudent exploration of his tongue an arousing, teasing echo of something deeper and darker at the core of her that throbbed and ground with need in shameless response.

Her breath sobbed when he raised his mouth enough to lick along the cushiony softness he'd made of her lush lips, to tease and tantalise their moist arousal with his tongue as if he couldn't get enough of her. Then it was his turn to groan as she darted her tongue inside his mouth, to chase and tease and put into practice all he'd just taught her.

Now wouldn't he be surprised if he knew I was only as adept in the amorous arts as he's just shown me how to be? she mocked herself silently.

He was a drunkard, a hardened cynic, and now she could add accomplished seducer of women to the slate against him. And he thought her barely one step away from a doxy touting for custom in the Haymarket. Even under the addictive spell of his kiss, Louisa managed to sigh. To him she was a willing mouth and an eager body and suddenly that was insulting everything there should be between lovers. If she were what he thought, she'd still have a heart and soul, however broken and damaged, and she wanted to be more than a reluctant itch to be scratched then added to a list of women he'd taken, then all but forgotten. He was more than that as well, for all he looked as if he didn't care to be.

There was a depth of sadness under all that to hell-with-you manner, what suddenly seemed almost a wasteland of loss behind his cynical self-mockery. If letting him take her to their mutual satisfaction meant no more than a quick tumble in the hay, then she couldn't do it even to evade a legion of Charltons. *No*, a mocking internal voice said, *because you want too much from this conundrum of a man for that, don't you, Louisa?*

The question taunted her as his large hands cupped her shamefully aroused breasts and threatened to incinerate other wants with the sheer sensual need for more. Her eager nipples pebbled under the wicked stimulation of his suddenly very sensitive fingers and she felt as if she might burst into spontaneous flames. Temptation tore into her at the very thought of learning more, of letting him take her and render her unmarriageable between one moment and the next, but she fought it. Those who loved her might hope she wavered because of proper, belated, maidenly shrinking at the irrevocable step between virgin and woman, but that was nothing to do with it. It was because he was too embittered to wake up next to her in the morning and make the loss of her maidenhead feel right to either of them that she couldn't take that step and walk him over a precipice.

It would solve so much, but then he'd know Eloise La Rochelle was as big a lie as the brilliant and icy Miss Alstone was to the *ton*. Perhaps she was the biggest fool in London to pass on seduction by such a master of the amorous arts, but she met Captain Darke's clearing gaze and knew her instincts were right. He could be all her tomorrows and her sensual fate, or just a regretted possibility, but she wanted more than a brief but blazing seduction that would probably haunt her for a lifetime. Did she hope for protracted and lingering seductions to come, perhaps? Not marriage—to her that was as impossible as fairy dust—but she couldn't kill whatever held her back by melting into his kisses and solving one problem with an even greater one.

'I see how you hook in your prey now, Miss La Rochelle,' he said with a shake of need in his deep voice that spoilt the steeliness of his would-be taunt.

'I don't hook them, as you so elegantly put it—they catch themselves, Captain, then I take my pick,' she lied.

'If you think to net me, then you've rarely been more wrong,' he grated out in a fine, frustrated fury.

'I'm a woman, Mr Darke, and therefore very rarely wrong at all,' she taunted him with a sidelong look at his still-heaving chest and the flush of hard colour burning on his high cheekbones. She wriggled her hips and boldly abraded his impressive manhood with her lithe body to prove it.

'In this instance you're so glaringly mis-taken I'm surprised you can't find the good sense to admit it,' he informed her stiffly and snapped the spell their bodies were slower to relinquish than their minds by pushing her roughly away. Turning his back on the wanton sight of her, draped against the hard edge of the kitchen table, he groaned in unmistakable self-disgust.

Louisa stayed where she was, mainly because her legs were still shaking so much from want and shock that she doubted they'd hold her up if she tried to move. 'Yet you'll remember me, Captain Darke. Even if I was about to let you put me outside like a stray cat, you'd still take the fire we've just lit between us back to bed with you and burn mercilessly for me all night long, deny it as you might,' she taunted dangerously, recklessly prodding at his temper for some reason she couldn't even put into words for her own satisfaction.

Maybe part of her still wanted to goad him into seducing her until she forgot anything else. She wondered uneasily at her own folly and tried to look as if his revulsion at the very idea of ever touching her again couldn't possibly hurt her.

'I might well, but why draw back from a promising new keeper when you seem to be without one while my youthful employer is at sea, Eloise?'

'To make you more eager, of course,' she explained, as if it was perfectly obvious to any masculine idiot who hadn't pickled his intellect in brandy.

'Just how eager do you expect your lovers to be? Is seeing me so burnt up by the lure of paradise between your finely displayed legs that I'd have promised you everything I have, short of a soul I long ago sold to the devil, not desperate enough for you?'

'Obviously not,' she parried, doing her best not to blush at the thought of what they would probably be doing right now if she hadn't drawn back.

She imagined they'd somehow be striving for a fulfilment her body ached for with a merciless, hard knot of frustration at the centre of her that felt as if it might never relax on being denied what was natural and right between lovers. 'Lovers'—that was the key. It was what they didn't have—not one sliver of love flowed between them, so none of it would be right, however hot and needy they were for each other. Although she would never marry, she wouldn't let herself fully love a man outside it unless she really did love him. That seemed about as unlikely as Captain Darke falling at her feet and swearing undying, unswerving devotion to a woman he despised, for all he claimed to want her so hotly.

'What else *do* you expect of a man, then, if that's not enough?' he asked.

'Affection,' she told him rather forlornly, knowing she'd probably never gain it from this guarded, isolated man. 'And a little respect.'

'Very hard qualities for a female in your profession to find, I would have thought,' he mocked her almost angrily, as if no woman had a right to demand so much of a man she was thinking of taking to her bed, always supposing they managed to get that far.

'Hard ones to seek anywhere, Captain Darke, let alone on the streets,' she said, with what she knew would look like too much knowledge in her dark-blue eyes as she met his hard gaze.

'Aye, I'll grant you that much bravery, or should that be impudence rather?' he said reluctantly and she didn't know whether to feel smug or guilty.

She reminded herself he was so drunk she could probably have pushed him over with one hand when he first staggered across the open door of that bedchamber and made her jump nigh out of her skin. If she'd pushed him away hard enough at any time during this surreal encounter, he would very likely have fallen in a heap and gone back to sleep as sweetly as Kit's watchman, and nothing they'd done in the last half-hour had caused a stutter in Coste's impressive snoring. The world ticked on and she and Captain Darke ticked with it and suddenly it felt as if their bittersweet interlude had been little more than a wicked daydream. She put a hand out as if to grasp it, but a picture of him ardent and wholeheartedly wanting her with every sense evaporated under her touch. Such fantasies weren't for the likes of them; she knew too much and he'd learnt too much for that sweet pipe dream to ever come true.

'I'd curtsy to acknowledge your extraordinary graciousness,' she told him in the hard, cynical voice she thought Eloise would use to protect herself from her enemies, 'but somehow I've forgotten to be suitably servile these last few years.'

'Aye, it's easy to grow accustomed to luxury and money. Harder than I hope you'll ever know to manage without them when they've become such a part of your life you can't imagine losing everything,' he said and she wasn't fool enough to think he was worrying about her future.

'I started out with nothing more than the clothes I stood up in, Captain, but you fell a lot further, I think?'

'You may think what you wish, but don't expect me to confirm or deny your fantasies,' he told her abruptly, the story of his sorry downfall obviously forbidden ground.

'I can pick out the nob in a crowd any day of the week, so don't try to pretend you're not one, Captain.'

'Then be content with being right and leave it at that, my dear.'

'Again, I'm not dear to you in any way, Captain Darke. Let's stick to the truth as often as we may.'

'And if that's as often as usual, it won't be heard much.'

She shrugged and reminded herself how little she wanted him to know her true self, even if she would dearly love to know his. 'So be it,' she said carelessly.

'Not much point in me asking what you're really doing here then, I suppose?'

'Not much,' she confirmed with a nonchalance she hoped masked her shudder at the thought of what she'd escaped tonight—and how she'd done it.

'Well, I suppose we're done with each other for now then, at least until morning.'

'Yes, I really suppose that we must be, Captain.'

'For good, if I had my way, Miss La Rochelle,' he informed her gruffly enough for her to know he still wanted her and bitterly resented her for it.

'Now your way would be downright boring and I make it a rule never to be so tedious that gentlemen of my acquaintance truly prefer my room to my company,' she fantasised cheerfully.

Perhaps from now on she would be herself, as she'd seldom dared to be while she had tried to move amongst his true kind as if she belonged—and blatantly did not. Whatever it cost her to be the girl who'd belonged nowhere in particular once again, that girl was who she was. And to be that person she had to sleep. At least she'd be safe from the predators who stalked the night-time streets, so until it was too early for Charlton and his ilk to be abroad, she could allow herself the luxury of sleep and hope she'd have resolve enough to take up her new life come morning.

She took the candles he carefully didn't offer her and lit a new one off them, after fetching some from Kit's dusty and unused drawing room, handing the guttering ones back to him and giving him a significant look she recalled her mother darting at her when she wanted her to go to bed and saw no reason to tell such a grown-up girl to actually go there. By saving herself the fact and almost the feel of his all-too masculine gaze on her nether regions, outrageously outlined as they were by Charlton's breeches, she had to watch his lithely masculine legs, narrow hips and lean body as he effortlessly scaled the stairs ahead of her instead.

She decided she was turning into some sort of female satyr and felt herself flush at the wicked thoughts the sight of his muscular form roused in her rebellious body. Tonight she'd felt powerfully male limbs so intimately against her own and not even wanted to flinch away; she'd known the astonishing novelty of actually yearning for the thrust and rhythm of that very particular man deep inside her, to show her what no words could ever tell her about the wild, sweet potential of it all. Never mind her unwanted success among the polite world, tonight she'd gone from schoolgirl to woman and never mind the physical fact of her virginity, still exactly as it had always been.

Tonight Captain Darke had taught her to truly want; even now part of her did so as she undressed in Kit's second-best spare bedchamber, did her best to perform a brief *toilette*, then blew out her candle and slid between cool linen sheets. She shifted in protest against that unfulfilled need as she stretched luxuriously on the feather mattress and decided her terrifying climb to freedom had been worth every precarious step. Tonight she'd found out exactly why Charlton Hawberry wouldn't do as her husband, even if she wanted one. Now all she had to do was find out the Captain's quirks and qualities if she was to take him to her bed and maybe even her heart. That thought sobered her, as she considered the impossibility of Captain Darke ever returning so huge and compelling an emotion as love, even if she had no more desire to be trapped into marriage than he did.

Could any woman reach the last traces of gentleness and vulnerability that must still exist under all that armour of indifference and cynicism, or why would that armour need to be so strong? A colder, less ardent soul than the one he'd sought to bury under layers of pack-ice, or drown in a brandy bottle, would survive without the embittered shell Captain Darke had grown to survive, but could she get inside it if all she found out when she got there was how much he refused to trust his emotions? And how on earth would she ever persuade him she was worthy of his trust if he found out when he took her to his bed that Eloise La Rochelle was as big a lie as hard, embittered and dangerous Captain Darke?

Hugh woke reluctantly and groped for his pocket watch even as he bit back a loud moan at the brightness of a new spring day and the lying promise of a London sky washed clean of all its sins, until it besmirched itself again with the smoke and stink of a great city. He might be less cynical about the day, he supposed, if the sharp sunlight wasn't falling across his eyes unveiled by shutters or curtains, just as he'd so often fooled himself he liked it. Might be, but he doubted it, as full memory of the night before kicked in again and another shot of agony tore across his aching forehead at the very thought of Miss Eloise La Rochelle, who was very likely waiting to torture him over the breakfast table at this very moment. If she could find it under all the detritus he and Coste had deposited there, of course.

Rubbing an exploring hand over his villainously rough chin, he winced at the idea of having kissed even that intrusive and annoying gadfly of a woman in such an ungentlemanly state, even though he'd been drunk and driven by some unholy need he still couldn't fully comprehend by the light of day. She might not be a lady, might not have been accustomed to respect and good manners from her seducers before she encountered his friend Kit and decided to hang on to him with both hands, but Hugh had once been a gentleman so it was a matter of honour not to harm a woman of any stamp. He should have taken a second shave of the day to insure that he didn't hurt her soft skin, if only he'd known he'd be kissing such a wanton siren last night. 'Failed again, Hugh,' he scolded himself cynically. 'Proved yourself a rogue once more, as per expectations.'

Not bothering to even make the effort to cling to well-bred restraint in the face of so many failures, he hauled himself out of bed and gave vent to a heartfelt groan as his own heartbeat pounded fists of pain into his suffering brain at the sudden movement. Reaching blindly for the water jug, he gulped a lukewarm draught directly from it and groaned as he waited for the thundering in his ears to abate and the pain in his temples to dull to a bearable throb, then splashed water on to his face to try to relieve the ache behind his eyes.

'Damned petticoat-led idiot,' he castigated himself as he glared at his bleary-eyed reflection in the fine mirror his friend had furnished this guest bedchamber with, as he dried his face on the fine towel provided for more appreciative visitors than he was proving to be. 'And just what would you think of me if you could see me right now, my friend?' he speculated as he contemplated Kit Stone's outspoken disgust at the spectre he'd made of himself.

And that was before Kit could even begin on the subject of kept women and which of them was keeping her. Hugh shook his head, despite the fierce clash of pain it cause, frowned fiercely at his reflection, then realised he didn't even want to meet his own eyes in the mirror any more, let alone imagine holding his friend's dark and yet somehow steely gaze when he finally came home and took back his empire and his woman from such faulty hands as Hugh Darke's had proved to be.

'Abel Coste! Where the devil are you?' he

went to the door and bellowed, in the hope his drinking companion of last night was in a better state of preservation than he was himself this morning, which would hardly be difficult, given that he felt as if he'd been trampled half to death by a herd of wild horses.

'Whatever is it?' his unwelcome visitor demanded impatiently from below.

'I want Coste,' he snapped back.

'Well, you can't have him, he's busy.'

'Since you certainly don't need a shave, I can't imagine how,' he mumbled disagreeably, but she obviously possessed hearing a cat would have been proud of.

'And if you were planning to let him shave you, then you must be even more addled than I thought, considering the sorry state he's in this morning,' she told him, as if she was some sort of stern maiden aunt rather than a brazen hussy.

She was still looking like a barbarian princess in her ill-fitting breeches and that ridiculous black shirt, her silken mass of dark chestnut hair falling down her back like a promise of all kinds of sensual delights. He knew she was no better than she should be, yet she made him ache to feel the luxurious wonder of her against his naked skin while he played idly with that wanton hair as they lay, momentarily sated, in each other's arms. The last thing he needed was this burning desire to make her scream with desire and passion such as she'd never known before, and now he came to think about it, a mild shout of satisfaction might well blast the top of his head off and do permanent damage to his feeble brain just now.

Damnation take it, he shouldn't even think of her *in extremis* like that. Not only was he in no state to pleasure even the most undemanding of houris, but he was also an ungrateful bastard who suddenly really wanted to at least try to drive her wild with mutual lust and see if such exquisite gratification could cure his hangover.

How could he even think of turning on the man who'd rescued him when everyone else had left him to rot in the gutter by trying to steal his woman? He'd better convince his baser self he didn't want the confounded woman as a matter of urgency, then at least he'd be ready to conduct Kit's business for the day instead of standing here fantasising about seducing his mistress.

'I wasn't planning on letting Abel or anyone else near my throat with a razor,' he drawled in a deliberate echo of the insufferably cocky aristocrat he'd once been, 'but to shave myself properly I need hot water and Coste is much better at lighting the range than I am.'

'You must be atrocious at it then, since he made such a sad business out of it with all his moaning and groaning and constant "oh deary, deary me, but I don't feel at all well," that I found it a good deal quicker to deal with it myself,' Miss La Rochelle told him so disapprovingly he was reminded of his sister's steely-backboned governess in a particularly formidable frame of mind. He made the mistake of grinning over an image of his gadfly in breeches, instructing the daughters of the nobility in good manners and proper behaviour. 'It wasn't in the least bit funny to be expected to light your confounded fires for you as well as sober up the only help you seem to have left in the house in order to get some breakfast,' she snapped.

She then subjected him to a hostile glare that should reduce him to abject penitence. Wise enough to know it would be counterproductive to tell her that her ire was a boon rather than a bane to his aching head, he kept a grin from his lips with a mighty effort and did his best to look crushed. In his experience, the only way to deal with a female on the rampage was to agree with whatever she said and go his own way when her back was turned.

'Of course not,' he agreed. 'It's probably a disgrace as well—did you forget to tell me that or have my aching ears left out some listening?'

'Men have a very peculiar sense of the ridiculous,' she informed him with regal contempt, obviously not inclined to gratify him by rising to his baiting.

'And most women don't have one at all,' he let slip, then corrected himself. 'Except for the odd honourable exception, of course,' he told her with a would-be placating smile that must have come out as a mocking grin since she glared at him, before marching back to the domestic regions. He didn't even have time to muse on feminine unpredictability before she was back with a steaming jug.

'Here's your hot water and don't scald yourself,' she ordered him as she thrust it into his hands. 'I suggest you make yourself decent before you come downstairs, if that's not too much to ask of a man with trembling hands and a brandy-addled constitution like yours,' she told him before she rounded on her heel and strode towards the kitchen while he gazed owlishly after her.

'Managing female,' he muttered darkly to himself.

'I heard that!' she shouted back improbably and he amended her hearing up to bat-like sensitivity and resolved to tell the truth about her only when he was safely on the opposite side of London in future.

He kept trying not to smile as he shaved more deftly than he could have believed possible when he woke up this morning, and had to force a suitable blandness on to his reflected features in order not to cut himself. Usually the sight of his own face froze any inclination he might have to smile, but this morning even that didn't seem as bitter a spectacle as expected. Last night he met a ladybird in the dark and now he was grinning to himself about her like a lunatic, despite a painful state he would prefer to deny existed that ought to be beyond a man in his condition. He reminded himself he couldn't have her, even if she wanted him to, and poured his cooling shaving water with its unattractive bloom of shorn whiskers and used soap back into the can.

Hugh set the jug by the door to take downstairs once he was dressed for a morning in the City, spent attending to his employers' business affairs and grimaced at the thought of the hours of checking tallies and reviewing accounts lying ahead of him. Somehow even the thorny task ahead of him couldn't blot out the dangerous sense of anticipation he felt at tangling with the woman downstairs one last time. He even caught himself whistling, before realising she would hear him. Eyeing himself—cravat decently tied and stockings and knee-breeches unwrinkled—he shrugged into a very sober waistcoat and gave himself a mocking bow. Today he was almost unrecognisable as the renegade captain of the *Jezebel* and resolved to avoid the haunts of the *ton* on his way to the City, lest someone recognise him even got up like a respectable cit. He shrugged off the prospect of being known for someone far less worthy, decided breakfast took precedence over old sins and let the smell of Miss La Rochelle's cooking lure him downstairs once more.

Chapter Four

'My guess is that you're a better cook than Coste or I will ever be,' Hugh observed as he strolled through the propped-open kitchen door.

'Which wouldn't be difficult, given the state of the saucepans and skillets left in the scullery,' the most unusual cook in England muttered irritably in reply.

'We never claimed to be domesticated,' he admitted with a casual shrug.

'You'd be arrested for fraud if you did.'

'Very likely, but where did you get all this?' he asked with a wave of his hand at the largesse spread over the end of the long deal table nearest to the closed stove.

Her self-imposed task had put an attractive flush of colour on her cheeks and he noted the surprisingly seductive scent of warm woman and the faint suggestion of a gloss of perspiration on her fine, creamy skin. Never having been the sort of man who preyed on his servants, he'd not subjected kitchenmaids to lecherous scrutiny in the past, but the sight of his employer's exotic mistress, dressed in her scandalous dark breeches with that absurd black shirt clinging to her all the more because of the light bloom of perspiration on her delectable body, was enough to make a monk ache with frustration, and he wasn't a monk. Wrenching his eyes from the spectacle of all he couldn't have, he made himself listen to her reply to his question through the thunder of his own blood in his ears and sought refuge behind the table until he had his body in a fit state not to betray him.

'I dragged your fellow debauchee out of his chair and pushed him under the pump until he stopped screaming like a stuck pig, then told him if he didn't find me the makings of a very hearty breakfast, I'd tell Kit what a useless excuse for a man he still is, then hope he was sent straight back to the gutter where Kit found him,' she explained, mercifully all without turning round to turn those shrewd dark eyes of hers on yet another faulty male.

Yet Hugh doubted she'd carry out her threat against his brother-in-iniquity; her shoulders were hunched against his scrutiny, but her very defensiveness argued against her. 'Where's Coste hiding himself now, then?' he asked, as he dared to come out from behind his barricade and pick up a slice of just-crisp-enough bacon from the stack keeping warm on the side of the hob.

'He's probably still trying to find a couple of scrubbing women willing to muck out the pigsty you two have made out of this room and the scullery, and another couple to dust and make good the rooms you haven't yet got around to spoiling. He insisted that he wasn't ready to eat yet,' she said gruffly.

'He won't know where to start.'

'I told him where to find a reliable domestic agency and sent a note along with him for the manageress setting out my requirements,' she said, turning about at last to sharply forbid him to take one more bite until it was all ready, otherwise mercifully keeping her eyes on what she was doing rather than on him. His more-obvious state of arousal had mercifully subsided, but it was his body and he knew very well it was only waiting for the flimsiest excuse to lust after hers once more.

'I expected I'd have to force you into eating anything this morning,' she said with an ambiguous twist of the lips that might have been a smile and something told him she'd been looking forward to it.

'Sorry to disappoint you, Miss La Rochelle, but I have a very hard head.'

'Evidently,' she replied coldly, as if he didn't deserve such a mercy.

He strolled into the scullery to leave his used shaving water and was astonished to find that she had washed all the crockery and glassware he and Coste had left scattered about the kitchen. Such an excess of energy made him wonder if she'd slept at all and whether she had embarked on this whirlwind of activity to put whatever came next for her out of her mind for a while. What was bold, bad Eloise La Rochelle afraid of? he wondered, and why did he hate to think of her facing problems so insurmountable that they might leave her cowed and fearful instead of her usual bold and brazen self?

Given her daring method of arrival last night, she certainly wasn't naturally timid and many things that would make even a bolder-than-average female quake seemed to leave her unmoved. So had she got herself tangled up in something dangerous as soon as Kit's back was turned and should he be making it his business to find out just what she'd been up to? He eyed the racks of dishes draining over the sink with a preoccupied frown and went back into the kitchen for his breakfast and a more sober and detached assessment of his uninvited guest than any he'd managed to make so far.

'You've been very busy indeed,' he said on returning to the kitchen.

'I don't like to be idle,' she admitted and he thought he saw a shadow darken her deep-blue eyes, then it was gone and she was glaring at him as if he might eat with his knife unless sternly watched once more.

'There seems very little risk of that,' he said and tried not to fall on the food she'd cooked like a ravening beast. 'Can I pour you coffee?' he asked, reaching for the pot at the same time as she did, flinching as what felt like a shock of lightning jagged up his arm as their fingers met fleetingly, then fell away.

He took a deep breath and stared at his hands, unaware until he saw his knuckles whiten that he'd clenched them into fists to stop himself gripping her slender fingers as if they were his lifeline. He loosened his fists and made himself glance at the bright morning outside the window, still gallantly promising something more than the usual London haze. Today he could enjoy the blessing of a fine morning, a useful occupation and a full belly—what more could a man ask of life? Sighing at the thought of all he *could* ask for, but no longer dared risk wanting, he turned back to watch her with raised eyebrows and a cynical half-smile.

'I am perfectly capable of lifting a coffee pot for myself, thank you,' she said sharply and he wondered if she'd been as disturbed by that startling bolt of connection between them as he had.

'I don't doubt it, after viewing the evidence of your industry,' he said mildly and ate his way through a delicious meal as the headache he knew very well he richly deserved began to drum at his temples once more.

It was probably caused by the tension of wanting her so urgently, but not being able to have her, he assured himself. An old familiar and purely physical burn that, as a captain used to months without female company, he knew all too well and had learnt to endure. This time, however, he somehow doubted that reading Shakespeare or studying his charts and plotting a series of possible courses to fanciful places would distract him from it, but at least experience had taught him that the sharpness of it would dull if he could find a sufficiently absorbing occupation. Yet could any distraction blot Eloise La Rochelle from a man's mind for very long?

'Thank you,' she said unexpectedly and sat and sipped her fragrant brew with what he guessed was feminine satisfaction in producing something edible when two supposedly strong men had been unable to do so between them. 'It's good to be busy once more,' she added and he wondered if a life of silken idleness had palled on such an unusual Cyprian.

'I'd be an ingrate if I failed to appreciate the fruits of your labour, even so,' he said as he laid down his knife and fork to pour coffee and add sugar to it.

'Should I pass you the cream?' she asked.

'No, thank you, I became used to going without it on board ship.'

'Don't most captains take a cow with them on long voyages?' she asked and he wondered if she'd studied the life of a sea captain because her lover often lived that life without her. The shock of pure venomous jealousy at the very idea of her pining for her lover brought him up short and made him glare at his own hand stirring his coffee as if it had mortally offended him.

'Sometimes there isn't enough room for luxuries,' he managed fairly normally.

'Oh, yes, merchantmen are carefully designed to make use of every available inch of space for cargo, are they not?' she replied, setting off that demon of envy in him once more and making him even more silently furious with himself.

'Men-of-war are just as niggardly with every spare inch they can gain, having a goodly quantity of ammunition and unstable gunpowder to stow, as well as a vastly greater crew to accommodate,' he explained.

'It must be strange for you to go to sea as captain of a merchantman after commanding in the Royal Navy,' she mused, blasting his attempt at replacing the general with the personal out of the water. He sighed as he lay back in his chair to sip his coffee and met her eyes warily.

'I never said I'd been a navy man,' he argued, almost groaning aloud at the defensiveness in his voice. It was still a wound he hated to have probed, which seemed foolish in the extreme compared to everything else he'd lost.

'How else to account for the naval officer's sword in the larder, I wonder?' she said with a pretence at scratching her head. 'Was Coste a dashing captain at Trafalgar, I wonder? Or perhaps he's really an admiral on half-pay, when not pretending to be Kit's hall porter and supposed watchman? No, I think the sword must be yours, Captain. I doubt Coste rose above able seaman in his entire career at sea and neither Kit nor Ben have served in the Royal Navy.'

'It's not so very different,' he admitted because it was easier than arguing. 'The sea can only be read or even guessed at by good navigation and a weather eye on her contrary moods. It's still my job to decide if it's wiser to sail before the wind or ride out a storm in safe anchorage. And at least I have a sound, fast ship that isn't an easy target for any enterprising French frigate captain, eager to build a fine and romantic reputation as a triumphant sea wolf.'

'And did you once roam the seas looking for such prey yourself?'

'Of course, that's what the Admiralty expects of flag officers not on blockade.'

'And were you good at it?'

'Naval captains must prove worthy of their

rank if they expect to stay at sea,' he said carefully.

'And some do so more easily than others, I dare say,' she said blandly, so why didn't he trust her smile?

'Perhaps,' he replied tersely.

'And you were one of them,' she said and he cursed himself for giving her a clue if she ever wanted to track him down.

At least the Admiralty hadn't ordered the breaking of the sword now resting in Kit's larder, or his speedy expulsion from the Service. He almost wished they had, so it couldn't follow him like a symbol of all he no longer was, but couldn't quite discard.

'Don't bother visiting the Admiralty to find out how and when they lost or mislaid one of their junior officers, will you? Their lordships don't encourage idle curiosity.'

'Who says it would be idle? And you're very defensive about a career you pretend not to care a fig for, Captain Darke,' she said shrewdly.

'Perhaps I hate having my life picked over for the amusement of others?'

'And I don't have time or inclination for idle gossip, Captain Darke.'

'Then you must be the most unusual female I have ever met.'

'Please don't think me artless enough to mistake that for a compliment,' she countered smoothly, yet he felt he'd annoyed her by lumping her with the more curious of her kind and tried to be glad of it.

'I don't think you in the least bit artless, I assure you, Miss La Rochelle,' he said with a cynical almost-smile she didn't bother to return.

'Clearly,' she told him, but he thought he saw a shadow of pain in her blue eyes before she gathered up their dirty crockery and bore it off to the scullery.

'You hardly need to be with so many charms already in your armoury,' he explained clumsily—why must he follow her into that utilitarian room when she'd given him an ideal escape route?

'Look what you've made me do now,' she chided fiercely as she jumped on finding him so close to her, splashed herself, then swatted angrily at the large wet patch plastering her dusky shirt to her torso with a glass cloth.

He did just what she asked and the cool scullery was suddenly close and stuffy as his gaze lingered on wet dark linen, clinging emphatically to wet woman and almost as closely plastered to her fine breasts and tightly furled nipples as he'd like to be himself. Hard and fierce and instantly emphatic, his painful erection would have informed him he wanted her any way he could get her, even if his hungry eyes weren't busy devouring her like a lover. Want flared hot and heady between them again, but on its heels came a dark memory of his younger self, home from the sea and pitifully eager for the woman he thought was his. At least his wife's betrayal had armoured him against mistaking lust for anything else. He assured himself that his annoying reaction to Eloise La Rochelle, or whatever she cared to call herself, was a physical thing he'd learn to ignore and nothing deeper.

'I wish you good day and expect you to be gone by the time I get home, madam,' he informed her stiffly and turned to pick up his coat from the chair he'd flung it on to earlier, shrugging into it as he cravenly bolted for the front door and freedom from wanting what he couldn't have.

At least it should have been freedom, except he had to halt stock-still on Kit's doorstep to breathe deeply and steadily as he thought hard about desolate arctic waters and relentless storms at sea. At last he was respectable enough to proceed through this confoundedly civilised neighbourhood without his very obvious need for Miss Eloise La Rochelle and her magnificent body instantly causing a scandal.

Not just her body either, he couldn't help but recall as he marched rather blindly along the wide streets to his destination. She had that acute, questing mind and an unexpected sense of humour to render her almost irresistible as well. He let himself consider the unique charms of such a contrary, intriguing woman for a moment and would have been horrified to know an unguarded smile quirked his mouth as he did so. Most of the time she was as knowing as any street urchin, full of self-reliance and used to hardship almost from birth, then she'd astonish him with an eager enthusiasm for life and suddenly seem as coltish as any *ingénue*. No, he assured himself, he was long past being a fit companion for any sort of innocent, even if it was Eloise the buccaneer. Once again, he fought his overactive imagination as he pictured her in that black shirt aiming a pirate ship at his sturdy merchantman, and discovered how much he'd relish capturing and taming such an unlikely opponent when she failed to overrun him.

'Idiot,' he chided himself as he nearly walked into a lamppost. A little restored to his usual stern self, he strolled towards Stone & Shaw's offices in the City, but was still too preoccupied with his eventful evening, sore head and unwanted visitor to sense that he was being followed.

Louisa paused when he did and wondered why she'd impulsively stuffed her cap on her head and shrugged into Coste's overlarge jacket, then ventured out in broad daylight to see where rude and disobliging Captain Darke was bound. She watched her own reflection in a shuttered window and tucked a giveaway strand of hair under the hatband of the silly hat she'd stolen last night. At least Charlton could live without his very odd suit of clothes, but she promised herself she'd replace Coste's jacket if she damaged it, then all her senses suddenly sharpened as she considered a wiry young tough who seemed as intent on staying on Captain Darke's tail as she was herself.

He was good, she grudgingly admitted that much to herself as she lurked in a doorway and eyed the innocuous-looking youth pretending to watch a street vendor chase off a starving little would-be pickpocket. Luckily she'd trained herself to be even better once upon a time and felt her old skills return as she fell into step behind both the Captain and his follower and neither of them even had a suspicion she was there. Spying a fancy footman, she was grateful Kit didn't insist on Coste going about in some fanciful livery, though, for she'd certainly attract attention if she'd been forced to steal a *chapeau-bras* and gold-laced blue jacket. She slouched towards the unfortunate dressed so ostentatiously and he gave her a pained snarl and shuffled his feet self-consciously, obviously believing her another annoying idler, silently jeering his ridiculous uniform.

Grinning at this confirmation that she looked nothing like fashionable Miss Alstone, or even Miss Eloise La Rochelle, Louisa swaggered a little in her disreputable breeches and worn and ill-fitting coat and pretended to be absorbed in the noise and bustle of Cheapside as follower and followed moved onwards. Hands in her pockets, she sauntered along at a distance from Captain Darke and his shadow, keeping enough space between herself and them to look as if she was aimlessly passing the time until more promising mischief offered.

She mused on the quality of the Captain's enemies and decided the boy was very good, and at the next crossroads she cast a disguised gaze about her to see if she was being followed in her turn. All was clear and as innocent as London streets ever were, so Hugh Darke's foes weren't that canny. Suddenly she wished more fervently than usual that her big brother would come home. Kit would soon find out who was so interested in his infamous captain and she suddenly felt inadequate for this suddenly very serious task, as well as uncertain why it seemed so vitally important that Hugh Darke should not be hurt by his enemies.

She'd followed him on impulse, unable to think of another way to fill in her time until Kit came back without sitting tamely in his kitchen, waiting for Charlton or her uncle to come and march her up the aisle. Now her impulse had changed from a way of idling away the day into a quest to protect the ungallant Captain's back. She wove a cautious track over to the other side of the street and blessed Hugh Darke for being tall enough to stand a little above the crowd and show her the way, even if he was several inches shy of her brother's lofty height and Ben Shaw must tower over him like a giant, as he did over everyone else she had ever come across outside a fairground sideshow.

Now Hugh Darke was entering the quieter street where her brother and Ben had their offices and she had to walk past it and head down an ally to avoid being too noticeable to him or his pursuer. Anxious all of a sudden that the young tough would use the sparseness of the area to attack Hugh, she sped to the end of her alley and out into the opposite end of the street, only to skid to a halt and have to duck into a handy doorway to avoid the non-descript lad coming the other way, obviously off to report to someone that the target was safe in his office now and beyond following. Wondering even more at such an odd sequence of events, she leaned back against the heavily made door at her back and decided she must follow the young thug, rather than do as instinct demanded and stay to make sure Hugh Darke was safe if he ventured abroad again. Doubtless someone else would keep watch over Kit's offices for the next few hours, but for now she might get a clue about who was behind all this if she could track the young bully to his lair or his current employer.

At the end of the chase she was very glad Kit and Ben weren't in London after all, for they would surely have had fits if they knew where she'd been today. First of all to the cheapest of pie shops the City rejoiced in, where she managed to loiter and look hungry as well as penniless until chased off by the infuriated owner with a fearsome ladle. Then the boy sauntered through the noisome rookery she knew from her youth was the haunt of thieves and pimps of the worst sort; even high on the rooftops as she'd had to go to follow him there, she had to tread as if on pins to avoid discovery.

The houses might be rotten as a blown pear, but they were full of people forced into degradation and misery and every room and attic seemed to heave with human souls even at this time of day. That was what she'd conveniently forgotten from her childhood spent with one foot in the underworld and the other in an almost respectable street on the edge of Mayfair: the stench and misery and hopelessness of poverty. It seemed criminal to her that anyone should be expected to actually live in such cramped, dank and stinking conditions, so close to one of the richest capital cities the world had ever seen. She ghosted across closely packed rooftops, jumped at leaning chimneys and soot-grimed walkways even the inhabitants appeared to have forgotten about and wondered at herself for ever being discontent with the well-fed and secure-seeming life she'd lived since she left all this behind.

Reminding herself she wasn't here to redeem her blemished soul, she followed the boy as he finally quit his native streets and again they were into quieter, wealthier areas and she wondered whether it might be better to come down from her unlikely perch and risk the broader streets with her now-sooty clothes and grimy hands and face making her remarkable in such a place. The apprentice tough ended the chase he didn't know he was involved in at a quietly respectable church, of all unlikely places. Louisa paused and watched with bafflement as the rough youth from the slums removed his apology for a hat and bowed his head, as he entered the church by a side door as humbly as if he really had come to seek salvation. Could she be mistaken about him after all, then? Was he really a lost soul in search of redemption, who just happened to have been going in the same direction as herself and the Captain this morning? Her once-honed instincts argued he was nothing so simple and she stayed to see if anyone else would come to such a sacrilegious meeting place.

Nobody went in or out until the boy came out and sauntered down the street looking singularly unrepentant. Torn between wanting to follow him and staying to watch for his confederate, Louisa tried to decide which would gain her more, then the door opened again and a soberly dressed gentleman stepped out of the church.

Something about that clerical-seeming figure below seemed wrong and she didn't know why the hairs on the back of her head rose in warning at the sight of him, but this was clearly a more important rogue than the one she now had to let go. Louisa eyed up her possible routes and hoped the man wasn't about to cross the wide square the church was set in, as she would either have to scramble across a good many rooftops to follow him, or climb down and risk being seen in the open.

Luckily he headed towards her rather than away, so they were soon in the maze of service streets and wide roads that made up the most exclusive part of the capital. Louisa's mind buzzed with possibilities as the sober figure finally entered one of the most prosperous squares through the mews behind it, then she scrambled to follow along the more generous roofs and was only just in time to see him disappear through French windows giving on to a town garden, as if he knew the house very well and could stroll in and out as he pleased. She pondered the man's position in such a household and wondered what to do next. No scruffy idler would gain access to such a house and how would she find out anything about the owner and his connections from such a humble position even if she did?

Marking the house on her internal map for future reference, she waited until a genteel bustle of activity made her realise it was the fashionable hour for visiting and any trail the man had left was about to be wiped out. He could have left in any of those coaches in whatever guise he usually wore, he might be someone she'd met at a ball or some soirée he couldn't manage to escape, she could even have danced with him in her other life. Horrified by the idea of being so close to a man who clearly wished Hugh Darke no good, she finally left very cautiously indeed and travelled a few streets at her lofty level before descending. She could find out nothing more just now, so she headed for a dealer in second-hand clothing that she knew from experience was the least likely to leave her scratching and cursing at someone else's parasites when she wore their wares.

By mid-afternoon Hugh had ploughed through his mathematical duties and was secretly relieved to get an urgent summons to the enclosed dock his youthful employers were having built to cut down on the organised pilfering of their cargoes. Hugh frowned as he pondered that pilfering and told himself it was normal, all owners suffered from the problem, which was why the East India Company had already built a closed dock and were probably planning more. Like Kit, he thought there was something more than chance behind their own heavy losses. It was all of a piece with the loss of one of his ships and the murder of its crew not already corrupted by whoever organised the infamous scheme a couple of years ago.

It had taken a deal of hard work and scrupulously fair accounting to repair the damage to their reputation and persuade Lloyds that Stone & Shaw were not behind the fraud. Rumours that the *Mirabelle* had not gone down after all, but was sailing under another name with an entirely different crew, had horrified her young owners and sent Kit on a quest to discover the truth and Hugh knew his friend wouldn't give up until he had every detail of the infamous scheme at his fingertips. Having an implacable yet invisible enemy of his own, Hugh knew how that constant but intangible malice ate away at a man's soul. At least he knew his foe was probably one of his late wife's legion of lovers, determined to make him pay for the unresolved crime that ended her life, but Hugh couldn't solve it and prove he wasn't a wife killer, so it had seemed better to take a captaincy from Stone & Shaw and stay out of the idiot's way rather than fight for his good name—a lost cause if ever there was one.

Chapter Five

Hugh frowned blackly out of the window of the hackney he'd summoned to get to Stone & Shaw's dock as fast as he could and wondered at the elaborate route the jarvey was taking. About to tap on the roof and inform the driver he wasn't the flat he probably looked today, he jolted in his seat as the hackney veered abruptly and threw him forwards with a jarring thud. Hugh was still rubbing his bruised temple and trying to reassemble his dignity when the door was thrust open and a familiar voice demanded he get down immediately and follow her.

'Why the devil should I?' he snapped back crossly.

'Because it's all a sham and you're being

kidnapped,' Eloise informed him shortly, tugging ineffectually at his sleeve. 'Please, believe me. I'm not sure how much longer my diversion will hold up,' she added desperately and he believed her, despite all her secrets and lies.

'I'll come, but only because this is the most unlikely route to my destination.'

'Good of you, now hurry up,' she urged impatiently.

Hugh took a swift glance about him and suppressed a grin as he took in the quality of her helpers. A one-legged sailor was sitting in the road, scrabbling for his wooden leg and loudly bemoaning the losses from his spilled apple cart in terms that must make even the assembled urchins blush, while an old woman berated him for a drunken and careless old fool. The urchins were wriggling about under the cab for the fallen and bruised apples and tangling up the traces as they darted nimbly out of the way of the jarvey's whiplash whenever he tried to fend off the sea of bodies suddenly surrounding his battered vehicle.

'Hurry,' Eloise urged and he gave her a long, distrustful look before deciding she'd gone to such a deal of trouble to get him out of that cab, he might as well humour her, if only to find out exactly what she was up to.

This time she was dressed in layer upon layer of disreputable clothes like a rag-picker's daughter, carrying as many of his wares as she could on her own back. It certainly hid her fine figure a lot better than her last disguise, he thought as he followed her into a maze of courts and alleys and had to concentrate hard to recall the way back should he need a hasty escape from her toils. Sensing his resistance, she tugged on his hand impatiently and drew him on as swiftly as she could. He could sense her apprehension through their locked hands as he felt a prickle of awareness shiver over his own skin and knew they were being watched from dark doorways and darker rooms. Unwillingly caught up in her drama, he made himself as silent and wary as he could and hoped he managed to seem the over-eager client to Eloise's part-time whore, although he wondered how such a client would know what delights lay under her false bulk.

He knew, even under all that ridiculous cover that must be making her sweat like a racehorse under her burden. Just the thought of her long, elegant legs under so many layers of hampering fabric—her dangerous allure threatened to slide under his guard once more and draw him into her net. He sweated himself now as she reached more commercial areas, full of workshops and small factories, and upped their pace as fast as she could without everyone coming out to watch them pass. It wasn't their speed that made his breath come short, it was the incendiary thought of finding a space where he could be alone with her to finally slake this feral passion for her, once and for all, that had him almost unmanned with longing. Stupid, he railed at himself—undisciplined, ill-starred and just plain stupid. She'd turned him into a lust-led fool in less than a day after haunting him waking and sleeping for three weeks before that. She always seemed to affect him as fiercely as water did baked lime and he wished he'd never laid eyes on the devious jade.

Now that they were closer to the river and among the warehouses where he was probably far more familiar with their surroundings than she was, he pulled away from her. Letting her take the lead only so he, too, could be sure they hadn't been followed, he sharpened his senses, made himself forget her as a woman as far as it was in him to do. Knowing suddenly that she was leading him to the small warehouse Kit and Ben had hired, then bought when they first set up a small business hauling coastal cargoes, he let her dart into the cover of its ancient shadow and fumble for the keys under her many layers of clothing. He opened his mouth to demand them of her, then closed it again when she hushed him and slipped the key furtively into the lock and turned it as silently as she could with both hands on the doughty iron.

Shrugging impatiently at her silent pantomime, he followed her inside and turned to help her close and relock the stout side door and inspect the gloom inside. He summoned up his captain's senses and sent them to explore that semi-darkness and came up with nothing but a cargo of finest coffee beans destined for the breakfast tables of discerning northern households, not very fresh air still haunted by sugar and spices and other exotics, a hint of mouse and worse. Even his sixth sense could find no trace of another human being, although there seemed an unacceptable quantity of non-human ones, which reinforced his opinion that Kit and Ben should demolish the venerable old building and replace it with something a lot more vermin-proof and never mind sentiment.

'Right, there's obviously nobody here, so I'll go no further into this business of yours without an explanation, madam,' he informed her grimly.

'Very well then, this morning I followed you to work.'

'You followed me?' he demanded, suddenly distrusting those finely honed senses he'd always prided himself on after all.

'I'm very good,' she boasted unrepentantly and how could he argue when he'd sensed not a single hint of her behind him? 'But so was the other person tailing you through the City this morning,' she added; this time he wondered if he had any senses left to him to have missed two of them trailing after him like a procession.

'The other person?'

'I used to know a parrot just like you, Captain,' she mocked him, but must have seen the warning glint in his eyes, because she suddenly looked as serious as anyone could wish, especially a beleaguered and apparently rather simple sea captain. 'He was a well-trained follower and belongs to a villainous crew.'

'And how can I trust you to recognise such a man?'

'You just can,' she assured him and met his

eyes unflinchingly, despite the dusty gloom thickening as daylight began to seep away from such dark places early.

'But can I also be sure of your motives, Miss La Rochelle, since you seem a little over-familiar with the workings of the London underworld?'

'You can,' she insisted steadily.

'For some extraordinary reason, I believe you.'

'Why, thank you, I'm suitably flattered, of course.'

'So you should be,' he told her dourly.

'Never mind all that now, we're in the devil of a jam and have to find the best way out of it.'

'I only have your word for that, so how do you conclude I'm in a pickle just because a man followed me to Stone & Shaw's offices in the City?'

'I followed him afterwards to a fashionable church where he met a supposedly clerical gentleman.'

'Which is odd, I admit, but perhaps the man is struggling for his lost soul.'

'And perhaps he's also raising flying pigs, because when they parted I followed the respectable cleric to a mansion in Mayfair and waited for over an hour before I got down off my perch to try to find out why he went into that house and departed arrayed in the height of fashion among his own kind.'

'Not a son of the church after all, then?' he asked whimsically, but his brain was whirling with ideas as he went over all the possibilities her story presented.

'Very far from it,' she said disapprovingly.

'You knew him, didn't you?' he suddenly realised, marvelling at her acquaintance with such fine gentlemen and instantly rigidly jealous of a man who could be a former protector of hers.

'Only later, when I realised whose house it actually was. I can't believe how convincing his disguise was, especially when he always seemed such an empty-headed fool when I met him at—'

She stopped, blank-faced and wary, as she bit back whatever it was she was going to say next. What a damned fool *he* was, he decided dazedly as he forced himself to assess Eloise La Rochelle anew. Her faultlessly unaccented accent, her unconscious elegance and that air she had of being a princess let out of her castle for a holiday and only pretending to be a female buccaneer, or even Eloise La Rochelle herself. An appalling suspicion crept into his obviously rather slow mind and he eyed her annoyingly calm countenance through the thickening darkness with hot fury clawing at his gut.

'You met him in polite society, did you not?' he asked coldly.

'How can you even think such a thing?' Louisa blustered, but ground to a halt as she met his steady, condemning gaze and decided the game was up. 'Yes,' she agreed stoically, trying hard to pretend having her clever disguise penetrated at exactly the wrong moment didn't matter in the least.

'Then you really are slumming it?' he asked stiffly.

'No, I'm looking for something real,' she told him in a raw voice that threatened to tug at his heartstrings, so Hugh hardened his heart against her and made himself re-examine the information he had about her and reach another startling conclusion.

'Say something unreal rather, Miss Alstone,' he said stiffly, trying to be cool and logical, yet struggling with hot humiliation, and a disappointment he refused to examine at the thought of her laughing up her sleeve at him. She'd deceived him every step of her way last night and again this morning. 'As far as I cared for anything or anyone in polite society, I gave Christopher Alstone's little sister the benefit of the doubt when I heard that you'd been named the Ice Diamond by the wags, my dear, but at least now I know how richly you must have deserved that nickname and can learn to pity your victims instead.'

'You never gave any fashionable female a second chance in your life,' she scoffed. How could he have not seen the haughty minx for what she was the instant she eyed him like an offended queen across Kit's office that first day?

'Now there you're more wrong than you'll ever know,' he said grimly, thinking of all the times he'd believed Ariadne, when only an idiot would take his wife's interpretation over the plain facts. 'I'm cured of it though, Miss Alstone, and if you made up this shameful tarradiddle for your own perverse amusement then I'll see you publically exposed and pilloried for it as you deserve to be.'

'I should have left you to your enemies, but oddly enough my sense of fairness wouldn't let me leave you to take your chance against such overwhelming odds. I'm rapidly changing my mind, needless to say,' she said, her face such a mask of polite indifference he couldn't read what lay behind it, and how he hated the mass of contradictions gnawing away at *his* supposedly stern composure.

'Good, I certainly need no help from the likes of you,' he snapped.

'You don't even know me.'

'I know enough.'

Hugh watched her lining up glib arguments to defend herself with and held up his hand to stop her. With his foul luck, and worse judgement, she'd be as convincing at it as his late wife had been. Ariadne had believed her own lies so steadfastly by the time she told them that she'd cheerfully swear to them, even when all the facts proved her wrong. Yet now she was dead and he was branded a murderer in all but proof. Dark grief, fury and shame threatened to swallow him up in the horror of that terrible crime once more, but he fought it back to hell where it belonged and hated this lying female all the more for showing him Hugo the Fool, the cuckolded husband, was still alive behind Hugh Darke's cynical disguise.

'I know you are the despair of your brother and sister, Miss Alstone,' he said coolly enough, for all that hot fury raged under his surface calm. 'Even I have heard that you lead half the otherwise sane men in polite society around by the nose with your beauty and various other perfections that elude me. It's just as well known that you don't care a snap of your fingers for a single one of them. You're a cold-hearted vixen who dismisses her suitors as if she's waiting for a prince or a king at the very least to decorate her cold brow with a crown, instead of the coronets you are apparently offered by the cartload every Season. And rather than make your long-suffering brother happy by graciously accepting one of those lords or their foolishly besotted heirs, you dance and flirt and charm them for your own idle satisfaction the one day, then give them a very cold shoulder the next.'

'My, I *am* a bad woman,' she said with deceptive mildness and Hugh realised he'd let some of his fury with Ariadne for being a liar and cheat and a lovely, dead, fool creep into his verbal attack on Kit's little sister.

'I don't care what sort of a woman you are,' he lied, 'but I'll certainly manage without your help from now on. Something tells me you'll lead me further into the maze just because you can, rather than show me the way out of it.'

'Don't you want to know who your enemy is, then?'

'How can I believe you? No doubt you have one or two inconvenient suitors littering your path to glory whom you would be very happy to rid yourself of at no cost to yourself.'

'I get worse by the moment,' she said with flippant amusement that only made him more furious with himself for being taken in by her, for believing her because he desperately wanted to, and for still wanting her so badly her refusal to accept any guilt for her actions threatened to charm rather than revolt him.

He'd fantasised about her in her lying disguise—heaven forbid he start doing so in her real one—that one day Kit and Eloise might have parted. It had gone, and he didn't even want to think about the appalling pictures that set up in his mind now he knew who she really was. One day, Eloise might have turned to him for satisfaction and seduction; only now that that was impossible did he realise how deeply she'd tangled him in her devious web. Never having Eloise in his bed to laugh with, to live with and to come home to, knowing she would expect no more from a hollowed-out creature like him, cut like a knife to the gut and he wanted to be done with her, to be hundreds of miles clear of her before the pain struck and the fury stopped hiding his hurt at yet another betrayal.

'Who is he, then?' he made himself ask distantly, thinking how much he'd once wanted to know that very thing and now it didn't seem to matter all that much.

'Now, which of my discarded lovers do I despise the most?' she mused, silently counting off on her fingers as if needing them to compile the best list.

Hugh clenched his fists against the urge to pound the old walls in a roaring frenzy because she'd used him for her own ends and he'd almost trusted her, until she proved him an idiot all over again.

'The first one to come into your head will do,' he said cynically, wondering exactly how many lovers she'd managed to draw in under the very noses of the *ton*.

'Oh, well, that would be you.'

'I'm not your lover,' he said starkly.

'Only because I chose a disguise that held you back, Captain Darke, you being a pirate of such peculiar honour as to never take his employer's moll, however much he might long to. If I hadn't hit on that particular alias, we would have been lovers by now and you know it. Imagine it—us two being lovebirds, liars, then sworn enemies together all in one day.'

'This is not a joke, madam.'

'No, you're right, it's not,' Louisa said desolately, stiffening her backbone and forcing herself to meet the hostility in his starkly austere gaze. There was no point defending herself against such revulsion, no reason to believe he'd ever change his bigoted, second-hand opinion of her. 'But it's more of a comedy than a tragedy.'

'And if only you knew how close one can be to the other, you might stop wilfully creating havoc wherever you go,' he muttered furiously, seeming to retreat into himself, to brood on something apparently even worse than wicked young ladies like herself.

'Which is rich, coming from you,' she accused and suddenly had all his attention as he glared at her with acute grey-blue eyes.

'What else do you know?' he demanded. As she flinched away from the steely purpose in his gaze and he stopped her retreat with a rough hand about her wrist, she doubted he knew it was tight as a trap on her soft skin.

'What else *could* I know, Captain?' she asked, doing her best to ice over her own eyes as efficiently as he had to stare at her as if he'd somehow scare everything she knew about him out of her by sheer force of will.

It was his gaze that fell and not hers, although she felt a sting of something she refused to analyse and blinked it back as she watched his eyes take in the tightness of his grip on her, before he unclenched his hand from her, then stepped back as if she'd stung him.

'I'm sorry,' he claimed hoarsely. 'I never meant to hurt you,'

'I expect you say that to all your women,' she responded bitterly, suddenly transported back to her childhood with a violent drunkard.

'Never,' he husked and despair and bitterness and something that might even be grief haunted his silver-shot eyes and that hard, dare-not-be tender mouth of his.

'Whatever have they done to you?' she whispered as she watched him fight back something terrible and felt helpless in the face of such horror and pain, despite all he'd just said and accused her of being.

'Nothing you would understand,' he scorned, protecting himself against any hint of pity. Perhaps it was his ordinary defence against shallow sympathy and spurious curiosity, rather than the deeply personal slight it felt like for a moment.

'Oh, of course not,' she forced herself to say as carelessly as if they were discussing an obscure subject outside the selfish remit of such a vain young lady.

'Does it still hurt?' he asked huskily.

'You should know by now that Miss Alstone, the Ice Diamond, is untouched by feelings of any kind, Captain,' she lied lightly and silently dared him to take a step nearer and breach that fragile distance between them.

Ignoring her, he took that step and cradled her wrist in his large hand, the hardness and occasional roughness of his palm pulling her deeper under his sensual spell, if he did but know it, and she silently despaired of herself.

'Yet you're not as unbreakable as you pretend,' he muttered as if the words were forced from that sensual, cynical mouth, before he sank his head and kissed her slightly reddened wrist and made her knees wobble with a rush of stubborn need.

Stiffening them against the too-potent appeal of a man who hated her one moment, then soothed and seduced the next, while probably still hating her, she resisted the silly urge to raise her other hand and smooth the over-long and distinctly shaggy dark locks he wore so well into some kind of order.

'No, I'm not yet quite unbreakable, I'm sorry,' she answered with a wry smile meant to defuse the sensual tension suddenly so alive in the growing darkness scented with old cargoes and coffee beans.

'Don't be,' he counselled as if he couldn't help himself.

'It's easier,' she replied as if she understood, when all she could currently think about was the jags of heat and longing for more that were afflicting her, even as he probably despised her more deeply than ever.

'I know, but not necessarily better,' he told her with a look of untold wanting and infinite sadness, before he abandoned her hand and kissed her full on the mouth once again instead, as if he couldn't resist the temptation of it.

It was a fantasy, she told herself; cynical Louisa Alstone who didn't believe in love or marriage, or any of the comforting illusions that got her fellow young ladies through life, and angry, disillusioned Captain Hugh Darke, who didn't believe in anything much at all. It was impossible and they would tear each other to pieces. Yet it was such a sensuous, irresistible seduction of her senses that she stopped thinking and blindly took whatever he had left to give. It was so luxurious, so heated and all engrossing that it felt infinitely better than anything else she'd been offered. Moaning her agreement, she opened her mouth as demandingly as he'd already taken hers and let her tongue tangle with his, so they could take up where they left off last night. At least tonight he knew she was nobody's but his, just for now.

Acknowledging the transitory nature of anything they could be to each other, she strove to make her agreement to it even more emphatic, by letting her hands explore his strong neck muscles and up to muss his already unruly hair and run her fingers through the sensual silkiness of it. His groan of whatever it was—agreement, encouragement, or just downright approval—made her breath come short and her mouth even more desperate as he cupped her face in his strong hands and drew her closer. He shifted and the threat of losing even this harsh magic between them made her keen a protest, then ghost her hands down his neck and soothe along his throat as she silently acknowledged he'd made himself vulnerable to her in this much at least. And it was enough for her, would have to be enough.

Chapter Six

Louisa felt the mighty muscles in her ungallant captain's broad shoulders shift under her touch and it made her feel sensually powerful. To spark such an instantaneous reaction from this guarded soul made her seem very special to herself tonight. She revelled in the sense of being outside time and normal spaces, locked inside this cocoon of darkness as the spring evening closed in all round them. Then she felt the full force of the fire he'd lit in her last night streak through her and settle burning almost as bright as the sun at the centre of her being until she shook with need. Lost for words to communicate what she wanted, even if he allowed her mouth the freedom to do it, she made an incoherent sound—half-moan and half-imperious demand—and sighed her relief into his kiss as his hands sank to knead her neat *derrière* and draw her closer to his mightily aroused manhood. She did her best not to give away her awe and that furtive heat it sparked inside her at the very feel of what she did to him, but it was hard not to just sink into his arms and beg.

Typical, she managed to spare the time to think, as far as she could think with his mouth on hers and her body so fascinated by the proximity of his. *Typical that he is as deep in thrall to whatever it is driving us together, apparently against our wills, yet he still manages to hang on to his essential apartness while I must melt all over him like heated sealing wax.*

How could she want any man so much it blasted through her much-vaunted self-control and breached that cherished separateness of hers, especially this one? She sensed that the craving making her hands shake as she laid them against the warmth and masculinity and sheer nerve-singing fact of him was exerting just as strong a pull on him, if not even stronger, but he still had control enough not to moan with need or tremble with frustration and this bittersweetest longing. A curiosity burned within her to know more; one he certainly wouldn't believe she had any need of, now she'd let him think she'd managed to accrue a procession of lovers with the critical eyes of the *ton* on her, the hawk-like watch of her elder brother, even from afar, and her aunt and uncle's very critical eyes on her as they waited for a reason to denounce her and rid themselves of a charge they never wanted for aught but the money she brought with her in the first place.

The man was undoubtedly an idiot if he believed a word of that silly implication of hers. She could only suppose it was her inner demon of curiosity and the sheer sensual excitement within her that made her claim to be something she wasn't yet again and get away with it. He might hate her eventually if they went on, but he was the only man she'd ever met who made her want him mercilessly just by inhabiting the same space, whatever space, even this dark, comfortless, unlikely meeting place. A siren voice whispered that he wouldn't have been so easy to fool if he hadn't wanted to believe her and do this, so she let herself believe it for a space borrowed out of the real world. It was a chance that wouldn't come again—an interlude apart from the real Louisa and her unlikely lover. A chance she

intended to take, then afterwards she'd somehow find a way to forget it and stick to her
chosen course through life, even knowing
what she'd be missing.

In the heat of this particular moment there
seemed nothing to hold her back from following his lead and exploring the very different,
masculine, grace of his leaner hips and round
to learn how his buttocks differed from her
own by being sparser and more taut with
muscle. Now why had she never dreamt how
arousing satin-taut skin over strong male muscle and bone could feel under her fingers as
she dared to send them just that bit lower and
search for the sensitive join of his leg to the
pared-down curve above? Evidently he liked
it almost as much as she had when he drew
his teasing fingers along the lusher line of her
feminine curves, before raising those wickedly
knowing hands to soothe and rouse and tease
her breasts into begging so shamelessly for his
touch she could feel it, even through the layers
she'd donned for this misadventure.

Torn between memory of how little he
actually liked her, however much he might
want her, and the promise of a lovemaking
she'd never forget in all her long and spin-
sterly future, she abandoned the memory

and embraced the promise and Hugh Darke. He would have delved under all those layers for buttons and access to her tightly furled nipples demanding his touch and his mouth as they remembered last night with a mind of their own. No, let him do that and she'd lose this. Let him think what he was doing for long enough to undo all the layers she was wrapped in and remember who she was, and she'd lose this one moment of enchantment among their usual disenchantment. It felt like an odd, mutual innocence at the moment and she even wondered at herself for thinking so.

She put thinking aside for later and whispered a demand for faster, a wanton command that he stopped wasting time and got on with it, as if all the worst rumours were true and she already had a pack of secret lovers and knew exactly what she was doing now. Trying not to dread that particular falsehood on his tongue, she pulled him closer to fit lush lips to his and felt need overtake reason as his kisses became even wilder and more arousing. He lifted her with one hand round her slim waist and the other beneath her buttocks until she was cradled into him like the most precious of beings, as he walked her towards those very convenient sacks of good Brazilian coffee beans. Wondering how he found his way so unerringly in the ever-deepening darkness, she felt him hesitate, begin to think about this, about him and her again and, even as he set her down on the lowest stack of sacks, pulled him down after her, to tangle him up in kisses before he stopped this wondrous banquet of the senses.

'I want you,' she murmured in a breathy voice she hardly even recognised as her own. 'Now,' she added with an instinctive, feminine demand that he seemed quite unable to resist.

'It's almost too late to stop already, but are you sure?' he managed in a husky voice she loved, because it revealed just how true his desire-rasped words were and added a layer of extra enchantment to their seduction of each other.

'Never surer,' she told him, stopping his mouth with quick, frantic kisses so heated and needy that he groaned into her mouth in response as she felt him bunch up her second-hand skirts and petticoats and then there was the cooling April air, first on her bare knees, then her smooth thighs and ever upwards to expose the betraying hot wetness at the apex of those thighs.

'Hot and sweet and all mine,' he whispered

possessively in her ear as his teasing fingers found that unmistakable welcome and explored it until she let out an emphatic, very articulate moan for more and he rubbed and caressed and melted the until-now secret place he'd found, and to think that she hadn't even known she needed his touch there so badly until now.

'Yours,' she agreed recklessly as she felt pleasure almost beyond bearing pool and fight for release within her, but he removed his teasing fingers just before it became inevitable and took her word for it as he swiftly undid his breeches' flap with one deft hand whilst holding his weight above her as he stripped his nether garments off in a fluid shove, before smoothing her willing buttocks deeper into the oddly comfortable beans at her prone back and parting her legs a little farther.

Louisa felt the nudge of his fiercely aroused member against her aching, heated core and knew this was the last chance to go back to how she'd been until now. Separate, aloof, alone. No, it didn't sound in the least bit worth clinging on to in the face of being together, frantic and needy for each other. So she let her thighs fall either side of his narrow hips and lay a little farther back to bid him very welcome.

'Witch,' he murmured and his voice was a caress, even while it sounded as driven and latently powerful as the feel of him between her legs.

'Pirate,' she sparked back, imagining his face intent and intense above her in the late-afternoon darkness and somehow finding it even more seductive that they could see little of each other but shadows.

'Blissful, wonderful witch,' he added as he surged into her in one long thrust she knew was far too powerful to let him hesitate as he beat against the shock of her virginity. 'Devious, lying, idiotic, enchantress of a woman,' he gasped in protest as he tore through that slender barrier and centred himself at the very heart of her as if that was where he belonged, despite himself and her one-time resolution not to have this ultimate wonder in her life, before he loomed out the night and undermined it.

'I am now,' she said complacently, 'but I want more', and shocked even herself by riding the flash and burn of pain so determinedly that the novelty and fullness and sheer wonder of him inside her threatened to set her on the road to madness if he didn't move, do something to assuage this burning need for more that still rode her like the most exquisite goad of half-ultimate pleasure, half-heavy, almost painful need.

'You'll get it, but only if you stay still for a while,' he gritted, holding himself motionless with a mighty effort as he fought the primitive urge to slam into her until he'd climaxed and emptied himself into her as relentlessly as the beat of life itself.

Even then she flexed internal muscles around him experimentally, as if she hadn't even known she had them until now and threatened to enchant as well as unman him. Minx she undoubtedly was, but vixen as well? Somehow he doubted it as he felt her adjust about him with an almost trusting innocence, a giving in her usually steely composure and armour of humour that touched him a bit too deeply for comfort. Letting his awesome arousal overcome a need for something more than even this most sensual of couplings, he dared let himself move at last and let out a long groan of satisfaction as he felt her strive to match her rhythm to his.

Now, in the moment, he knew she was his as no other woman ever had been. He was her only lover, the only man who had ever moved inside her like this, striving against the beat and demand of outrageous desire in his head and heart to take her slowly, to ride her to the sweetest of oblivion. For now, all he needed to do was to make this wonderful for her, then it would be wondrous for him as well. He let her feel his desperately rigid manhood stretch and fill her and blocked out the silken marvel of her fitting him as if she was made for him alone. Not since he was a hasty boy with his first eager, just a little bit more experienced girl had he needed to fight his body quite so hard for mastery. Not with his mistresses and certainly not with his wife, but then, Ariadne hadn't been virgin any more than any of his other lovers had been, until now. Louisa Alstone was the first woman who'd ever allowed him to be first and he must guard himself against the privilege and wonder of that marvel, when he was rational again. For now he luxuriated in it as he felt her move with him, begin to breathe more deeply, to clench even more exquisitely about his manhood and, at last, he knew she was ready for more.

Breathing hard to keep that more from releasing him before time into his own selfish pleasure, he occupied himself with meeting her deepest of blue eyes in the darkness, although he could see only the quick shine of them in this almost-blackness as she opened her eyes in wonder and lure at the feel of him moving within her. Next time he'd make sure they had their eyes to add to the other four senses, so they could drive each other even more insane with how they were together. He blotted out the thought that there would be no next time by stroking harder and deeper into her as he felt her begin to spasm, felt the bow of her body even before he heard a deep heavy breath fill her straining lungs as she let it out, on a long wondering moan of delight. At last he could slip his tethers and he plunged head-long into the greatest, most satisfying completion he'd ever experienced.

Hugh felt his whole being spasm in ecstasy as she plunged into the unknown, then flew under him and their individual peaks of utter delight were as dangerous as they were giving. As he drifted into absolute release, complete satisfaction for what felt like the first time in his life, a part of him exulted and worshipped her, even as another woke up and groaned in disbelief. At their destination for a lovely, peaceful moment it felt generous, shared, too much to let go. Then let go he did and finally descended from absolute delight into almost complete horror when he realised exactly what he'd done by taking up her invitation to seduce her so eagerly, then failing to draw out of her before he climaxed and damned them both for a pair of over-lusty fools.

Coming back to her workaday self at last, Louisa allowed herself a delighted little wriggle and let herself be pleased he was still inside her, even after she knew that he'd experienced the ultimate release with her. He sank against her pleasured torso for a sweet moment and she let her arms come up to grasp him, then fall to her sides as he groaned as if in agony. Horrified that he wasn't as warmly delighted with life and his lover as she was with her only one, she suddenly felt chilled and all too distant again. He regretted what they'd just done and she wanted to cry so badly she had to clench her fists until she felt her nails bite into her tender palms. She'd grown too soft for this sort of disappointment; she fought not to expect anything of him other than what she'd already had and did her best to reassemble the Ice Diamond, before he could voice his misgivings. Suddenly she hated that brilliant, heartless creature with a passion even he might not be able to match, but it was an old familiar shield from a hurtful world and, at the moment, all she had.

'Thank you,' she made herself say, as if the most significant-seeming minutes of her life so far didn't matter all that much after all.

'Thank you?' the contrary monster echoed as if she'd spat poison at him.

'Yes. I shall never marry, you see, so you relieved me of a burden of curiosity I had no wish to carry for the rest of my life.'

'How useful of me,' he replied as if the words nauseated him.

'Yes,' she made herself say blandly, 'it was, very useful.'

Suddenly she felt so utterly vulnerable lying here, stretched under him like a wanton, and shifted restlessly, telling her body it had to let go of the glittering fantasy of ever doing that again, with anyone. Then he seemed to find a rampant need of her after all, when she'd thought him spent for the rest of the night and for ever done with her. She felt him roll his hips suggestively within the cradle of hers and, to her shame, something ravenous and desperate awoke in her as well. Breath stuttered from her lips before she could calm it and she heard his grunt of satisfaction, just before his mouth descended on hers in a kiss that allowed nothing for the tenderness of her bee-stung lips or the newness of sensations as his arousal hardened inside her once more.

Once more she drank in the scent of him, the abrasion of springy masculine hair against her clutching fingertips as she curled her hands into his heaving chest for want of any other purchase on his sweat-slicked body. Whatever he said, she heard the driven sound of his approving, then demanding murmurs as they climbed another summit when she'd thought herself at the top of this particular mountain. Every sense screamed for satisfaction as her eyes searched the darkness for a clue to his feelings when he made her shudder with driven desire, made her cry out for more as he rode her with a tenderness for her once-virgin body that made tears glaze her eyes and allowed her to be glad he couldn't see her after all.

She sank and rose and twisted and thrashed under him with need and this time she knew where they were bound and tensed for sheer delight as the warmth and golden release of body on body, heart on heart, overrode everything once more. Convulsing helplessly as he drove her mercilessly on and on, until she was left breathless and sobbing for breath and for sanity. He buried his dear, ruffled head in the curve of her vulnerable throat and let her feel his mouth open on a long, silent shout of rapturous possession.

'Was that useful of me as well?' he gasped when he finally managed to pump enough air into his lungs to speak. 'I'd hate it if you found your one, and apparently only, lover to be inept or unmemorable.'

'Don't worry, I don't suppose I stand much risk of forgetting that if I live to be ninety,' she murmured gruffly.

With a great sigh of goodness-knew-what emotion, he rolled away from her at last and rested at the side of her as if he didn't have energy to get himself any farther. *Not because he can't bear to forsake your arms, Louisa*, a hateful voice warned as he drew in long gasps of air and she felt his lungs expand, even as she had to grasp her hands tightly together above her head in order not to reach out to him. She so wanted to smooth his tense features, to linger over his mightily muscled shoulders and caress his labouring chest that only her own exhaustion stopped her springing up and putting the width of this shady warehouse between them.

'Nice to know something about me is likely to prove memorable.'

'There's nothing about you that isn't,' she reassured him before she'd even thought about it. 'Not that I could ever forget so objectionable a man,' she added hastily as she sat up at last, hoping he hadn't read something into her words she couldn't let herself admit, even in her own head.

'Of course not,' he said remotely, as his breath settled and she felt his powerful limbs tense for action.

Luckily he couldn't see the hand she held up in protest for the darkness that loomed between them. Still she knew the moment he stepped away and began to don his clothing, scrabbling in the dark for the odd garment she'd cast into the wider darkness in the heat of frantic desire. She reluctantly began the task of trying to reorder her own appearance, shucking off an outer layer of dull and overlarge garments because they wouldn't be needed now. It was too dark outside for him to need a disguise now and she doubted he'd consent to hide his undisputed masculinity under even so sketchy a veil as the extra clothes she'd kirtled about her waist.

'Even as I hope you're getting dressed and concealing yourself from me before you rouse me to insanity once more, you're undressing yourself, Louisa Alstone. What a very contrary female you truly are,' he commented out of the gloom and she had to bite back on a sigh of regret, for all that lovely intimacy, that wonderful forgetfulness of herself in him.

She smoothed down her remaining, nondescript skirts and wished that, just once, he could have seen her in her elegant evening finery. She'd be groomed to perfection, she let herself fantasise for a brief moment. Her hair would be brushed into immaculate disorder, every shining lock curled and pinned to show the fiery glow within its apparent darkness. Her gown would fit as only an exclusive Bond Street modiste could shape it and it would be made up of the finest cross-cut silk crepe to cling and lovingly outline her much-vaunted figure. Apparently she was not too tall or too short and would have been the epitome of elegance, if she wasn't so cold. She allowed herself a wry grimace for the rosy glow her brother's money cast over her as far as her needy suitors were concerned.

'The top layer was meant to be for you,' she managed to tell him when she could make it sound as if it didn't matter.

'For me—devil take it, woman, do you take me for a molly?'

'How could I?' she muttered under her breath, but he heard her all the same.

'You certainly know different now, if you ever did,' he confirmed smugly.

'Would you like me to provide you with a testimonial?'

'Thank you, but your brother would undoubtedly kill me, so I'll pass on that.'

'As well, perhaps, but the clothes were meant to be a disguise.'

'Good heavens, I think you really mean it. You really are the oddest female,' he told her as if he had more important things on his mind and she seethed in the darkness as she fumbled for the key under her skirts and then searched about for the wretched thing on her erstwhile resting place.

'Looking for this?' he asked, suddenly in front of her and she felt as much as saw the outline of the cleverly wrought key held out to her.

'You stole it?' she accused rashly.

'Just as you must have done,' he confirmed lazily. 'It's always as well to be prepared, as you undoubtedly know.'

'You took it while you were busy seducing me?'

'Not exactly while, more afterwards, and I

dispute your definition, since you seduced me as surely as I did you. Don't try to denounce me as the despoiler of innocence when you begged to be deflowered. No—correction, you convinced me you were as experienced as the lovely Eloise and had nothing left to deflower. Which of us do you think anyone would believe, once they knew you kidnapped me and lured me here in a questionable guise, my dear Miss Alstone?'

'I have no intention of broadcasting my seduction, so if that's what you're worried about, Captain Darke, stop plaguing me with slanderous suggestions and be reassured that I'll never tell a living soul.'

'Yet Mother Nature has a way of catching out the most secretive of lovers. So what about any child we made tonight?' he asked all too seriously and her heart stuttered in its tracks at the bare idea.

'It would take more than that to make one,' she managed to say scornfully, even as part of her marvelled at the very notion.

'No, sorry,' he said with a fine act of lighthearted indifference, 'unfortunately I can't close my eyes to the fact that it often takes a good deal less than we just managed between us.'

'Well, there's certainly no need for you to sound so smug about it.'

'That's not smugness, it's resignation. We must marry, my dear.'

'Over my dead body,' she managed to whisper between gritted teeth.

'I admit it's not what either you or your brother would have wanted, but I'll not have a child of mine running about the place, blithely learning petty theft and fraud at its mother's knee.'

'I can't be a mother,' she gasped as if the very idea pained her, which it did, acutely. She let the insult pass her by as she stood horrified by the suddenly very-present possibility that he might be right.

'I think we may shortly find that you can, like it or no,' he mocked her.

'No, no, I mustn't,' she said, hugging her arms about her suddenly trembling body and trying not to come apart in front of him. 'No,' she whispered again in horror at the very idea as she sat suddenly back down on her much-maligned coffee sacks and rocked backwards and forwards at the desperate possibility of it.

'I've heard of being wise after the event, but this is ridiculous, Miss Alstone,' he told her. When she didn't reply, but continued to rock blindly, as if she'd forgotten he was even there, he moved to kneel beside her and hold her still.

He was almost tender as he soothed her and whispered meaningless words of comfort as he felt the dry sobs that shook her, for all her faint attempts to put the usual armour of indifference back in place.

Chapter Seven

〰️

'I can see how a lady like you might be horrified by the bare notion of bearing my child, but I promise it won't be as bad as you think, Louisa. We will contrive to look after it somehow between us, and even if I'm not the husband you would have chosen, I'll try to be an easy one on you and a good father to our children, whenever they should come.' Hugh Darke was promising her all the time she tried to take in what had happened and how stupid she'd been to make him think he had to vow anything to her, let alone marriage.

'You don't understand,' she wailed, ineffectually hitting a would-be fist against his rock-like chest as he tried to take her in his arms in an embrace of pure comfort that was so tempting she had to find a way to make him let her go.

'I understand that you're a lady and a very lately ex-virgin and I'm just a common sea captain, but I could say we've made our bed and now must lie on it, if only we'd ever got that far.'

'It's not that, and I'm not a lady anyway,' she said vaguely, for it seemed as if they were moving through a dream and she was looking much further back at a reality he couldn't even guess at.

'That you are—the whole world knows Miss Alstone is a Diamond of the *ton*, and only the highest born and most beautiful in the land gain that accolade.'

'The Ice Diamond, the Untouchable Alstone?' she scorned incredulously. 'You should be the first to pour scorn on that epithet from now on.'

'I'll call out any man who seeks to argue with your icy reputation in public, even while I'm enjoying the real, warm human woman in my bed,' he reassured her and if she hadn't been bound up in her own misery she would have surely relished his partisanship, as well as his apparent desire to revisit her bed, however makeshift it might prove to be.

'I never wanted to make my début among the *ton*,' she told him blankly, as if not quite sure who she was talking to and all of a sudden she felt him take her misery seriously and draw back to try to see her face in all this frustrating darkness. 'I certainly never intend to marry and did everything I could to make that fact clear to my family. I would not accept any gentleman's offer of marriage, could not,' she explained desolately as if she was in the dock instead of his arms.

'Since I'm in a very good position to know you were a very proper maiden lady, then why not, Miss Alstone?'

'Oh, for goodness' sake, call me Louisa,' she demanded with a sudden return to her usual forthright manner and, for a brief moment, she felt horror recede and the world rock back on to its proper axis for the first time in years. Then it was back again, that old revulsion at herself, the familiar, terrible worthlessness of what she'd done, so long ago.

'Why will you have no husband or child to love, Louisa?' he demanded imperiously and suddenly she knew he had easily as much noble blood pumping round his body as she could claim to have inherited from the Earls of Carnwood.

'I can't tell you,' she whispered, back in that nightmare. 'Whatever will you think of me if I do?'

'How can I say, until you actually tell me what troubles you so deeply? We can hardly say or think much worse of each other than we already have, now can we?'

'No,' she admitted hollowly, thinking back to all the names she had called him, all the harsh opinions he'd already voiced about her.

'Then what does it matter to you what I think of you? If you won't marry me and insist on bastardising our maybe child, then I'll certainly think far worse of you than you currently do of yourself, I can safely promise you that much at least.'

'How comforting,' she managed to say almost lightly and decided he might as well know the worst about her, if only so he'd agree to walk away and forget her.

'Tell me, it can't be worse than a secret I can't bring myself to tell you in return,' he soothed ruefully, but she couldn't imagine anything worse than her own dark misdeeds.

'It was back in the years before I became a lady,' she warned him.

'Before you were born, you mean? I can't say I approve of the axiom that the sins of the fathers are to be visited on the sons, or in this case the daughters, so I know that you were always a lady, my dear.'

'My father certainly had a full hand of misdeeds to hand on, even if that was all he left us.'

'So I have heard, but as I say, I can't see why that ought to blight you, any more than it has your brother and sister.'

'Only me,' she said so low he had to bow his head to catch it and she felt him so close to her again that her heart seemed to ache over that last inch of space between them.

'No, you're an Alstone just as surely as they are. Your parentage is stamped all over the three of you for anyone to see.'

'Oh, my mother was ever faithful to him— despite his rages and his false promises and the hundreds of ways in which he didn't deserve her devotion. But once upon a time there were four of us children, and it's my fault that there aren't four of us any more.'

'How can it be? You must have been a child yourself when you lost your brother or sister, for I never heard of another little Alstone going to live with your aunt and uncle after your parents' deaths.'

'I was thirteen years old when Maria and

I went to our uncle's house to be turned from little savages into proper ladies, at least according to him. Maria was sixteen and eager to please, as well as good and dutiful, so she found it far easier to be "civilised" than I did and settled to it without complaint.'

'Which you most certainly did not, Louisa, if I know anything about you at all,' he said with a smile in his voice that made her knees weak. Again she longed to breach that small gap and lean into the comfort he was offering, but somehow forced herself not to. 'You were a child and no wonder if you were rebellious,' he continued, her unexpected advocate. 'You're an Alstone when all's said and done, are you not? I never came across one yet who wasn't as proud as the devil and impatient of the rules—apart from your sister, of course. Even I can see that Mrs Heathcote is almost as good as she is lovely and perhaps provides the exception to prove the rule.'

Another man who had evidently fallen very willingly under her lovely blonde sister's gentle spell, Louisa decided with unaccustomed bitterness and hated herself all over again. 'Aye, Maria is the best of us wicked Alstones,' she said, 'and I am the worst—I carry my father's loathsome stamp right through me.'

'Don't talk such damnable nonsense, woman, you have the Alstone looks and believe me, they are quite spectacular enough for the rest of us mere mortals to cope with. There's a glorious portrait of the Lucinda Alstone rumour insists enchanted Charles the Second even more than usual in the Royal Collection and you can believe me, because I've seen it, that you're even lovelier than she was. It's lucky I found you before Prinny did, really,' he added and she almost smiled at the absurdity of his cocky reassurance.

'Oh, really—lucky for whom exactly?'

'Me, of course, since you're going to marry me. For him as well, I suppose, since I won't have to threaten him with *laissez*-majesty when I go after him with my horse pistols for leering at my wife, so long as he never has the chance to leer at you in the first place.'

'How do you know he hasn't done so already?'

'Has he, then?'

'Just a little, but he called me a pretty child and tickled me under the chin before Lady

Hertford became restless and dragged him away.'

'Sensible female,' he approved smugly and she felt the comfort of normality he was trying to create for her and also a lurch of feeling she hadn't armed herself against. Dangerous, she decided with a shiver, and sat a little straighter, almost next to him as she was.

'They say he was once handsome and quite dashing,' she mused so that he'd hopefully forget he'd been trying to plumb her deepest, darkest secrets.

'According to my mother, he was as pretty a prince as you'd find in any fairy tale, until he became so fat and petulant you can't help but wonder if he'd have been better finding something to do, besides feel sorry for himself.'

'You know a lot about him,' she said suspiciously.

'Any Londoner in town when he was still Prince Florizel, and not fat as an alderman, could tell you that much.'

'But your mama wasn't just a London bystander, was she, Captain?'

'Never mind my mother, we were discussing yours.'

She sighed deeply and felt the shadow of the past loom until even the deep darkness of this windowless cavern seemed to be touched by it.

'She was far more beautiful than I am in her youth, but stubborn as any mule and somehow saw some quality in my father nobody else ever did. Mama never raged about her reduced circumstances or let us children think we were in any way less because we didn't have servants and fine clothes, or aught but a few second-hand books she managed to squirrel away from my father somehow or another. I deplore her blindness towards my father, for there was never a more selfish or ruthlessly vain man put on this earth than Bevis Alstone, but I can't bring myself to blame her for it, because she genuinely loved him. In the end I think she thought of him as a particularly naughty child.'

'How humiliating for him,' he said gently and she suddenly supposed it had been, so perhaps it was an unfortunate marriage on both sides and her mother would have been far better loving a better man and he a worse woman.

'He didn't kill her, though, I did that,' she finally said bleakly. 'And Peter,' she added as if purging her soul of all her bitter crimes at once.

'Of course you didn't,' he told her before she could add another word.

'How do you know?' she asked indignantly, almost as if she had to defend her right to the worst crime a human could commit against another of her kind.

'You haven't got it in you to harm a new-born kitten, let alone a woman you obviously loved and any kind of brother, even if he took after your sire in every vice available to him, which I doubt, since the rest of you certainly do not.'

'Well, he didn't, anyway. Peter was a dear, good boy; if he was a little slower than the rest of us, he loved more to make up for it. You never came across a more endearing soul than him and even the thieves and thugs in our near neighbourhood wouldn't have hurt him, although we only lived on the edges of a rookery and Kit and I would never have taken him inside for fear of what they would do to him there. He was five years younger than me, so Kit and Ben and I ran riot and played catch-me-if-you-can through St Giles while Maria and Peter stayed home with Mama and minded their lessons.'

'And Kit is five years older than you at the

very least, so you were not running wild with him at thirteen years old, were you?'

'No.' She shook her head slowly, shuddering at the thought of what she'd done and why. 'He left for the sea when I was seven or eight, but whenever he was home I'd follow him everywhere. Even he stopped trying to prevent me doing so, once he realised I could climb like a monkey and run as fast as the wind from any pursuit, so there really wasn't much point in him trying to stop me when he knew I'd get out anyway, and find it all the more sport to track him and Ben down when I did. I hated the times he and Ben were at sea and how I hated my father for reducing us all to such straits that Kit couldn't go to school as Mama longed for him to do. I couldn't endure the thought that Kit might be lost at sea, while Papa gamed and drank and demanded good food and warm clothes, even if we had to go without so he could present a smooth face to so-called "good" society. I've since discovered anything remotely akin to society turned its back years before, but at the time I hated "society" almost as much as I hated the gaming hells for letting him in.'

'Understandable in the circumstances,' Hugh Darke said.

'I was worse than he was, easily as selfish as he was,' she condemned herself. 'Anything Mama asked me to do, I ignored. Any task I had to perform because we were too poor for any of us to be idle, I did with ill grace and escaped from the boarding house my mother ran as soon as I could. Then I went into the rookeries and the mean streets around them, so I could play at being all the things girls and boys my own age were forced to do in order to put food in their bellies.'

'In your shoes, I'd have done the same.'

'You'd have been off to sea with Kit and Ben and left me more alone than ever, in my own eyes at least.'

'Well, if I'd been born a girl I dare say I'd have followed in your footsteps, then,' he assured her with a smile in his voice she suddenly wished she could see.

'You're a better man than me,' she said on the whisper of a laugh. 'Make that a better woman,' she added; for a moment, none of it felt bad after all.

'Best make it neither. I'm very glad I'm a man and you're a woman, but I still know I'd have felt as frustrated and rebellious in your situation as you did, Louisa Alstone. You're spirited and clever and if you managed to survive alone in such a harsh world, then you're evidently extremely resourceful as well.'

'Don't make me into someone better than I deserve, Captain,' she cautioned.

'And don't make yourself into your own demon.'

'No need for that, I killed Peter and Mama,' she remembered bleakly and all temptation to take herself at his inflated value disappeared.

'How?' he asked and she marvelled that he didn't draw his arms away or try to set her at arm's length.

'Kit and Ben had gone back to sea again and I hated losing their company and the exciting adventures we had, so I ran off one day when I'd finished my daily ration of sewing and chores about the house. It was high summer and the nights were almost as light as the days, so I climbed out of a bedroom window and stayed away all night. I found a roof in Mayfair to sleep on and it was a good deal cooler and more comfortable than our bedroom under the eaves in a rotten old house that should have been pulled down half a century ago. Then I decided to run back through the streets before the world was awake, just for the devilment of it. Except this time I ran through the wrong ones and picked up the typhus fever,' she said, then stared blankly into the darkness as she finished her tale. 'It killed Peter first and then I don't think Mama could fight it for her grief at losing him. Maria was only ill for a couple of days and I recovered in time to know what I'd done and wish I hadn't. Maria and I bungled along somehow, running the boarding house as best we could with Mrs Calhoun and Coste's help, and Papa came home every now and again when he had nowhere else to go. Then Kit came home with his share of a cargo in his pocket and arranged for Maria and me to live with our uncle and his wife. So Kit has paid for our keep and education ever since and I stayed there and tried to make up for the terrible thing I did, but nothing could wipe out that particular sin.'

'You did nothing wrong, you idiotic woman. I can understand a grieving child taking on a terrible burden of guilt, but surely not even you are stubborn enough to cling to it now, in the face of all logic and mature consideration?'

She shrugged, knowing he couldn't see her, but they were so close she could feel the frustration come off him. It was both unexpected and kind of him to try to absolve her of guilt. It also confirmed he had all the instincts, as well as the upbringing, of the gentleman she now knew him to be.

'If I had only stayed at home as I should have done that day, Mama and Peter would probably still be alive today,' she said sadly.

'And if any number of things in history had happened in a different order we might not be standing here tonight, futilely discussing ifs and maybes. You know as well as I do that disease is rife in the slums of this city, especially in the summer, and anyone could have given them that illness. Would you expect the butcher or baker or candlestick-maker to carry a burden of guilt for the rest of their lives if they had carried it into your home?'

'No, but they would have spread it in innocence, not after disobeying every rule my mother tried to lay down for my safety and well-being and probably worrying her sleepless all night as well.'

'So you were headstrong and difficult— what's new about that, Louisa?' he asked impatiently and for some reason that made her consider his words more seriously than sympathy might have done.

'Not much,' she finally admitted as if it came as a shock.

He chuckled and she kicked herself silently for feeling a warm glow threaten to run through her at the deep, masculine sound of it. 'I doubt very much those who love you would have you any other than as you are, despite your many faults,' he told her almost gently.

'But Peter's dead,' she told him tragically and if he couldn't hear the tears in her voice at the very thought of her loving little brother, now six years in his grave, she certainly could and bit her lip to try to hold them back.

'And just how do you think your brother Kit and Ben Shaw would have felt if they came home to find you or your sister gone as well? Such epidemics are no respecters of what is fair and unfair, Louisa. None of you deserved to die or to bear blame for deaths that happened because the poor live in little better than open sewers at the heart of this fair city. Blame the aldermen and government ministers who allow such abject poverty to thrive in what's supposed to be the most advanced nation in the world, but don't be arrogant enough to take the blame yourself. And don't you think your mother would hate to hear you now? It sounds to me as if she loved her children very much, so she'd certainly not want to hear you talk like a fool and refuse to bear children yourself, just because she's not here any more and your little brother couldn't fight a desperate and dangerous illness that can just as easily take strong men in the prime of their lives.'

'I still shouldn't have gone.'

'No, but all the other times you climbed out of your window and ran wild through the streets you probably should have been sewing samplers or minding your books. It sounds like the natural reaction of a spirited girl, denied the pleasures and luxuries of the life you should have had, if your father wasn't selfish and shallow and self-obsessed. Taking the burden of guilt for what happened when it clearly belongs elsewhere is arrogant, Louisa. All you were guilty of was a childish rebellion that you would have grown out of, once your brother was able to provide you and your family with the sort of life you should have lived from the outset.'

'He was so sad, Hugh,' she confided with a sniff to hold back her tears that he somehow found deeply touching. 'At night when he thought Maria and I were in bed and asleep I would hear him weep for them. Then Papa came home one night, drunk as usual, and they argued and raged at each other until Papa stormed off into the night and swore not to come home again until Kit was back at sea.

They found his body floating in the Thames two days later and only my sister was ever soft-hearted enough to think he'd drowned himself out of grief for my mother, when he was so drunk he probably couldn't tell the difference between high water and dry land. Yet it wouldn't have happened if he hadn't argued with Kit and I hadn't done what I did.'

'And no doubt Kit feels guilty about that as well, being made in the same stubborn, ridiculous mould as you and the rest of the Earl of Carnwood's rackety family. There's no need for you to take on his regrets as well as your own, since I never met a man more able to own his sins and omissions than Christopher Alstone.'

'I suppose you could be right.'

'Of course I am. Now, kindly inform me what you were planning to do to me once you had me guyed up in that ridiculous disguise and let's have done with your imagined sins.'

'That's it? I am to consider myself absolved? You should have been a priest.'

'Maybe not,' he said with a laugh that would have been self-mocking if he wasn't so busy mocking her. 'But nothing you did or didn't do in the past has made you unfit to be a mother, Louisa. Probably just as well, since we're

going to be wed and will doubtless bed each
other at regular intervals, very likely before
we get to the altar as well if you keep glaring
at me like that,' he threatened half-seriously.

'How do you know I'm glaring at you?' she
asked haughtily.

'Instinct,' he told her succinctly. 'I can't
promise you much, but I will promise not to
treat you as shabbily as your father did your
mother,' he added gruffly.

'That would be nice of you, if I had the least
intention of marrying you.'

'You will have to, my girl, since I refuse to
spend the next three months or so not meeting
your brother's eyes or hiding from Ben Shaw's
mighty wrath while we wait for you to decide
if I've just got you pregnant or not. Consider
it the wages of sin and take that guilt on your
shoulders if you must, but at least let's have
no more Cheltenham tragedies while you wait
it out as my wife instead.'

'So far I hear only what you want and nothing about me, but the answer to your question
about the disguise is that I don't really know.
I can't go back to Kit's house because my enemies will be looking for me by now, and I
wanted to get you away from the man who's
trying to trap you until we could defeat him

somehow, which was all very stupid of me, I suppose.'

'Undoubtedly it was,' he agreed gruffly.

'You could probably go back there safely yourself,' she encouraged him and felt his suspicion on the heavy air as clearly as if she could actually see his frown.

'While you do what in the meantime?'

'I have plenty of plans for my future. It's you I don't know what to do with.'

'I think we just demonstrated that you know *exactly* what to do with me,' he said, sounding as silkily lethal as he must when examining any of his crew brought in front of him to explain their sins.

'And you dislike being thought fit for only one purpose as much as I do?'

'When did I imply any such thing, woman?'

'With every word you drawl at me as if you're right and everything I say proves how bird-witted I am.'

'Only when you're talking rubbish,' he muttered impatiently, as if driven to the edge of reason by addle-pated arguments, when she ought to accept his words as proven fact, then do as she was bid.

'It's hardly rubbish to say we're both unsuited to marriage and even more so to marrying one another.'

'Yes, it is. We'll do very well in our marriage bed, something we just proved to each other beyond all reasonable doubt.'

'So my doubts are unreasonable and that's all there is to marriage?' she asked with a theatrical wave at the coffee stacks she was quite glad he couldn't see. The very thought of them made her blush now they were discussing seduction and his peculiar idea that it automatically led to marriage.

'Ah, now I can see why you were truly so unsuited to the *ton*nish ideals of marriage *à la mode*. You, Miss Alstone, destined as you are not to be a miss for very much longer, are a romantic.'

Stung by the accusation, when she'd always thought herself such a cynic, Louisa was about to loudly dispute such a slur when she made the mistake of wondering if he could be right.

Chapter Eight

'I have never felt the slightest need to sigh and yearn over a man,' Louisa lied defensively, 'and least of all over you, Captain Darke.'

'Good, because I'm not worth wasting a moment's peace on,' he said curtly and a fierce desire to argue that statement shook her, but she fought it with an effort she must think about later.

'I'm not going to marry you,' she said as definitely as she could.

'You're such an odd mix of cynicism and vulnerability, my dear. I'll probably spend a lifetime trying to understand you,' he said, as if he hadn't heard.

'It will be a lifetime separate from mine,' she insisted for the sake of it more than out of any passionate certainty. She was so busy feeling hollow inside at the idea that the sounds she was waiting for from outside hardly seemed important any more.

'Why the devil is a ship docking hard by, Louisa?' he barked at her and she felt his frustration as he gripped her as if he'd like to shake her.

'It's come for me, of course—what's the point of having a brother with his own shipping empire if I can't call on it when I need to?' she replied coolly.

'You don't trust me to keep you safe, then?'

'It's not a matter of trust,' she argued uncomfortably.

'Now there you're so very wrong, Miss Alstone.' His voice was so low she did her best not to hear it as he turned to the master of the coastal brig she'd summoned here once the tide was right. 'What the devil do you want?' he barked when a shadowy figure unlocked the riverside door and stood outlined against the night.

'My sister,' Christopher Alstone replied grimly, opening his dark lantern and making Louisa blink. 'So what in Hades are you doing here?' he demanded.

'Kit!' Louisa exclaimed on a huge sigh of

relief and confusion as she ran into his arms. 'I missed you so much,' she told him fervently.

'It's mutual, you confounded nuisance of a female,' he informed her abruptly, even as she felt at least half of his attention slide to Hugh Darke and his muscles stiffen like a fighting dog scenting a challenge. 'What have you done to my sister?' he ground out, as if he knew exactly what they'd been doing, but surely even her powerful brother couldn't see through walls?

'Nothing,' she said impatiently. 'And what are you doing here?' she asked, standing away from him to examine his deeply shadowed face.

'I asked first,' he said silkily, his eyes not moving from Hugh and she wondered if these two warriors were about to try to kill each other over her.

'And you're clearly as annoying as ever,' she sparked back, determined not to be side-lined and silent while they decided her future between them.

'Clearly,' he agreed with that flinty lack of temper she knew from experience was his most effective weapon in an argument. 'An answer, if you please?' he demanded starkly

and Hugh Darke moved Louisa aside to confront her brother.

'I was trying to persuade her to marry me,
until you interrupted us,' he said, as arrogantly
challenging as if he'd just thrown down a
knightly gauntlet and fully expected to have
it thrown back in his face.

'Oh, good,' Kit said mildly and Louisa felt
her rage soar almost out of control at the exact
moment his seemed to deflate.

'Good? Do you really want this idiot to
marry me?' she raged.

'Why not? Lots of other idiots have asked
you to do so and they only mildly annoyed
you. At least this one seems to have found a
way of holding your full attention while he
puts the question, even if I don't like anything
else about him being shut in here alone with
my little sister.'

Drat him, but why did her brother have to
be so uncannily perceptive? Because he was
Kit Stone, she supposed: precociously success-
ful, driven and even more stubborn than she
was.

'Speaking as the idiot in question, I don't
care about your ruffled pride and your reputation for icy detachment, Miss Alstone. I
just want you to agree to marry me, so your

brother doesn't have to beat me to a bloody pulp and we can all go home, before eating our dinner and getting on with our interrupted lives with no more of your infernal melodramas,' Hugh told her impatiently.

'Which is exactly why we should *not* marry, since your dinner clearly matters to you a lot more than I do,' she said, rounding on him now that Kit seemed more an amused bystander than her avenging guardian.

If she let herself think about the volumes that detachment spoke about her brother's belief in Captain Darke's bone-deep sense of honour, she might start respecting the devilish rogue herself and she knew precisely where that would get her—marched up the aisle before she came back to her right senses again.

'On the contrary, I'm exactly the right husband to deal with your wrongheaded ideas and headstrong ways. Any other man would be driven demented by your starts inside a sennight.'

'He could be right,' Kit observed traitorously.

'And I'll be flying to the moon any moment now,' she scorned, but the idea of arguing with Hugh Darke for the rest of their born days suddenly seemed a little bit too promising.

'I'll take you there, Eloise,' he whispered in her ear and she wondered how he'd managed to creep so close behind her that she was all but in his arms once more, and in front of her brother as well.

She shuddered with what she told herself was revulsion, but he'd reminded her how it felt to soar in his arms, to strive for the very moon and stars, and she sighed in besotted anticipation of doing it all again.

'Not until you've put a wedding ring on her finger, you won't,' Kit warned as he eyed them very suspiciously once more. 'And what's all this Eloise business?'

'You really don't want to know,' Hugh said with a return to his austerely apart, piratical-captain look as he withdrew his warmth and strength from her.

Louisa shivered at no longer feeling him next to her—how could she know if her scent and sound and touch were as deeply imprinted on his senses as his were on hers? He was so detached all of a sudden it was as if she'd dreamt that feverish interlude in his arms when neither of them seemed able to hold anything back from the other. She was almost glad when Kit decided this was neither the time nor the place for such an important discussion and put aside that comment to pick over later and eyed her pale face with brotherly concern.

'I probably don't either, but let's get Louisa out of here. We can deal with Eloise and the details of your wedding in the morning.'

'No, I can't go home with you, I need to get away,' Louisa argued, an illogical sense that she needed to escape nagging at her even now she had two powerful protectors instead of just the one.

'Why?' her brother asked.

'Because Uncle William has been scheming to marry me off to a worm of a man, who probably offered to share my dowry with him, and both of them will be hot on my trail by now.'

'He'll answer to me for it, then, but why would that mean we can't go home?'

'The insect abducted me and kept me in his bedchamber for a night and a day and made sure my uncle and aunt saw me there, so they could exclaim loudly about my wickedness and their scandalised feelings. They forbade me their roof, unless I instantly married the repulsive toad, which I refused to do needless to say.'

'That need not worry you, Miss Alstone. He

won't pollute the world for very much longer,' Hugh Darke gritted between his strong white teeth and, given the fierce look in his eyes, she believed him.

'How would your killing him help me? You would have to flee the country and I would still be the centre of a fine scandal, all the more so if I was stupid enough to have married you in the meantime. It would seem as if I ran off with you after growing bored with him.'

'She's right, Hugh,' Kit intervened as Hugh Darke rounded on her with his best master-of-all-I-survey glare. 'You need to leave the worm to me,' Kit added, offering that caveat to soothe the devil of temper so very evident in Hugh's furious gaze and stirring hers instead.

'No, he'll only dirty your hands,' Hugh gritted furiously, quite lost to reason, even if her brother only had more masculine folly to offer. 'What's his name, this insect-worm?' he asked fiercely.

'Do you think I'm fool enough to tell you that, when you will only add to the scandal already surrounding me by calling him out?'

His hands closed about her arms, as if he wanted to shake some sense into her and she condemned her senses for leaping to attention, even at his angry touch through her second-hand jacket and gown. For a betraying moment she swayed towards him, as if her body and her senses were begging for a kiss despite her growing fury.

'He must not get away with it, Louisa, I can't let him,' he gritted as if her lost reputation mattered to him more than it ever could to her. As surely as she knew Charlton would walk away if she was teetering on the edge of a cliff, she knew this man would plunge off it himself, if that was what it took to save her.

'Don't you think me capable of making him sorry he was even born, then, Hugo?' Kit said almost gently.

'I do, but it should be my job. No, make that my pleasure.'

'It can't be and you know why,' Kit said obscurely and Louisa's ears pricked up at the veiled curb in that short sentence. Then she felt the reminder bite into the man still holding her arms as if he didn't know quite what to do with her.

Hugh jerked away from her, seeming horrified that he'd ever laid hands on her in the first place and watched those very hands with revulsion, like a very masculine Lady Macbeth, after she'd driven herself mad with murder and ambition and couldn't wash the imaginary blood off them.

'I know, so how can I wed your sister? I forgot what I am in the heat of the moment,' he whispered and it was as if he and Kit were talking about something deeply important she wasn't going to be told.

'Whilst I suspect I don't want to know about the heat of that particular moment, we both know there's nothing to stop you marrying. The rub will come if you fail to make my sister happy afterwards and I'm forced to kill you,' Kit told him implacably, and any illusion she'd suffered that he was resigned to what had taken place between herself and Hugh tonight melted away like mist in the July sun.

'That would go quite badly with me, either way,' she muttered mutinously.

'Not as badly as you knowing the truth about me would,' Hugh said, looking glum about her predicted unhappiness and softening her heart, if he did but know it.

'I told you my tale,' she challenged him, and if Kit chose to think it was the one about her abduction and lost reputation, then so be it.

'And you think mine is that simple—just a

few words and a rueful smile at how easy that was to get out of the way and go on?'

'As mine was?' she demanded, furious with him for brushing aside her fears and peculiarities as if they didn't matter.

'I didn't mean...' he blundered on.

'Never mind what you meant, never mind your secrets. I haven't got all night to spare for arguing with you. I'm tired and hungry and downright weary of rescuing ungrateful, lying, mistrustful idiots from their enemies. If neither of you intends to take me somewhere safe and warm and feed me, pray give me a hand up on to that brig of yours, brother mine, and I'll get the master to drop me off at the nearest port downriver where I can buy myself a bedchamber for the night and a decent meal.'

'Not in a hundred years, sister dear, and he's long gone. I thought half of London must know he was casting off and none too happy to be going in the middle of the night, given the amount of noise he made about it.'

'I didn't hear him,' she said stiffly and actually caught herself out in a flounce as she spun round to glare at her would-be bridegroom and dare him to comment.

'Neither did I,' he admitted meekly.

'Lovebirds,' Kit added sarcastically and

Louisa wondered if she ought to kick one of them, even if it was just because they were men and couldn't help being infuriating any more than they could voluntarily stop breathing.

'What are we going to do, then?' she demanded.

'Go home,' Kit told her implacably and, since there was nowhere she'd rather be, she allowed him to bustle her out of the warehouse and along narrow streets and alleys he knew even better than she did in the dark, then out on to wider and marginally more respectable streets where he hailed a cab, then sat back to watch the night-time streets roll past as if they fascinated him.

'Where have you been, then?' Louisa finally asked her brother, remembering she ought to be furious with him for disappearing as he had.

'Here and there,' he told her shortly.

Simmering with temper because it was better than letting her tiredness and uncertainty take over, she put her mind to Hugh Darke's many mysteries as the little house in Chelsea and a degree of physical comfort beckoned at last.

'Just as well you didn't get back last night,'

she muttered as they arrived and her brother helped her down while Hugh paid the jarvey.

'I'm not going to ask why not until I've had my dinner and a soothing shot of brandy,' he said as he ushered her up the steps and rapped sharply on the door.

'Hah! That's a lot less likely than you think,' she observed with a sidelong glance at Hugh that made Kit frown as Coste cautiously opened the door.

'Let us in, you idiot,' Kit ordered sharply.

'Didn't know it was you, now, did I?' Coste mumbled as he stood back to do so.

'You would have done if you actually made use of the Judas hole I had put in for once,' his employer informed him as he used Coste's candle to light those in the sconces round the cosy dining parlour they had got nowhere near last night. 'Is there anything edible in the house?' he demanded and put a taper to the fire laid ready in the hearth for good measure.

'Aye, sir. Miss Louisa gave me money for food and a couple of cleaning women. We've a good pork pie and a ham and all sorts of fancy bits of this and that. There's treacle tart, apple pie and gingerbread, too, but not so much of the treacle tart as there might be,' Coste said with a reminiscent grin.

'And you two somehow managed until now without my housekeeper and a kitchenmaid?' Kit asked mildly enough.

'Well, I was going to tell you about that, Captain…' Coste trailed off, casting a look at Hugh that begged him to take over explaining their misconduct.

'We two bachelors proved too rowdy to satisfy Mrs Calhoun's strict standards of behaviour and she took herself and her daughter off before there was any gossip about them being here with two rowdy bachelors like us,' he obligingly admitted, nodding at Coste to make himself scarce while he still could.

'I warrant she did,' Kit replied grimly. 'Don't forget to bring that pie and a pint of porter along with tea for Miss Louisa,' he urged his retreating manservant and watched Hugh with cold eyes. 'I trust my sister was not caught up in that rowdiness,' he added with such mild iciness that even Louisa shivered in her seat by the fire.

Hugh shifted in his chair as Louisa carefully stared into the flames and Kit sighed rather heavily. 'Later,' he said portentously and Louisa felt as if the two men were once more having a silent but fierce conversation she didn't understand, and that they had no intention of explaining any of it to her.

Hugh Darke wasn't in the least bit over-shadowed by her powerful brother. Despite her captain's apparently subservient role in Kit and Ben's empire, he acted as Kit's equal and her suspicions about his true place in the world crept back and left her wondering why he took orders from even so compelling, and success-ful, a pair as her brother and Ben Shaw. She furtively surveyed her brother and her lover in turn, noting the similarities in their elegantly powerful builds and proud carriage. They were both dark-haired as well, of course, but that was about the end of any similarity be-tween them and Hugh Darke was certainly the more mysterious and contrary of the two, even judged on appearance alone.

He had that strong Roman nose that looked as if it had been broken at some point in his varied career; emphatically marked dark brows frowned above his challenging silver-blue eyes and yet his mouth could have be-longed on a poet or a troubadour, if not for the stern control he kept it under. She knew how sensitive it could feel against hers now, but the containment of it argued he'd been through a very hot fire to become the steely-eyed captain

he was now. A younger Hugh Darke would be
almost too handsome and appealing for his
own good; she imagined this complex and
contrary man carefree and laughing, and was
glad to be spared that pristine version of him,
since she was far too impressed with the current one to need any more encouragement.

Louisa gave up on reading Hugh's thoughts
and tried her brother's instead, seeing nothing
but an austere lack of expression on his face
that made him exasperating, even as she let
herself realise how much she'd missed him.
Grief and guilt had hardened her against loving anyone easily, but now she could let it go
at last and remember her little brother as he
was and it was as if her family had been given
back to her. Kit was darker than the rest of
them, of course, but Peter had looked so much
like her it had hurt to look at herself in the
mirror when he died. Who would ever guess
that Captain Darke could give her little brother
back to her as he was, instead of the reproach-
ful angel guilt had painted him? She owed him
a debt for that, which added to her confusion
as they all sat in weary silence, carefully not
discussing her eventful day.

Coste finally carried in a rattling tray, deposited it on the nearest table, then went back

for her tea. It wasn't a very elegant repast, but they made short work of slices of pie and ham with the mustard and fresh bread and some pickles that looked much less ancient than the ones that had confronted her last night. After a while she refused anything more, sitting back to sip her tea and watch Kit and Hugh eat as if they hadn't done so for a week.

'The amount of food you gentlemen require to sustain life will never cease to amaze me,' she observed at last.

'Whilst we coarse males are continually astonished by how little a lady can maintain herself upon,' Hugh returned with an unexpectedly boyish grin that somehow managed to warm her more effectively than the now-glowing fire.

'Since I don't subscribe to the idea that ladies should eat before they dine in mixed company, so we appear to possess the most bird-like of appetites, Captain Darke, perhaps I'm not a lady,' she said with a shy smile.

'I've always thought that a true lady doesn't need to try to be one myself, Miss Alstone,' he replied and surprised her into blushing at his implied compliment.

'You'll be sipping ratafia and exchanging remarks about the weather next,' Kit interrupted impatiently and Louisa decided she'd much prefer to put off the conversation he wanted to have until morning, except then she'd toss and turn all night worrying, so it was probably as well to get it over with.

'Very well, what do you want to know?' she asked.

'So much I hardly know where to begin, but the name of your worm will do to start with. Then we can discuss everything else and what must be done about it once we've dealt with him,' her brother said grimly.

Louisa annoyed herself by looking to Hugh for support and he nodded as if he was only waiting for that detail before storming off into the night to wreak havoc as well. 'No,' she said and prepared to be very stubborn rather than let him risk his skin once again.

'All I need do is enter any fashionable lady's drawing room tomorrow afternoon and flap my sharp ears towards the nearest whispered conversation and I'll find out in five minutes,' Kit threatened and she knew he was right. Such a juicy scandal would not even be silenced when the lady's sharp-eared brother was in the room if the story really was running about the *ton* like wildfire.

'Promise me first that neither of you will try to kill him?'

'Does the man's safety mean so much to you then, Miss Alstone?' Hugh Darke said coldly.

'No, but my brother's does and even you are too good a man to soil your hands on a nothing like him,' she told him fiercely and it was more than he deserved after the icy disdain he'd just glared at her.

'My apologies, ma'am,' he said stiffly.

'His name, Louisa?' her brother demanded.

'First your promise,' she replied stubbornly.

'Very well, I promise he can live until morning.'

'Not good enough, I'll not have you banished for duelling or hung for murder either. I've already lost one brother and certainly can't spare another.'

Kit looked thoughtful at that reminder, then nodded reluctantly. 'I'll find another way to punish the wretch, Lou, but don't ask me to let him get away with what he's done to you, for I just can't do it.'

'And you, Captain Darke?' she asked implacably.

'And I what, Miss Alstone?'

'Are you going to promise not to chase my

would-be husband down with the carving knife?'

'I have a perfectly good sword handy, as you no doubt recall.'

'There will be no swordfighting, no furtive and stupid duel with pistols at dawn and no pretend-casual encounter at some club or at a mill, or anywhere else for that matter. If you don't promise not to kill the man, I shall inform my uncle you two are on the rampage and the worm will be long gone before you get anywhere near him.'

'Justice can be swift indeed, Miss Alstone,' he argued.

'That's exactly what I'm worried about, you stupid man. Do you think I want any more deaths on my conscience, after carrying such a burden of guilt for so long?' she said and made herself let her pain at the very idea of losing him show in her gaze.

'I promise,' he murmured, his eyes silently telling her it was only because of that burden of guilt that he reluctantly gave in.

'And what exactly are you promising me, Captain?'

'To find another way to make his life hell,' he said with a grim smile.

'I don't mind that, then. Mr Charlton Hawberry abducted me and, since he made my life hellish for a spell, whatever punishment you come up with might at least stop him doing it to some other female.'

'Although I never heard his name before, he even sounds like the villain out of a melodrama,' Hugh exclaimed disgustedly.

'I told you he was a worm, didn't I?' she offered mildly.

'He sounds more like some obscure breed of fly that needs squashing. Will you give me that promise back so I may do so, Miss Alstone?'

'No, and need I remind you that I rescued myself from him, which must have gone some way towards swatting the horrible man and will have to do for now.'

'I'd still dearly like to know how you managed it.'

'As would I,' Kit told her with a keen look that made Louisa wish she hadn't used her misadventures to divert them from their manly wrath.

'I waited for the right moment and got away from him,' she said airily.

'How?' Hugh barked as if he had every right to examine her.

'I found the only way to evade his bullies

and his revolting company that he'd neglected to close off and took it.'

'Describe exactly how you did so, then,' Hugh said implacably, as if very near the end of his tether. She wondered fleetingly why Kit was sitting back in his chair and letting his captain interrogate her, then decided she might as well get the tale over as quickly as possible and it didn't matter which of them asked the questions.

'I climbed out of a window,' she admitted, because it could be any window, on any floor. She realised her mistake as soon as she recalled telling them she was imprisoned in Charlton's bedchamber, and they knew as well as she did that most of the narrow town houses hired for the Season had their principal bedrooms on the second floor, three storeys and a basement above the ground.

'With the aid of a rope of some sort, I trust?' Hugh asked roughly, as if the very idea made him imagine all sorts of terrible consequences in retrospect.

'Um, no,' was all she could manage as she shifted in her seat by the fire and avoided both their gazes as she recalled her truly terrifying escape.

Chapter Nine

'**D**evil take it, Louisa! You're not a wild girl clambering about the slums like some sort of human spider any more. You're supposed to be a lady,' Kit objected, which might have seemed bad enough, if Hugh hadn't gone as silent and lethally furious as a tiger grabbed by his tail.

'If I'd meekly sat there waiting for rescue, then I'd be well and truly wed to the insect-worm by now,' she defended herself rather half-heartedly, as she remembered that appalling climb across the front of a house with fewer handholds than a sheer cliff might fairly be expected to have.

'Not for long,' Hugh finally said with a hiss of pent-up fury that made her wonder if he was a gentleman of his word after all. Of course he was, she concluded as she met the barely contained rage in his icy-blue gaze, he wouldn't be so irate at having given it if he wasn't.

'You wouldn't have cared if I was wed to him or not, since you hardly knew me then,' she reminded him, but it didn't restore him to his usual cynical self somehow.

'I would have cared because you're Kit's sister, but it would be my pleasure to beat Hawberry to a pulp now. And adventurers don't start molesting females because it suddenly occurred to them, Miss Alstone, so I very much doubt if you are the first one he's ever used such despicable tactics against.'

'I'm not a victim,' she insisted fiercely.

'And I never met a female less likely to be anyone's dupe than you are, my Eloise. He chose his target very badly this time,' he asserted and at last she saw something in his silvered-blue gaze that could have been admiration.

'Eloise?' Kit asked as his sharp ears and even sharper brain picked up on that unfortunate nickname again. 'Who the devil is this Eloise?'

'I am,' she said as uninformatively as possible.

'Oh, good,' Hugh said irrepressibly and she glared at him.

'You keep out of this,' she demanded and her glare was even more furious as his smile became wolfish and his gaze almost molten with heat at the memory of Eloise and her bold ways and even bolder tongue.

'Spoilsport,' he muttered a little too intimately and, if he wasn't conscious of Kit's eagle-eyed gaze shifting between them suspiciously, she felt it acutely.

'Later,' Kit promised ominously and Louisa caught a typical masculine resolve to punch each other until they both felt better flash between them and was tempted to stamp upstairs and let them get on with it, but she didn't want either of them hurt.

It puzzled her how deeply Hugh Darke's well-being had come to matter to her in such a short time and she fought a fluffy reverie on the intriguing subject of how instantaneously she took fire whenever he was near. It was almost as if someone had laid such a strong enchantment on them that they were helpless to resist it, but she was such an unlikely heroine of a fairy tale that she reminded herself who she really was and glared at them both.

'No, you don't,' she insisted sharply. 'There's enough to worry about without you two pummelling each other bruised and bloody just for the fun of it.'

'You think we'd have fun?' Hugh said, so blandly innocent she was sure of it and decided she understood the opposite sex even less than usual.

'Yes, I do,' she replied and silently dared him to argue, 'and never mind Charlton, how do we find out who's behind today's plot against you, Captain Darke?'

'What plot?' Kit demanded.

'There was one, however he tries to convince you otherwise. I foiled it and your captain was most ungrateful at being rescued from his enemies by a mere woman.'

'Only because your sister thinks she's justified in taking intolerable risks with herself any time she decides to pry into matters that don't concern her, Alstone. A note to inform me of your suspicions would have done the job just as well,' he accused her, turning the full benefit of his angry scowl on her rather than Kit.

'There wasn't time,' she told him defiantly.

'Yet you found plenty of it in which to organise a rather showy ambush and procure yet another disreputable disguise for yourself, let alone an even more absurd one for me?'

'Would you have believed me?' she asked after a long moment while his gaze on hers seemed to demand an explanation she couldn't give, when she didn't really understand why she'd had to secure his safety so personally in the first place.

'Probably,' he finally breathed as if in response to a far deeper challenge.

'That wasn't good enough, you see, I had to be sure.'

'And if my lion-hearted sister decided you needed to be rescued, believe me, Hugo, rescued you were going to be,' Kit intervened with what looked astonishingly like an approving smile.

'Clearly,' he responded, looking a little dazed by the notion that he mattered to anybody.

'Don't you want to know who I rescued you from?' she demanded.

'You might as well ask her, Hugh. My sister seems to be a mine of unwelcome information tonight,' Kit said with a glance of fellow feeling at Hugh Darke that made Louisa want to kick some inanimate object and flounce out of the room, except that would only make them more smugly masculine than ever.

'I have a legion of enemies,' Hugh said wearily.

'You might have a new one,' Kit said, offering up cold comfort.

'New or old, he certainly puzzled me, Captain,' she said, wanting to comfort him for his surfeit of foes for some odd reason.

'He's bewildering me at the moment, because I haven't the least idea who he is, so why not part with his name, whoever you think he is, and let your brother and I add him to our list?' Hugh said indifferently.

'What list?' she asked.

'The one of all the people we're supposed to punish for their sins without actually laying a finger on them, remember?'

'And a very civilised form of retribution it will be, too,' she said virtuously.

'Tell him who it was then, Lou, so you can go upstairs and rest before you fall asleep in your tea,' Kit advised and suddenly she felt the weight of the last night and day's worth of adventures bear down on her.

'I racked my memory for hours afterwards, but I'm nearly sure I've finally managed to match the house to the man, although I still can't quite believe it can be right,' she told them.

'For goodness' sake, just give us your best guess and then go to bed,' Hugh demanded impatiently.

'It's not a guess,' she said with as much dignity as she could muster while battling against the after-effects of her demanding day. 'I tracked the man who met your follower back to a house in Grosvenor Square. When he ran down the front steps nearly an hour later I could tell he was one of the *ton* from his dress and that air of owning the world you aristocrats seem to be born with.'

'You should, since you have it yourself in spades. Now cut line and get on with your story, Louisa,' her brother said shortly.

'It took me a while to work out who he was because it's so unlikely, but I went to a ball there once so I'm sure it was the Earl of Kinsham's house. The man who had Hugh followed, Kit, was his lordship's son and heir, Viscount Rarebridge, and what earthly reason could he have to do that?' she said, barely able to believe it herself, so no wonder if they didn't either.

'The deuce it was!' Hugh exclaimed softly,

taking her word for it, even while he visibly flinched at that name, as if the knowledge hurt.

'Why would a man like his lordship have you followed?' she asked.

'I heard whispers that he was one of them,' he muttered half to himself, 'but I never let myself believe it.'

'One of whom?' she demanded.

'My wife's lovers,' he explained bleakly and she felt her knees wobble with the stark shock of his words.

'You have a wife?' she whispered and wondered numbly how words could actually hurt on your tongue.

'What?' he asked, almost as if he'd forgotten she was there.

'Your wife?' she asked more firmly, rediscovering her temper under the goad of his impatience.

'What wife? Oh, that one. No, my wife has been dead these three years and more,' he replied rather vaguely, somehow not defusing her temper when he couldn't seem to grasp what he'd done to anger her in the first place.

'You have a lot of explaining to do,' she informed him haughtily.

'Later,' he said, as if she was bothering him with foolish trivialities.

'Now, unless you want me to march round to Grosvenor Square this minute and ask Lord Rarebridge why he's so intent on pursuing you myself.'

'That I don't, it would be most unseemly' he said primly.

'Then tell me,' she insisted, trying to look as if she was metaphorically picking out the right bonnet and gloves for the trip.

'My wife took lovers. I stopped counting after the first one I found out about and left for my ship,' he said so brusquely she knew he lied and every name on that list had hurt him. 'Unfortunately, my father wouldn't believe Ariadne anything other than the innocent she played so convincingly and she continued to live under his roof when I was forbidden it for slandering such a fine example of English womanhood. Better for her sake perhaps if she hadn't, since she died there next time I was home on shore leave and raging about the neighbourhood like a wild bull, telling anyone who would listen to me about the injustice of it all, while they no doubt considered my plight a rare piece of entertainment. Looking back at the rash young idiot I was then, he seems so young and silly that I marvel at my own folly.'

'How did she die?' she asked, certain from the shadow in his eyes there was far more to his wife's death than the blunt facts he'd told her so far.

'She was found strangled with one of her silk stockings and my elder brother lay dead outside her bedchamber door. He'd been shot in the back as if he was in the act of fleeing her bed and I, the wronged husband, was presumed to have found him there and murdered him in a furious rage. My estrangement from my wife and family was hardly news in the neighbourhood and I was the only suspect.'

'How could they even think it?' she asked, crossing the room to touch his arm and draw his gaze back to here and now; anything to take the stark bleakness from his blue-grey gaze and set mouth at the thought of that terrible night.

'If not for an old friend vouching for me, I would have hung, Miss Alstone.'

'Idiots,' she condemned roundly and he managed a half-smile before looking remote again and carrying on as if he had to tell her the worst before he faltered.

'I was so blind drunk that night that I'd

collapsed in the taproom of the local inn and been left there to sleep it off for half the village to see. According to Dickon Thrale, the landlord and my childhood friend, he left me lying there in the hope I'd wake up and realise what an idiot I was making of myself. I recall almost nothing of that night, but he certainly saved my life. Yet, because Dickon and I ran wild together when we were young, many in the surrounding area refused to believe I didn't wake up, escape, commit murder, then crawl back to the inn to pretend I'd been there all along. Apparently there were signs that whoever did it must have climbed up the outside of the house to reach my wife's bedchamber, so eventually my inability to even stand upright unassisted that night was accepted and I was declared innocent, if stupid and dissipated. Even now I sometimes wonder if I did it and my friend lied to save my skin, so I can hardly blame the whisperers for persisting in their claim that I had got away with murder twice over.'

'You might fight with your brother, since you're a man and it seems to me that's what men do, and I'm quite sure you bellowed at your wife when you found out what she was up to with other men, but you couldn't hurt a woman or shoot a man in the back if your life depended on it, Hugh Darke,' she informed him impatiently, wondering how he could even dream he ever would.

'How could you know that?' he demanded equally impatiently.

'Because I know you.'

'You know Hugh Darke, or you think you do after a very short acquaintance, which has hardly given you enough time to plumb my darkest depths.'

'No, I know you. Whatever you care to call yourself, whoever you've been since you left your own home and old way of life, there is an essential core of honour and almost brutal honesty about you I would be a want-wit not to recognise.'

'How can you know anything significant about a man you met one day ago? Come, Miss Alstone,' he mocked as if her belief in him might become a danger in itself and therefore must be avoided at all cost, 'I'm quite sure that you, of all people, know better than to trust your first impressions of anyone. You know society presents a smiling face in public and it's really naught but a mask.'

'Would that insight be gained over the years I ran wild through the slums of this unfair city of ours, do you think, Captain? I admit the ones I spent with my so-called equals were a good deal less varied, but you're right in thinking they taught me to recognise a person's true nature, under all the pretty sham the *ton* use to disguise their power and ambitions, so I really don't follow your current argument.'

'Both your lives should serve to warn you I'm not a man to be trusted,' he said roughly, as if she were being obtuse and not him.

'Whether you're striding about your quarter-deck or in your cups, you're the man you've made yourself and, whatever else I might think of you, I'll never believe that man a murderer. I met one or two of those in my youth and you don't have either the heartless steel or the casual cowardice to make a good killer,' she assured him, holding his gaze as she stepped closer to make her point, matching his hard palm to her soft one in a silent declaration of her faith in her lover.

'I've killed for my country,' he told her blankly, as if he couldn't bear to be thought too much of, but he didn't remove his hand from hers.

'You were only there to offer and join battle

with our enemies. Please don't take me for a fool, Hugh.'

'And please don't take me at all, Louisa, not now I've remembered who I really am and how little chance I'll probably have to pretend I'm Hugh Darke for much longer,' he asked, looking as if he truly regretted it when he removed the warmth of his palm from hers and retreated a step or two.

'Perhaps you consider I'm not a good enough match for Hugo Kenton, then?' she asked as coolly as she could, contrarily feeling as if the promise of their shared future was being withdrawn, just when she'd almost got used to having it there.

'Of course you were bound to work out who I really am,' he said bitterly. 'How many men are openly cuckolded by their wife, then accused of murdering her as well as their own brother? I should have known you'd soon pin me down, Miss Alstone, moving in the circles you do.'

'Yes, you should,' she said impatiently, 'and you're still innocent.'

'Only until I'm proven guilty, and no doubt Rarebridge is congratulating himself on getting one step nearer to doing that right now.

He probably wants to examine me properly and disprove Dickon's evidence.'

'You believe every man your wife slept with to be innocent apart from yourself then, Captain? I'm not as sanguine about his purpose as you appear to be and it must be very convenient for the real murderer that you took the blame for his crimes on your own shoulders as if you deserved it. The men he set on you are not poor and simple souls, intent on making a little money by tracking down a renegade for a man with more gold than sense. They come from a gang who will do anything for money, up to and including murder.'

'Believe her, Kenton, my sister used to amuse herself by following the worst and most suspicious villains she could find, for the sheer daredevil challenge of staying on their tails without them knowing about it,' Kit said grimly and Louisa was surprised he'd known what she got up to when he wasn't there to check her wilder starts. 'I had to get her out of the stews for more reasons than the obvious one of not leaving my sisters in such a place once they began to mature.'

'At least physically,' Hugh said sceptically, his gaze hard on her as he realised what dangers she'd run, now and then.

'Never mind that—do you believe me about the nature of the company his lordship is keeping?'

'I believe what you say is worth a clear-headed investigation.'

'How very flattering of you, Captain, I'm almost overwhelmed.'

'It is, if you did but know,' he said with a rather weary smile. 'I promised myself when Ariadne died that I would never listen to another woman swearing she was telling me only the truth, when my wife lied as compulsively as she breathed. Now I'm considering a man I once called my friend could want me dead or be willing to let me hang in his stead, all on the say-so of a lady.'

'How very remarkable of me to persuade you of anything so vexatious, being a woman and all,' she drawled, hanging on to her temper by a hair's breadth.

'Clumsy of you, Hugo,' Kit observed. 'And loathe though I am to part you two lovebirds, it really is high time my sister went to bed. Climbing out of windows, scaling three-storey buildings, carousing with rogues like you and tramping about half of London at a dizzying height must take it out of a woman, even if she is my intrepid sister. Are you sure you can match her, Kenton?'

'Quite sure you'll insist I do, whether I want to or not,' he replied with a withdrawal of all emotion that made Louisa feel very weary indeed, and resolved not to wed the man, child or no, if he couldn't make a better fist of wanting her.

'We'll see,' she told them both, with a militant nod as she quit the room with a cold look for Hugh and a warning one for her brother ordering him not to follow her.

'That certainly told us,' Kit said ruefully as the door snapped to behind her.

'Little firebrand,' Hugh replied with a wry smile.

'And if you ever manage to persuade her to marry you, my sister will be as true to you as honed steel for the rest of your mutual lives. She doesn't know how to be anything but loyal to those she loves, confoundedly restless little minx though she is.'

'Who said anything about love?' Hugh argued, although the very notion of gaining Louisa Alstone's suddenly seemed infinitely desirable, rather than the cursed trap it ought to be to a man with his history.

'If you don't propose even trying to love my sister, I might have to kill you after all, Kenton,' Kit warned him, with none of the drama and fuss a lesser man might put into such a threat, and all the cold purpose it would lack on such blustering tongues.

'What man lucky enough to have even a chance of winning your sister wouldn't fight his best friend for her? If he had aught to offer but a filthy scandal and a sword of Damocles hanging over his head, of course,' Hugh made himself answer just as coldly, feeling as if he was bidding farewell to an impossible dream he would regret losing for the rest of his life.

'Then it's high time we got on and cleared your name, Hugo. This limbo can't continue much longer, under the circumstances.'

'And do you think I haven't tried to do just that?' Hugh responded gruffly.

'Not hard enough, or those damned rumours would have died a natural death the day you were declared innocent by the magistrates. Louisa is right—while you half-believe you could have done it, there's no reason to probe the matter more deeply. Are you going to honour her belief in you and do what you should have done three years ago, man? It would help the rest of us if you weren't more interested in finding oblivion in the bottom of the nearest bottle while you're about it, but if you insist on turning aside from your obligations, no doubt my redoubtable sister will continue her crusade to clear your name anyway.'

'God forbid!' Hugh said with a shudder, easily picturing Louisa Alstone doing exactly that. His frown softened into a silly grin as he considered the extraordinary outcome of his latest attempt at losing himself in a brandy bottle.

'When I found you drunk and disorderly in the gutter all those years ago, you hadn't shared too much with my sister,' Christopher Alstone warned him austerely. 'You'll fight your demons this time, Hugh Kenton, or you'll fight me.'

'How did you know?' Hugh asked unwarily, his thoughts on the extraordinary intimacy he'd shared with the so-called Ice Diamond, which proved what a pack of witless fools the beaux who misnamed her so in their cups truly were.

'Don't be ridiculous; even if it wasn't written all over your faces when I arrived, I recognised you two were lovers the instant I saw you alone together. Why else do you think I sent the *Kindly Maid* on her way in such a hurry, before the crew got the slightest drift of what the two of you had been doing while my back was turned?'

What could he say to the man who took him in and gave him work when the rest of the world turned their backs? God, but Kit Alstone must be regretting his kindness now, and how could he blame him?

'I'm sorry, Alstone, there's no excuse for what I did. It was the act of a villain and a braggart and all they say of me under both my names I have just proved all too true. I can't seem to keep my hands off your sister and the devil's driven me from the instant I laid eyes on her, and I'll confess to you that I've dreamt about her night after night, like some mawkish youth, until I tried to drown the very thought of her in brandy and still failed. She only made it worse by materialising out of the night when I was several sheets to the wind, looking like a pirate queen and the embodiment of every idiotic fantasy I ever had about her. I've no excuse for how I behaved, not even when the very sight of her makes me forget every last scrap of honour and integrity I thought I still had.'

'When *did* you first lay eyes on her?' Kit asked, suspicion sharp in his dark eyes once more, and Hugh could hardly blame him, since he'd made it sound as if they'd been carrying on a clandestine affair for weeks while his back was turned.

If anyone laid his greedy hands on his sister, he'd take him apart with his bare hands. So why was Kit Alstone watching him so keenly, instead of slamming his fists into his face and making him regret the day he was born? He'd not be able to offer any resistance when his employer had every right to beat him to a bloody pulp for taking his sister's maidenhead, then threatening to walk away and leave her to deal with any consequences of their heated, hasty coupling alone.

'When I docked three weeks ago. I found Miss Alstone alone in your office, glaring at me with those extraordinary indigo eyes of hers and looking like every unattainable fantasy I ever dreamt after too long at sea, and she was quite evidently there to see you and not me.'

'And she encouraged you to think she was my lightskirt, I dare say?'

'How could you know that?' Hugh was surprised into asking before he realised he'd just confirmed Kit's suspicions about his wayward sister, when he'd been doing his shabby best to protect her from the worst of her brother's wrath as well.

'She's my sister, don't forget. Louisa has been a delight and a challenge to the rest of us from the day she was born and has more steely determination in her little finger than you'd find in half a legion of proper young ladies in pursuit of a peer's coronet. My sister hates to be thwarted, nearly as much as she dislikes being left out of any mad adventure that's brewing. It's only because I know what devious schemes and tall tales she's capable of thinking up that I'm not dismembering you slowly and painfully at this very moment.'

'That's something for me to be grateful for then,' Hugh said solemnly.

'Did you still think she was this mysterious Eloise when you…?' Kit's voice trailed off and Hugh saw a tinge of hot colour on his cheeks that matched the one he could feel burning across his own at the very thought of what they were discussing. For a moment he was tempted to lie and say yes, but he owed Louisa more honesty.

'No, I'd smoked her out shortly before that.'

'Then why the hell did you do it, man? You knew very well she was not only a lady, but my little sister by then, so even if she somehow misled you about her virginity, which is the kind of ridiculous lie I wouldn't put past her if it suited her, you must have known I'd flay you alive, then use your worthless hide for a waistcoat if you didn't marry her very soon after being fool enough to take her at her word.'

'I couldn't *not* touch her,' Hugh finally admitted in a rush of baffled emotion, as if the very words had been racked out of him along with the inexplicable feelings behind them. 'I can't keep my hands off her, or my mouth or… No, you don't want to know. I admit that I lose control of my senses and my mind and my very self when I'm alone in the dark with your sister and let's leave it at that, shall we?'

'Yes, let's,' Kit said with suspicious geniality. 'Which will give us so much more time for planning your wedding, don't you think?'

'I'm a nothing, who can't even use the name I was born with. Do you really think your sister would be better off wed to a potential murderer than bearing a bastard alone, Alstone? I'm not sure I do, especially when I could be taken up for murder and hung if Dickon and the villagers recant their story, or someone manages to cast enough doubt on it in order to justify a trial. Better if Louisa went off somewhere anonymous to have my child in secret, if there is one, then later adopt it as some obscure little orphan cousin, rather than marry a dangerous brute like me.'

'When are you going to explain all this self-pitying drivel to her then, Hugo? Just so I can quit the scene and leave you to take the furious edge of her tongue because, by God, you'll richly deserve it. I don't say it's what I wanted for her; I won't even lie and tell you the idea that you might prove the ideal man for my feisty little sister had ever occurred to me before you made it a *fait accompli*, but now your marriage is imperative, at least I'm more hopeful about it than either of you seem to be.'

'She deserves a better husband.'

'True, so make yourself better, unless you want to be slowly dismembered after all?'

'If only it were as easy as merely wanting to deserve her,' Hugo said, sadly shaking his head over how very far from the ideal husband he would always be.

'It could be simple enough, if you'd only get on and fight for your reputation and the life you should have led these past three years, rather than lying down for everyone to trample over as if that's all you deserve.'

'And that's supposed to be easy?'

'When you consider the alternative of telling my sister you're not going to marry her, even though you might have got her with child, I think you'll find that it is. You are innocent of murdering your wife and brother, Hugo, but clearly you lack the courage to prove it—so what exactly do you expect Louisa to say when you explain to her why you can't marry her after all?'

'Put like that, the whole business appears much simpler,' Hugh admitted.

'Because you fear the rough side of Louisa's tongue?' Kit asked coolly.

'No, because I hate the way she squares up to take the next blow on her stubborn chin without letting anyone see how much it hurts her. I don't know why you thrust her into society when she clearly didn't want to be there, Alstone, but the *ton* doesn't seem to have done her any more good than it ever did me.'

Somehow Hugh sensed that he'd said something right, purely by accident, and some of the tension left his friend's lean frame and the atmosphere in this now-stuffy room seemed a little easier all of a sudden. Perhaps he could make a success of himself after all, or at least enough of a success to give Louisa the sort of life she richly deserved, if not the husband he would have wished for such a fiery, loyal, misjudged lady as his Eloise had proved herself to be.

'That's because neither of you ever learnt how to handle them, Kenton,' his future brother-in-law was telling him and it behoved Hugh to listen if he really wanted that unlikely future with an equally unlikely bride. 'My sister is far too proud to admit she needs anyone's approval, let alone that of a pack of finicky strangers inclined to look down their long noses at Bevis Alstone's brood, and it strikes me you're not a sight different to her. I know you were lionised as a hero even before Trafalgar and your captaincy came along to make you even more bigheaded, so falling from such dizzy heights was harder for you than a man like me who never had much grace to lose in the first place. Now you're so wrapped up in living down to your dark and desperate reputation that you can't see there are good people among the *ton*. I'd probably include you in those honourable exceptions, by the way, if you hadn't sunk to being one of my ship's masters through your own inaction.'

'What a spineless fellow I am, to be sure.'

'No, but you probably need to prove to

yourself and my sister that you're not, if you're ever going to be happy together. I trust you do intend making Louisa happy, by the way?'

The question was suddenly sharp and Hugh reminded himself exactly who he was dealing with and how ruthless Christopher Alstone could be, as he considered that question as soberly and honestly as he had it in him to manage at the moment.

'I would be honoured to wed your sister, if I thought she wouldn't suffer by such a close association with me,' Hugh admitted cautiously, not willing to look deeper into his feelings whilst it seemed such an unlikely outcome.

'Good, I'll let you live until morning so you can ask her properly then,' Kit said casually and held open the parlour door so that Hugh had no choice but to take the candle thrust at him and go up to bed as well.

Chapter Ten

Louisa awoke the following morning in the bedchamber that was fast becoming familiar and wondered what Mrs Calhoun would have to say about that state of affairs, once she arrived back at her post to find Louisa living in such close proximity with dissolute Captain Darke. Not quite sure what to make of it herself, she climbed out of bed and found a can of cooling hot water on the washstand she only hoped her brother had brought in, instead of the man she must learn to think of as Hugo Kenton. Somehow the idea of Hugh seeing her asleep and unguarded made her shiver and she told herself it was because she wasn't yet so committed to the man she wanted him to know how she looked first thing in the morning, either asleep or barely awake.

The Kenton baronetcy went back a good deal further into history than the Alstone family earldom and, since she recalled hearing that the current baronet only had two sons to his name to begin with, Hugo Kenton would be a baronet one day, whether he liked it or not. Or he would if he was cleared of suspicion for his wife's and brother's murders, since no murderer could gain from his crime. She didn't feel like the future wife of a potential baronet. She didn't feel much like daring, mysterious Captain Hugh Darke's bold and brassy lady either.

Except for the odd twinge of soreness at her most intimate core, she didn't feel much different from the Louisa Alstone who'd risen from this very bed only yesterday morning. Yet she knew deep down that she was drastically different all the same and not just physically either. As she washed and dressed in garments much more suited to a young lady than Charlton's silly dressing-up clothes or the cast-offs she'd bought yesterday, she considered that difference distractedly. What if she was in the process of becoming a mother at this very moment? Could the tiny seed of a new human being, hers and Hugh's child, be growing in her belly right now?

She rubbed a wondering hand over her flat stomach and felt awed by the very idea of taking responsibility for something so much greater than herself. The idea of a tiny being, partly from her and partly from its potent father, was too much to even think about when it might only be alive in her imagination. Yet the possible product of that hasty, driven coupling between her and Hugh Kenton might dictate her future—all their futures. Odd that love and consideration for a being that might not even exist should drive two such unlikely people into marriage. But what if there really was to be a child and she refused it a father as strong and brooding and torn by ridiculous self-doubts as her impossible, piratical lover?

Pushing all such possibilities and questions aside for consideration later, she wound her hair into a simple knot on the back of her head, decided she was as neat as she'd ever be without the help of a maid and went downstairs to find out if she had to cook breakfast again this morning.

Apparently she was to be spared the task as Mrs Calhoun had miraculously reappeared, obviously from somewhere much closer than

Maria and Brandon's rectory, and was directing operations with a long ladle in her hand, as if she fully expected to conjure something remarkable at any moment.

'You two can go and sit in the breakfast parlour and wait for Miss Louisa to join you like a pair of civilised gentlemen for once,' she scolded as Hugh repeated his trick of the morning before and stole a piece of crisp bacon from the dish she was preparing for what looked like a formal banquet rather than a simple breakfast.

Louisa felt a clench of something dangerous squeeze her heart at the intimacy of coming to know her lover in so many ways other than the obvious. A smile she sincerely hoped nobody saw curved her mouth while she wondered what it would be like to learn as many of his odd quirks and habits as he'd ever let anyone know as his wife. If he didn't feel any more for her than a passing lust and a guilty conscience at having seduced an over-eager virgin, then she was never likely to know more about him than she did right now. The very idea of that brutal separation from a man who was already beginning to mean too much to her killed her smile before she hardly felt it on her lips, ready to betray her.

'No need, Mrs Calhoun,' she said brightly enough as she stepped forwards, 'I'm already here, so why can't we all eat together as we did in the old days?'

'I know what's due to a lady, even if she doesn't seem to have the least idea herself,' Mrs Calhoun informed her sternly.

'And if we agree to take that old argument of yours as a given, dear Mrs Calhoun, why should we three sit apart from the rest of the household like a trio of bodkins? If you're intending to tell me Kit sits in lone state whenever he has no visitors to entertain, then you must have become a lot less truthful since last we met,' she told her mother's one-time cook-housekeeper with an affectionate smile.

'You're as bad as that one yonder,' Mrs Calhoun told her with another wave of that expressive ladle of hers towards Hugh, who did his best to look innocent and failed, as well he might.

'Oh, no, I challenge anyone to turn your kitchen into a midden quite as quickly as Captain Darke managed to do when you were gone,' Louisa said with a militant frown he pretended not to notice.

'There you are, Master Kit, I told you he was a heathen.'

'Did I argue with you?' her employer asked as if it was nothing to do with him what went on in his own household, so Louisa scowled at him as well.

'No, but only because you know I'm right. Just as I was right to take Midge away for a while as well, for all he'd not lay a finger on her, even when he's in his cups. I wasn't having a lot of nasty-minded gossip about my girl doin' the rounds, just because she's not as clever as she might be and his nibs is as handsome as the devil and almost as bad.'

'Why, thank you, ma'am,' Hugh said with a would-be modest smile. 'I thought you were immune to my charms, but you know very well that you will always have my heart,' he added with a soulful look and his hand theatrically over the place where it ought to be, if only he had one.

'My cooking has your heart you mean, you black-hearted rogue, you. Now get along to the breakfast parlour like I told you to and take Miss Louisa with you, for I've no time to put up with either of you under my feet this morning when Midge and I already have more than enough to do getting this place set to rights again.'

'I can help you,' Louisa offered.

'That you can't, young lady, and it strikes me as how you've got more important things to do than pretend to be a housemaid this morning,' the formidable dame told her ominously and Louisa wondered if her ex-virgin status was written across her forehead for all to see, then told herself it was just a guilty conscience that made her blush and do as she was bid.

'You are in deep disgrace with our domestic tyrant,' Hugh told her unhelpfully.

'Not as deep as you must have been when she first set eyes on the state you got her precious house in while she was gone.She must have wanted to skin you alive then, even after my efforts to improve matters a little.'

'It's not her house, but your brother's.'

'Believe that if you must,' she muttered as her brother followed them into the room and all chance for a satisfying private argument about nothing in particular was lost for the time being as they ate their meal in uneasy silence.

'A word with you both, if you please,' Kit said shortly, once Hugh had thrown down his napkin and Louisa gave up even pretending to eat more than a few bites of her breakfast.

Since she thought Hugh as intent on avoiding those words and drifting on with everything unresolved as she was, she categorised both him and herself cowards and strolled towards Kit's book-room without an argument. The disadvantages of having fallen among gentlemen occurred to her as they bowed her ahead of them and she could almost feel Hugh whatever-he-was-calling-himself-today eyeing the sway of her hips and wolfishly appreciating any glimpses of her slender legs afforded by her soft muslin skirts brushing against her body as she walked. She let herself marvel at such an unlikely fashion pertaining in modern Britain, when it was far more suited to somewhere much hotter and more leisurely, to distract herself from the thought that it felt powerful to know she held Hugh's attention so completely it was almost something she could reach out and touch.

'What is it now, Kit?' she asked impatiently when they reached his comfortable study and she lost the advantage.

'You two,' he said abruptly and she raised her eyebrows. 'You will stay in this room together until I have a decision one way or the other out of you about your marriage. Hugh—you will forget your late wife for a moment and consider what you and my sister can have instead and whether you truly want to live without it. Louisa—you will stand and listen to what he has to say like a grown woman and not a little savage just dragged in off the streets against her will, then you will answer him only after some of that mature consideration you keep telling me you're capable of, at least if you wish me to ever take a single word you say seriously ever again.'

'Oh, I will, will I?' she flamed, but it was wasted because he hadn't waited for an argument and shut the door on them with a decided snap instead.

She strode over to the window and plumped down on the seat cushions to stare moodily out over the small garden beyond and waited to hear what Hugh had to say with a sinking heart.

'He's right, you know,' Hugh told her moodily.

'I know,' she said with a sigh, 'but don't expect me to like him very much for it just at the moment.'

'Which will make a change from disliking me, I suppose.'

'I don't dislike you.'

'That's a start, then, so perhaps we can

proceed to the business in hand without the accompaniment of raised voices or fisticuffs?'

'No, I don't wish to be an item on a business agenda.'

He sighed. She remembered Kit ordering her to be reasonable and sighed herself, before meeting his unreadable gaze as serenely as she could make herself. Not her best move so far, since she only had to look into his eyes for the intimacy of last night's dark loving to ambush her with all sorts of possible futures. Having little experience of deep emotion between a man and a woman, she couldn't tell if it was only lust that burned under the acute intelligence in Hugh Darke's silvered gaze.

'No, I don't suppose you do,' he conceded, 'but we must decide what to do anyway.'

'At this exact minute?' she asked, not sure why she wanted to procrastinate when the very thought of him ever marrying anyone else was unendurable.

'Yes, and a great deal hinges on your reply to my proposal, Louisa.'

'Hugh Darke for one,' she said, feeling oddly cast down by the idea of losing a man who never was. 'If I don't agree to marry you, then he will have to disappear, will he not?'

'His days are numbered, whatever you decide,' Hugh said, with a rather bitter twist to his supposedly careless smile at the idea of losing his alter-ego.

'Because of your association with me?'

'No, because of the choices I must make, Eloise or no.'

'Please don't try and comfort me with clever words, Captain. If not for what happened last night, you would be able to sail under Kit's colours for as long as you chose to do so, would you not?'

'Maybe I would, but how honest would that have been of me, I wonder?'

'Oddly enough, honesty and honour don't figure high on my list of priorities, Captain. I'd choose survival and as small a lie as necessary over them any day.'

'Witness your blatant inability to walk away from a friend in trouble, or not lay down everything you are for any stranger who happened to be in trouble? Don't make yourself out to be someone you're not to me, Louisa. At least grant us that much honesty with each other, even if there's to be nothing more.'

She paused and watched him cautiously, alert for any hint of mockery or doubt in his suddenly very austere countenance; she could see nothing but sincerity there, so she let herself ask the question at the heart of all this.

'We really shouldn't marry though, should we, Hugh?' she said very softly at last. 'Not people like us,' she added with real regret.

'People like me, you mean? What have you ever done wrong, Louisa?'

'I've always been difficult and intransigent and I don't suffer fools gladly or fake laughter when I only feel boredom, and that's just to start with,' she confessed.

'Sounds like heaven to me,' he quipped and suddenly she felt a deep shaft of pain open up at the idea that their marriage could indeed have been wonderful.

'No, because if you were to marry me, it would make re-establishing yourself in society twice as hard as it would be with a better wife,' she warned.

'Now you're being ridiculous, and mawkish with it,' he condemned roughly, as if he truly believed it.

'Then I'm astonished you want to marry me, but I was forgetting, wasn't I? You really don't want to marry me at all. We got carried away by propinquity and now you feel honour bound to wed me, despite the fact that I deliberately misled you about my virgin status.'

'I might have restrained myself a little more if I'd known,' he told her in that dark-velvet voice that sent hot shivers racing down her spine like little splurges of lightning, 'but not to the extent of letting you find an excuse to leave me, not once I knew this damnable wanting was mutual.'

'Does it have to be damnable?' she whispered, achingly aware that this incessant need of each other felt very far from it to her.

'What do you think?' he murmured back as they stared into each other's eyes as if their very lives depended on reading the right answer to that question.

'I have to hope that it doesn't,' she managed, refusing to drop her eyelids and shelter her thoughts and dreams from his gaze. 'It doesn't have to be paradise, I won't beg for love or even offer it until I know if that's what I feel for you, but it can be more than hellish between us, don't you think, Hugh? It's certainly more than I ever imagined feeling for any man already.'

'Oh, you sweet idiot,' he said with a twisted smile she could feel as much as see from such close quarters.

'Because I have hopes?' she asked, rather hurt that she'd come so far from her resolution never to marry to meet him with those hopes for something more, only to have them thrown back in her face.

'Because of who I am,' he said starkly, pain in his eyes now and such sharp distaste for himself in his deep voice that it somehow made her want to cry.

She blinked very hard, knowing he would see it as pity when it was a far more complex emotion than sympathy for a wronged man. 'It's only because of who you are that I'm even considering marrying you, Hugo Kenton,' she said, putting enough distance between them to look him fully in the face while she admitted it.

'When who I am should send you screaming to your brother for any alternative he can come up with to save your good name?' he replied, as if he'd like to be cold and almost amused enough to put her off him, but somehow couldn't quite bring the lie on to his tongue or into his eyes.

'No, because who you are is an honourable man who cares about others and would die protecting someone he loves if he had to. If I am ever to be a mother, and it's a great surprise for me to find out how very much I want that status after all now you've put the idea in my head, then I want that man as father of my children, Hugh,' she countered as strongly as she could.

She stood back and saw him battle between hope and dread and opened her eyes a little wider to stem the heat of tears that really threatened this time and would probably ruin everything. No doubt he'd seen enough tears to flood the Nile from his unfaithful wife and she refused to use such a weapon to win even the shallowest argument between them, because of that wretched woman's counterfeit sorrow and an innate sense of fair play.

For the same reason, she told herself, she kept a tender smile off her mouth by biting her lips, because no doubt he'd seen enough of those to distrust even the gentlest of curves on a female mouth. At this rate she would end up pretending to be emotionless and suddenly she knew that fighting not to be like Ariadne Kenton would ruin their marriage, if they made one, as surely as floods of tears and a constant parade of lovers. If Hugh married her, he would get Louisa Alstone: stubborn, difficult and as disobliging as the *ton* and almost everyone else seemed to find her. Giving a sharp nod to confirm her determination never to lie about her emotions, either way, she met his eyes with a challenge in her own.

'We began this argument last night, while you still had the scorch of how we were together biting at your conscience. Now we are arguing backwards and I'm sick of it, Mr Kenton. So, do you want to marry me or don't you?'

'If I were any other man but the one I am, then, yes, I do.'

She clicked her tongue with impatience at such a leaden declaration. 'Doesn't sound like it to me,' she informed him shortly.

'Then will you marry me, Miss Louisa Alstone?'

'What about all your ifs and buts, Captain?'

'To the devil with them, as long as you know I may never be exonerated from the scandal hanging over me and can accept it?'

'I can,' she said, knowing he had the might of Kit and Ben's stubborn wills behind his case as well as her own whether he liked it or not now, and that, whether they ended up married or not, that backing would continue.

'Then will you wed me, woman?'

'Yes,' she agreed on a sigh even she didn't understand.

'Good, then perhaps we should inform your

brother of our decision, so it may be got on with as soon as possible,' he agreed and she felt as if she was back to being that item on his agenda of things to do today.

'Perhaps we should,' she agreed rather listlessly.

'I promise not to be a drunkard with you, Louisa,' he said stiffly, when she'd thought the topic of their marriage closed off and done with for now.

'I asked you for no promises,' she replied as her memory dragged up all the abject ones her father had made her mother, then broken as easily as if they'd never been spoken as soon as he went out of the front door.

'Forget your father. I will never take more than three glasses of anything in any one day again, for my own sake if you don't want it to be for yours, Eloise. It's high time I stopped hiding in a brandy bottle; it had got vastly tedious, even when I wasn't getting myself into trouble with outrageously behaved female pirates.'

'Rake,' she accused obligingly.

'Not any more,' he argued with a would-be saintly smile.

'Eloise would be highly disappointed to hear that,' she murmured in a throaty purr as she brushed against him with a provocative, stray-cat rub that she hoped left him as instantly aroused as she was herself.

'Then perhaps we could make an exception for Mademoiselle La Rochelle?'

'And Captain Darke?'

'He can play, too, if you think we can find room enough in our marriage bed for both the rogues.'

'Somehow we'll find it, Captain,' she assured him with a mock-innocent smile and felt reassured by the wicked glint in his eyes at that intriguing idea.

'Are you intending to be happy then, little sister?' Kit asked when they eventually ran him down in the stables, checking on his restless team as well as the swift riding horses he kept for both necessity and pleasure.

'Yes, we think so, don't we, Hugh?' Louisa smiled, turning to look into silver-shot blue eyes.

'I'm going to be, so I dare say your brother and his best friend will take it in turns to beat me to a pulp if I fail to make you so too, my lovely,' he said and she was so glad he didn't quite call her 'love' that she smiled and did her best to look as dazzled and sweetly happy as any newly made fiancée.

'St Margaret's in three days,' Kit told them implacably and that was that.

Chapter Eleven

'So besides arranging my wedding for me, what else have you been about?' Hugh asked his employer as soon as Louisa had been dragged off to discuss wedding finery by a surprisingly enthusiastic Mrs Calhoun and he'd run Kit to earth in his book-room.

'Business,' Kit said uninformatively.

'Personal business?'

'Very,' Kit told him with a bland look that would put most men at a distance.

'So whose personal business have you been engaged on?' Hugh persisted.

'Yours, since you're about to become part of my family.'

'Damn it, Kit, don't you think I can deal with it myself then?' Hugh said, knowing very well what business it was and how he wished the whole dirty affair was dead and done with, along with his old life.

'You have had three years to do so and now it's become urgent.'

'Why? By some miracle your sister believes me innocent, you and Ben would never have given me one of your precious ships if you thought I was going to murder the first man who crossed me, so why the sudden haste?'

'Because your father is dying,' Kit told him sombrely and Hugh had to turn away and pace over to the window to stare bleakly out and hide his feelings.

'I wouldn't have thought I'd care after he ordered me to go to the devil alone, but oddly enough I seem to all the same.'

'We all have that conundrum to deal with, my friend,' Kit said gently.

Hugh turned to meet his steady gaze, recalling what Louisa had told him of her father's death. 'I was luckier than you. He was a good parent to all three of us, once upon a time.'

'Yet at least I knew what to expect of my sire.'

'Nothing?'

'Precisely, but we digress, Hugh. My demons are for me to fight, as and when I choose to do so; yours won't wait any longer.'

'The lawyers will certainly scratch their heads over the succession, given the estrangement that had existed between us for so long, but surely nothing has changed? I still didn't murder my wife, or my brother, and nobody can prove that I did, any more than I can shake off these rumours that I'm guilty.'

'It might stir them up and make the magistrates take notice, whether they want to or not. There are whispers about calling in the Runners to ask you and your friend the innkeeper sharper questions than you faced at the time.'

'Who puts them about, Kit? Who the devil is doing this? My second cousin, Arthur Kenton, is the only other heir and he's eighty if he's a day. Unless he's wed his housekeeper in the last three years and produced a legitimate brat in his old age, he can't have any real interest in the Gracemont estate or the title.'

'No, he's perfectly happy for you to succeed, so long as you don't wed another empty-headed demi-rep.'

Hugh gave a gruff bark of surprised laughter as he could imagine old Arthur saying those very words. 'You've seen him, then?'

'Him and most of your other living relatives,' Kit admitted and when Hugh considered his mother had been the youngest daughter of a family of eight, it suddenly seemed no wonder his employer had been away for so long. 'Including your father, of course—you will find him very much changed, I suspect.'

'I might, if I had the slightest intention of going anywhere near Gracemont Priory while he's still inhabiting it. He ordered me never to "befoul any of my roofs with your presence while I still have breath in my body" the last time I saw him and I fully intend to obey him, in that if in nothing else.'

'I never met a man more sorry for what he did in the heat of his grief for your brother, if that's any consolation to you?' Kit said.

Hugh stared bleakly back at him as he struggled with the full horror of the moment when his father had made it clear he thought his younger son guilty of murdering his elder one, even if the rest of the world had been forced to absolve him and must now rely on rumours to damn him with.

'Maybe I didn't do it, Kit, but I still married Ariadne Lockstone and brought her into his house, so that her latest lover could strangle her, then shoot my brother in the back one dark night.'

'And you did that deliberately, did you? Wed a gently-bred whore, just so you could destroy your brother and your father's peace into the bargain?'

'No, of course not. I wed her because I was a big-headed, besotted fool who thought he'd captured the sweet-natured little beauty all the other men in the *ton* wanted. I had no idea half the rakes on the town had already been in her bed and the other half would very shortly follow in their footsteps. No wonder she latched on to the only fool with money and a convenient career overseas who was still fool enough to beg her to marry him.'

'Not your father's fault either, Hugh. Maybe he should have thrown her out of his house when he found out the woman took lovers like most women change their clothing, but perhaps he'd decided to wait until you applied for a legal separation through the proper channels.'

'He was the one who forbade me to do so. That would have been far too public an admission of failure and Marcus would provide him with legitimate heirs, so any by-blows my wife chose to inflict on the family must be tolerated rather than leave his precious name tarnished by such a scandal,' Hugh said bitterly.

'You can never know if he would have decided to endure that humiliation or not now, for all he was wrong to try to dictate your life. All he cares about now is having you home again, if only so you can care for your sister and the people on his estates when he quits this world.'

'That sounds like him, too. You've been very busy on my behalf.'

'He sent for me,' his friend explained dispassionately.

'He sent for you? No word to his own son, but he must send for my friend and employer? Was it to tell you what an unsatisfactory heir he has to put up with and how heavily it presses on his soul and his conscience to leave all he's ever cared for in such unworthy hands?'

'No, he spoke to me of his bitter regret at being so lost in grief and shame that he pushed you away and let you think he believed you guilty of a crime it just isn't in your nature to commit.'

'That would be because he did believe it— my father told me to get out of his house and never come back, my friend. Don't make me doubt my ears and eyes as well as everything else. To hell with him and Gracemont—if it tumbles down tomorrow I won't give a tinker's damn,' Hugh lied.

'Soon it will be yours; you can demolish it if you hate it so much.'

'To hell with that! I'll not see my sister homeless and our people left to starve,' Hugh raged in a fine passion, until he realised what he'd just said and plumped down in one of the comfortable armchairs by the fireplace and glared at the makings of a fire laid there as if it held all the answers he wished he had.

'Here, drink this,' Kit demanded, setting a glass of fine brandy at his elbow, then ghosting out of the room.

'Hugh?' Louisa asked softly as she met his frowning eyes with puzzlement in her own, so at least Kit hadn't told him what an idiot he was before sending her to soothe his savage brow, now his so-called friend had forced him to face his true feelings for his old home and the inheritance it sounded as if he'd be receiving all too soon.

'A promise no sooner given than broken,' he told her bitterly, raising the brandy glass at her in a mock toast before downing the contents in one swallow.

'Only if you intend to consume the rest of

Kit's decanter as well, and I told you I didn't want that promise.'

'Nor any of the other ones I have to give,' he said gloomily.

'No, I want them, Hugh, but first it would be good if you could learn to mean them before you make them.'

'Why not?' he said recklessly. 'No doubt I'll argue black's white soon after, as your confounded brother tricked me into doing before he sent you to calm the beast.'

'He's my confounded brother and it's my privilege to misname him, not yours. Anyway, Kit can only manipulate you into saying whatever it was you didn't want to say if you allow him to. You should know by now how sly and slippery he can be when he's intent on doing good to those who don't want to be done good to,' she said unsympathetically.

'How can I agree with the second part of that without breaching your prohibition from the first?' he asked with a fleeting smile that acknowledged how difficult and stubborn he was probably being. 'My father is dying, Louisa,' he told her in a rush, saw pity in her deep-cobalt gaze and rose impatiently to his feet so he could pace restlessly and not meet them again until it had gone.

'Ah, Hugh?' she asked softly, as if she wanted to find a way of comforting him, but didn't know how, and something seemed to break inside him as he fought back what he considered unmanly tears at the loss of a man who'd once looked him coldly in the eyes and sworn his second son was as dead to him as his first.

'He ordered me out of his house, told me he was ashamed to own me as his son and ordered me never to try to contact him or my little sister again, and now he's dying, Louisa.'

'And you love him, despite all he's said and done?'

'Yes,' he managed between gritted teeth as he strode up and down Kit's fine Turkey carpet, fighting the full effects of that admission with the only action available to him.

'Which makes you a better man than he ever was,' she said gently, halting his restless pacing by simply standing in his path.

'I don't think it's a competition,' he said on a shaken laugh and walked straight into her arms and felt them close about him as if it was exactly where he'd needed to be since the moment Kit told him Sir Horace Kenton had finally hit an obstacle he couldn't wilfully ignore or order out of his way.

'It's not, of course, but did you and your brother never have a friendly one between you? I know that we all did for our mother's approval,' she said gently and he smiled, grateful for the reminder of how much he and his brother and sister had loved each another, once upon a time.

'Now you mention it, I believe we did. It was scattered to the four winds as soon as I entered the Navy, of course. Hard to keep up a rivalry about who had the most sugar plums and the least number of stern lectures on our heathen ways with a few thousand leagues of ocean parting us.'

'And you loved him dearly as well, didn't you?'

'Yes, but I could still have harmed him, Louisa. You know all too well how savagely a drunkard can lash out in his cups and I was very drunk the night my wife and brother died, and remembered very little about it the next morning.'

'From my experience you're not a violent drunk, Hugh,' she said softly, raising a hand to gently frame the side of his face. 'A man's true character comes out when he's in his cups and you were certainly in yours the night I encountered Captain Darke for the second time.'

Merely feeling her slender fingers against his skin sent a shiver of awareness through him and reminded him exactly how he'd felt when she appeared out of the night. 'You were lucky I didn't fall on you like a savage right there and then, given the ridiculous state I was in about you. I'd dreamt about you every night, cursed you every day when I woke up rampant and unsatisfied and wanting you like some sort of satyr. I'd only got myself so inebriated in the first place in order to forget you for an hour or two, and there you were, standing there like the answer to my wildest fantasies and making me forget I was at least raised a gentleman.'

'Did you really dream about me?' she asked, as if the idea trumped everything else and was almost wonderful to her.

He groaned and managed a rueful smile even as he put some very necessary distance between them to keep himself from showing her exactly what he'd dreamt about her all over again. 'You really don't have any idea how enchanting you actually are to the opposite sex, do you, Miss Alstone? Which is almost unbelievable, given that you've been the toast of St James's since you made your début in society.'

'Oh, I don't give a fig for all that,' she said dismissively, as if she didn't even like to be reminded of it, and Hugh decided he'd never met a woman with less natural vanity. 'All it takes to please those gentlemen is for a female to have a moderate fortune and all the usual appendages in the right place, plus a set of features that might look well on their daughters, should the lady breed such inconvenient creatures in the quest for an heir. It's all about bloodstock and very little to do with hopes and dreams, Hugh.'

'True, but what about those hopes and dreams, Louisa?' he said seriously; his appalling lack of self-control meant she had little choice but to marry him now, and he should at least have known about them before he spoilt them.

'I didn't know I had any until yesterday,' she said.

Fighting the feeling that it would be both wondrous and awesome to be the source and solution of Louisa Alstone's dreams, he raised an eyebrow in a silent question he couldn't bring himself to ask out loud.

'Then I found out that I wanted your fire and passion and consideration as well as your strength and integrity, Hugh, and that I'd been fooling myself all those years in thinking that I couldn't make a family with a man who could offer me all that.'

'Along with a name almost as black as Lucifer's to go with it?' he made himself ask bleakly.

'If the world is stupid enough to give you one, then, yes,' she assured him steadily, meeting his eyes as if she believed in his innocence absolutely. It was heady and flattering and he fought down an unworthy sense of triumph that this astonishing, brave and truly beautiful woman believed in him, despite all the horror and spite talked about him.

'The world has a way of intruding on life, Louisa, and I'm a guilty man in the eyes of most of it,' he warned.

'Then we'll have to make them see you as you really are.'

'Don't work me up me into some sort of damaged hero, Louisa. I'm not the stuff martyrs are made of, or heroes for that matter.'

'Of course you're not, but nor are you capable of murdering your wife or your brother, and I don't care what the rest of the world says. I don't even care if you doubt yourself, Hugh, because I know you didn't do it.'

'I was so furious, so hurt and ashamed that

I couldn't satisfy my own wife, Louisa,' he whispered at last. 'Ariadne needed men, not just one man; she had to have their attention as much as food and water and air to breathe. I hated what she made herself, hated what she'd done to me, but most of all I hated the way my brother watched her with contempt and a hint of lust while she preened and flirted with them all. After months at sea, brooding over the idea that my brother might be tupping my wife in my absence, I was already half-mad with jealousy and grief even before I got home and my father accused me of being a cruel husband, who drove his innocent wife into the arms of other men with his harsh temper and unnatural coldness.'

'More fool him, then,' she told him with a rather wicked smile that said he was certainly not cold or harsh with her. 'And, as you were proven to be laid out insensible a few miles away at the time of their deaths, how can you be so stupid and arrogant as to believe you hurt them in the face of the evidence? You would sooner have shot yourself in the back than your brother, whatever disgraceful state you were in at the time,' she told him as he gave up on distance and held her more tightly than he probably realised.

Louisa felt him struggle with his emotions and wished he'd just let go of them and trust her. Some instinct told her that he was too damaged by what had happened that awful night and afterwards, to fully confide in a woman he was marrying only because the world would consider he'd ruined her if he didn't. This was no time to worry about her own abraded emotions, though; he needed comfort and she needed to offer it to him.

'I couldn't fight my father's accusations,' he admitted tersely. 'The idea I could have killed Marcus while out of my senses on brandy and fury seemed to blast my very soul black and deprive me of speech. My wife didn't love me, but that was nothing compared to re-membering how jealous I'd been of her and my own brother. I let her infidelities make me a drunken fool lost in a brandy bottle and if only I'd been stronger, Louisa, if only I had bothered to insist on a legal separation, both of them would probably still be alive today. I couldn't admit so finally that I'd failed my wife and my family and look what happened to them because I was a coward.'

'She was the one who failed, you stubborn idiot of a man. If Kit and I have to catch the murderer behind your brother's death to make you realise none of it is your fault, then we'll do it just to prove ourselves right, you know? It's a family failing.'

'I have noticed,' he admitted with a faint smile.

Louisa hated the venal coward who'd let this good man suffer for his own crimes, but she had to be infuriated with him as well, in case she broke down and cried for him instead. 'You think you should have guarded your wife and brother from harm instead of getting drunk, don't you? You're not omnipotent, Captain Kenton, and I wouldn't want you for my husband if you were,' she told him sternly.

She felt him chuckle against her skin and some of the terrible tension seep out of his powerful body, felt the breath in her lungs freeze, then gasp out as the feel of him breathing so close to her made her knees weaken. He seemed to note the intimacy at the same moment and pressed a heated kiss to the accelerated pulse in the hollow at the base of her throat. Fire shot through her in a white-hot flash and she felt him harden in instant response. How totally he wanted her, she thought wonderingly, then he groaned and drew in a deep breath, before exerting his iron will over his need and hers, so he could hold her at arm's length and eye her reproachfully, as if she was Eloise again, a blatant seductress who was wilfully over-eager to be ravished by his passionate attentions.

'I can and will keep my hands off you for two more days, Louisa Alstone,' he informed her sternly, as if she was the one who'd recklessly turned comfort into passion and not him. 'It might nigh kill me, but I swear I'll do it,' he told her and met the challenge in her eyes with a laugh in his own. 'At least I will if you'll only help me by resisting this fever between us, rather than conspiring with my dratted body to make me a liar.'

'If we are really going to marry, then we share it all, Hugh,' she said seriously.

'We certainly share that,' he responded, his eyes not quite meeting hers.

'Not just the nights, but the days as well,' she informed him calmly, although her accelerated heartbeat told her how important it was that he understand her, even when he didn't want to.

'Are you planning to shadow my every move in future, then? It will certainly make for an unusual marriage; if not necessarily one I like the sound of.'

'I plan to share your problems, as you will mine,' she made herself say calmly, knowing he was trying to use her temper against her.

'You'll probably cause most of them.'

'Don't push me away, Hugh,' she pleaded, although pride urged her to do exactly what he wanted and walk away from him and their marriage even now.

'I have to try, don't you see? A murderer's possessions are forfeit, woman.'

'But you're not a murderer, Hugh.'

'If that fragile alibi fails, then I'll be tried as one and, guilty or not, I'll probably hang as one.'

Chapter Twelve

Louisa shrugged, trying not to let Hugh see that the very idea of losing him made her feel as if she was suddenly made of ice after all, and might shatter into a million icicles if he so much as breathed on her the wrong way.

'Would you have me walk away from you, then?' she asked painfully.

'Yes,' he said, face set like a stone mask as his eyes didn't quite meet hers again and she knew he was lying.

A small splinter of warmth thawed the absolute chill afflicting her and threatened to thaw her into a supplicant, begging for something she didn't quite understand wanting in the first place. Whatever it was, she couldn't let it slip away.

'Liar,' she whispered softly.

His eyes turned from hers completely as he glared across the room as if he wanted to go back to his pacing in peace and fool them both he was better left to deal with this alone. Suddenly his strong mouth twisted as if in agony and his silver-shot blue eyes were full on hers as he stopped shielding himself from her at last.

'Guilty,' he ground out. 'I'm a liar and a thief. I fly under false colours and take what they value most from those I love. Pray not to love me; fight not to marry me, Louisa Alstone. Go to the ends of the earth to avoid me, but for God's sake don't let me destroy you as everyone else in my life has been destroyed.'

'Do I look like some silly little martyr looking for a cause, Hugh Kenton?' she demanded furiously. 'No, I damned well don't and if I'd grown up sighing over heroes in storybooks, or longing to be rescued by the knight out of a fairy tale it might be fair enough of you to try to warn me off like this. If you don't realise how well I know my own mind by now, then perhaps time will teach you better, but I won't walk away from you that easily. I refuse to deprive our child of a father who'd fight the devil himself for its safety and well-being, even if you can't seem to stomach the idea of me as its mother.'

'It's certainly not that, but there may not be a child,' he said as if driven to point out all the drawbacks of becoming his wife to her once again.

'And if there is, I'm certainly not running after you in a few months' time when it's obvious I'm your discarded lover. It's now or never if you intend to wed me.'

'Do you think I don't want to marry you, woman?' he growled as if she was doing her best to torture him.

'All the signs seem to point that way.'

'Then they're wrong. I want you as I never wanted another woman in my life before, Louisa Alstone. I think about you when I should be busy with so many other things that I marvel Kit's empire didn't collapse in his absence for want of attention. I wake up in the morning wanting you and go to bed at night racked with longing for you in my bed and at my board.'

'You've only known me for two days.'

'Two minutes were enough for me, and it's all of three weeks since I first set eyes on you, you impossible, stubborn, naggy-tempered witch,' he told her with such disgust that she felt obscurely pleased he considered her so ir-resistible he'd longed for her since that day in Kit's office as well.

'Me, too,' she admitted.

'You too what?' he said, running an impatient hand through his already wildly disordered dark hair.

'I wanted you from the first moment I set eyes on you,' she told him boldly.

'Ah, Louisa, how the devil am I going to get through the next two days without going completely insane with needing you?' he asked as if he thought it a very real possibility.

'You don't have to,' she offered shamelessly, refusing to drop her eyes and pretend to be a shrinking maiden when she was neither.

'You don't know your brother as well as you think if you're not aware that he'll tear me apart if I lay a hand on you again before I wed you.'

'This isn't the only roof in London.'

'It is for the next two days—now stop tempting me, woman. I need to marshal my senses, not have them scattered to the four winds.'

'Well, if we're not allowed to do that, we might as well put our energies into catching your enemy while we still have them,' she said with a steady look she hoped told him she wasn't going to be sitting at home embroidering wedding garters for the next two days.

'I suppose there is no point in me forbidding you to set foot outside this house on anything less frivolous than a trip to the dressmaker?'

'Absolutely none,' she confirmed smugly.

'I don't think you were a neglected child at all, Louisa Alstone,' he accused her crossly. 'You were obviously so spoilt that none of your unfortunate family dared to cross you in any way. I'd have been beaten and locked in my room for a quarter of the exploits you seem to have got away with without so much as a blink from those who should have stopped you.'

'They'd have had to tie me to my bed, but never mind,' she consoled him unrepentantly. 'Think how useful it will be when we have children,' she said virtuously. 'Between your sins and mine, they'll never be able to hoodwink either of us that they're all sweetness and light, while behaving like little demons as soon as our backs are turned.'

'Alluring though the prospect might be, I think it's time to talk about something else,' he said huskily and Louisa had to believe he found the idea of those little dark-haired devils of theirs as seductive and downright wonderful as she did.

'Very well, then, it's probably high time we called Kit back in to pool our knowledge and considered what to do next.'

He groaned as if he didn't like that alternative much either, but tucked her hand within the crook of his elbow all the same and they went to find her brother.

'Stubborn, ungovernable woman,' he said as they strolled towards Kit's sitting room.

'Arrogant, intractable man,' she replied placidly.

'Still minded to wed each other, despite all the quarrelling, then?' Kit asked absently, as they invaded his privacy once again.

'Yes, planning to drive each other demented for the next fifty years or so,' Hugh said with such smugness that Louisa's heart warmed and her smile softened.

'On the understanding it would be a shame to inflict such glaring defects of character elsewhere when we can nag each other to death instead,' she countered with a challenging look for her brother and her husband-to-be.

'I can hardly wait for you to begin a lifetime of annoying each other and leave me in peace, then,' Kit said with a relieved and surprisingly boyish grin as he rang for the finest burgundy in his cellar to celebrate.

They drank a toast to their astonishing new future and sipped the fine vintage as the full significance of it all began to sink in. One day, probably all too soon, Louisa realised, she was going to be a lady after all—a real one, with a title she couldn't ignore if she tried. It was enough to make her have second thoughts, until she looked at Hugh and realised he needed someone brassy and unconventional and badly behaved to stand beside him.

None of the sweet little maids he must have grown up with would outstare and outmanoeuvre those intent on throwing Hugh's past sins and other dark deeds at his head. It occurred to her that if he'd been the heroic gentleman of breeding and repute he must once have been, she would probably have refused him, however compromised she might be. He was the only gentleman she could marry; out of all those deluded enough to ask her, he was the only one she could risk being her true self with, she realised, as she watched him stare into the subtle depths of the fine wine in his glass as if it might be able to tell him how all this came about.

'We have to get Lord Rarebridge alone,' she announced to distract him.

'We?' Kit said mildly enough.

'I'm as deep in this as either of you,' she said, knowing the only way to fight her brother's protective instincts was to remind him how little she needed protecting, then perhaps he could convince Hugh.

'I know you'll stick your nose in and ruin everything if we don't include you, little sister, but I won't admit this is any of your business even so,' Kit argued.

'If the end result is what I want, I don't much care, and his lordship will rush to help a lady in distress, whatever her reputation,' she said to think up an alternative scheme before they crept off without her to catch Lord Rarebridge at his club or some other harebrained scheme that would result in one of them being hurt.

'Dearest Uncle William and the insect-worm have been silent on that subject; they went to ground as soon as your escape was discovered and are no doubt cowering in fear of my fury,' Kit said so impassively Louisa knew they were right to be terrified.

'I believe husbands take precedence over brothers,' Hugh growled unhelpfully and

Louisa was tempted to throw something at one of them or stamp her feet.

'So what about Lord Rarebridge?' she asked stonily.

'First the lord and then the lackeys,' Hugh drawled in quite the grand manner and she only just managed not to scream with frustration and count to ten, because she had got her way, hadn't she?

'You say the lady is injured?' Viscount Rarebridge asked the bewigged and liveried footman who had just rushed down the quiet path he'd taken to haunting in Hyde Park, whenever his father's town house seemed too full of his elder sister's enormous brood of children. Now this dratted manservant was bothering him instead, he wished he'd stayed home and endured the racket, but he reluctantly agreed to help the man assist a lady to a more populous area and summon help.

'She'll likely be dead by the time we gets there,' the fellow muttered with the sort of insolence he'd expect of a servant hired for the Season.

'And why should I believe there is a lady at all, my man?' he asked in a supercilious tone that made Kit Alstone itch to plant him a facer.

'Since she were wailing about her poor ankle fit to make a statue cry, I certainly ain't imagined her, mister,' he said, tempted to be done with all this play-acting and just scurry the popinjay along in his wake.

'There's something devilish familiar about you. Have I seen you before?'

'Not like this you ain't,' the footman assured him gruffly, 'and young Miss needs 'elp some time this week, my lord.'

'You're an impudent knave, and I've half a mind not to take another step with you,' Lord Rarebridge blustered.

Luckily Louisa let out a very convincing wail of distress from where she was no doubt sprawled impatiently on the ground as if she dared not get up, and Kit thrust the viscount in front of him and into the quiet corner of Hyde Park where his sister had insisted they would not be disturbed. Glad his friend would soon be responsible for his sister's wilder starts, and very sure Hugh would protect her far more fiercely than he could when he was busy on the other side of the world far too often, he nevertheless had to admire his sister's acting abilities as she allowed his lordship to assist her to get to her good foot and hop to a nearby seat, where she subsided in convincing agony to rub her perfectly sound ankle.

His lordship just hovered in front of her, looking acutely uncomfortable, and Kit's estimate of the man's intelligence went even lower when Hugh appeared at his side and the idiot just gaped at him as if he'd seen some sort of ghostly apparition.

'Good Gad, Kenton?' he gasped.

'As you say,' Hugh drawled.

'Don't blame me, Rarebridge, I was quite ready to call you out first and ask questions later,' Kit assured the reedy little peacock menacingly, when he'd removed the wig and tucked it into his pocket before running his hand through his hair and wondering aloud how any man put up with such an abomination for long.

'We mean you no harm, your lordship,' Louisa said as she rose from her seat on two perfectly sound ankles and Lord Rarebridge looked more hunted than ever.

'Then why contrive such a scandalous meeting, ma'am?' he asked sharply.

'Because you have been plotting against mine, if not against me,' she said softly and suddenly his lordship found himself wondering if females were as weak and in need of protection as he had always considered them to be.

'I think she means me, Rory,' Hugh informed him laconically.

'Never thought I'd hear you admit to being any woman's lapdog,' his lordship did his best to sneer, but seemed to know it was a poor attempt and Hugh merely stared at his erstwhile friend as if he didn't quite know who he was any more.

'But this lady isn't just any woman, as I'm sure you will agree,' Hugh argued very softly and the very mildness of his manner made Lord Rarebridge shudder.

'My apologies, Miss Alstone,' he said with a coldly correct bow in Louisa's direction as he finally recalled who she was, and that she had once turned down his half-hearted offer of marriage.

'Accepted, my lord, so long as you tell me exactly why you had my affianced husband followed halfway across London yesterday.'

'Good heavens, ma'am, how could you possibly know about that?' he asked without stopping to think how incriminating his words were.

'I tracked you and your very dangerous

tools down myself, my lord,' she replied as coolly as if admitting she was due to attend Almack's tonight to endure dry bread and butter and lemonade with this year's crop of débutantes.

'Don't be ridiculous,' he ordered impatiently.

'I'm not, but you certainly are,' she assured him, then felt as much as saw Hugh move to dominate his lordship's bemused attention without having to do anything so crass as push her aside or talk over her.

'Never mind the how, Rory, I want the why,' he said bluntly.

'I don't see why I shouldn't tell you,' he said rather spitefully. 'The wider world thinks of you as a murderer, even if they can't seem to get on and prove it.'

'So you set yourself the task of doing it for them?'

'I decided to discover the truth,' he said so virtuously that Louisa itched to be a man for a minute or two so she could vent her rising temper on this prancing fool without Hugh and her brother being able to stop her.

'I doubt you'll find it by looking in places like that, but if you're so convinced of my guilt a simple denial won't stop you,' Hugh said as if discussing the weather.

'It might. You refused to defend yourself when we all expected you to face up to whatever you had done when poor little Ariadne died, so your word as a gentleman that you didn't kill your wife and brother might go a long way with your friends,' the coward offered, as if he thought for one moment the rest of the world would accept Hugh's say so that he didn't do it, when a solid alibi apparently held no weight.

'And you intend to prove yourself a friend by using some of the worst rogues in London to track my movements? With friends like you, I'll soon be able to retire all my enemies, Rarebridge.'

'Damn it, man, have you any idea what you've done to your unfortunate sister? Poor little creature doesn't deserve the snubs and sneers she has to endure while she lives with the scandal you won't stand and face.'

'I've never thought of my sister as a poor little creature and I'll be very surprised if she thinks of herself as such, and where was I to face down the gossip, Rory, the dock or the gutter?' Hugh asked implacably and Louisa nearly cheered aloud to hear him fight for himself at long last.

'I don't know, but you shouldn't have disappeared like a fugitive,' Lord Rarebridge argued sulkily, as if his bluster was draining away and leaving him wondering what it was all about himself.

'I was too busy surviving to worry about how things looked to the rest of the world,' Hugh said bleakly and Louisa willed him to admit why he'd left his home so finally that his sister was doubly bereft.

'Where were you then, Hugo?' his lordship asked more moderately.

'At sea, in more ways than one,' Hugh admitted with a shrug and a rueful smile for Louisa that made her step a little closer to offer her support. 'I drank, gamed and fought my way round the less reputable taverns of London until I landed in that gutter. It took two strong men to carry me home and dry me out, then Mr Alstone and his good friend and business partner decided to put my seamanship to good use, instead of turning me back out to go to the devil as my so-called friends would have done. I have worked as a ship's master ever since, Rory, and I hardly think you and your kind would wish to associate with such men, nor we with you.'

'Why didn't you write to your sister, then?' his lordship asked, leaving Hugh's implied contempt for the likes of him unchallenged.

'Because my father forbade it and I could hardly ask her to go behind his back—all that would have got her was more ranting and raving about undutiful daughters than she already had to endure.'

'The devil,' his lordship said and sank down on the marble bench. 'It was all a lie, then,' he muttered mysteriously and seemed utterly deflated.

'What was a lie, my lord?' Louisa asked as patiently as she could, for she scented the stamp of the real villain behind all this at last, instead of this idle and foolish young man, so bored with his life he was looking for trouble to fall into.

'I received some letters,' Lord Rarebridge admitted reluctantly.

'From whom did these missives come then?' Hugh demanded impatiently.

'I don't know,' the viscount mumbled, evidently ashamed of himself for paying heed to such spiteful stuff now they'd shown up what a shabby thing his wonderful crusade really was.

'So you pursued an innocent man on the say so of a person who lacked the courage to own his name?' she asked incredulously.

'At first I tore them up or threw them in the fire,' he said defensively.

'But then…?' she encouraged him.

'Then he offered more detail that I couldn't help but take notice of, told me things only a witness to what happened that night could ever know.'

'Or perhaps the perpetrator of it all himself?' she snapped furiously.

'Good Gad, d'you really think so?' he asked as he shot to his feet as if stung, which he would be if there was any justice, Louisa decided vengefully, by a very virulent and persistent gadfly, that lived for a very long time and loved the taste of stupid young aristocrat so much it kept biting and biting.

'Hugo Kenton would never shoot a man in the back, let alone his own brother, so who else is there? If there were any true witnesses to those terrible crimes, they would have come forwards before now and I'm quite sure Sir Horace Kenton offered a large reward to encourage them to do so at the time.'

'You know, I do believe you're right.'

'How amazing,' she said acerbically and was even more astonished by him when he nodded solemnly, as if he'd just witnessed a rare phenomenon.

'So where are the letters now, Rory?' Hugh asked more gently, as if resigned to the dimness of this particular viscount and preparing to stand between him and his fiery fiancée for his protection.

'Letters?' he said, as if being asked where he'd left somebody's pet elephant.

'Yes, the unsigned letters that set you on my tail,' Hugh explained patiently.

'Oh, them,' his lordship said glumly. 'I lost them.'

Louisa locked her hands together in lieu of wrapping them round the noble idiot's neck and squeezing hard and even Hugh seemed to hold back with an effort from seizing him and shaking some sense out of him.

'Can you recall their content, Rory?' he asked calmly enough.

'Probably, if you give me enough time to think.'

Louisa felt Hugh squeeze her tense fingers in warning and stood back to let him deal with this oddly naïve young man. It made her wonder how old they both were, these former friends, and marvel at the differences between the pampered heir of an earldom and the battle-hardened second son of a baronet. Even without the trauma of the last few years, her Hugh would be twice the man his lordship could ever become and she wondered if Hugh's sister felt anything but contempt for such a straw man. The viscount clearly admired Miss Kenton, and probably had half an eye on the fact that she would inherit everything if her brother was arraigned, then hung for murder, but she doubted he had the brains to actively pursue Hugo without some more deadly hand pulling his strings.

'Come and see if you can put any of them down on paper for us then, Rory. It's very important that we have every shred of evidence we can find if this man is ever to be apprehended. Will you do that for me, old friend?'

'Course I will, Hugo, do anything for you, you know that.'

'I do, Rory, I know exactly what you'd do for me now,' Hugh told his one-time playmate and shrugged at Kit and Louisa as he silently acknowledged how true that remark was.

Chapter Thirteen

'Viscount Rarebridge and his ilk make you wonder how the aristocracy manage to keep such a determined grasp on both government and country,' Kit said ruefully as they waited for Hugh to finish writing his lordship's scattered memories in his pocket book and rejoin them.

'Do you think that idiot will remember anything much of what was actually in those letters?' Louisa asked anxiously.

'Aye, he's not got an awful lot in his head to distract him. It's probably my duty to inform his father what he's been up to so he'll drag him off to the country out of harm's way, so at least I'll be his new worst enemy then instead of Hugh.'

'Perhaps, but how do we get our hands on the true villain behind all this?'

'*We* don't, Lou, and don't waste that wide-eyed innocent look on me.'

'I'm involved; you can't pretend it doesn't matter to me and that I should stay at home and knit socks.'

'Heaven forbid, I've seen your knitting.'

'Don't laugh at me, Kit,' she demanded, knowing that if she let them, he and Hugh would cut her out of this whole business and she simply couldn't sit about waiting to hear if they had been hurt or arrested.

'I'm not, but do you really think it's going to help Hugh's sense of himself if you constantly fight his battles for him, little sister? Only an idiot would hide his past from his wife, but he must slay his own dragons, love.'

Louisa fumed in silence for a while, listening to the birds sing blithely and the distant sounds of children playing in the afternoon sun. The noises of the city were muted in this quiet corner of Mayfair and she reflected that only days ago she had been one of the chattering crowd in Rotten Row at the fashionable hour. How glad she was to be done with all that, although as Mrs Hugo Kenton, in town for a few weeks to enjoy the diversions of fashionable life, she might enjoy herself far more than being scurried from one ball to another by her aunt.

She certainly hadn't come across one man it would cost her a pang to leave behind when she wed Hugh. Some of her suitors had been handsome or fabulously rich or even both, and one or two were witty and keenly intelligent, but none of them had instantly held her attention as Hugh the pirate, or Hugh the poet, or whoever he truly was, could just by being in the same room. Marriage to Hugh could be an endless adventure if they got it right, so she supposed she would have to adapt her life to his if he was willing to reciprocate.

'I suppose you're right,' she finally admitted.

'That's more of an admission than his lordship's that a mere female might have come upon a fact by accident,' he teased her and she chuckled reluctantly.

'Am I a managing woman, Kit?' she asked, heard the wistfulness in her own voice and wondered what on earth Hugh Darke had done to her. No, Hugo Kenton, she reminded herself, and wondered even more.

'You might be, if you wed the wrong man.'

'I wasn't intending to wed one at all,' she admitted.

'Which is exactly why Hugo Kenton is the right man for you, little sister; he's certainly the only one who's ever caused you to swerve an inch from a course you'd set your mind on taking.'

'You make me sound so formidable,' she protested.

'No. How could I be so crass?' he teased her and she gave him an urchin grin and went back to listening to quiet sounds around them, not letting herself admit even in her head that she was listening for Hugh's near-silent approach until she finally saw him pace lithely down the path to meet them.

'Did you get anything more out of him?' Kit asked once they were back in his neat town carriage and on their way home.

'All he could recall, I'll show you once we're back in Chelsea,' Hugh said tersely and they lapsed into silence.

'Were we followed, Grimme?' Hugh asked the new groom at journey's end.

'Twice over, sir, first cove very obvious, second as quiet as you like,' Grimme answered and waited as if expecting an order to go after one or other.

'Not tonight,' Hugh finally decided. 'I know who sent one and we'll pick our ground before we take the other one on.'

'Aye, sir,' Grimme said and went off to attend to the horses.

'Are you ever going to tell us, then?' Louisa demanded the instant Hugh shut the door of Kit's study behind him.

'There's not much to tell,' he answered, gratefully accepting a brandy glass from his brother-in-law-to-be and raising it in a silent toast as he mouthed 'three' at Louisa to tell her he hadn't forgotten that promise after all.

'I should like some tea,' she informed him majestically and he didn't dare even think what he really wanted, not for another two days at any rate.

Kit confounded him by going off to order the tea tray from his housekeeper and Hugh eyed his own particular termagant with hungry patience.

'He trusts us,' he said at last.

'I suspect he trusts you rather more than me, knowing how your gentlemanly instincts trump my ladylike ones,' she said with a smile that admitted more than he'd dared hope for when she agreed to marry him for the sake of a maybe-child, but not quite as much as he'd dreamt of in those heady dreams of her sweet and hot and in thrall to him in every way a woman can be to a man.

'Stop trying to convince me and everyone else you're not a lady, my dear,' he advised her rather wearily and sat back in his chair to contemplate the fine cognac in his glass rather than the much more tempting sight of Miss Louisa Alstone, elegantly dressed and almost back to her Ice-Diamond perfection.

'Do I grow tedious, Mr Kenton?'

'No, only infuriating. Disappointed?'

'Not really, just a little bit scared,' she admitted and he resisted the temptation to snatch her out of her seat by the empty fire and into his arms, so he could offer comfort and chase the shadows from her eyes.

'You? I thought nothing frightened, Louisa Alstone.'

'Your family does, because I never planned to marry a gentleman; never bothered to study household economy so I could take over a great house one day, or learnt to love country life. I can't even ride properly, Hugh,' she ended, as if that was the greatest sin of all.

'No need to sound so mournful about it, my Eloise. You'll learn whatever you need to and ignore what you don't and if we end up at Gracemont Priory there will be a housekeeper and butler to manage the house and bailiffs and a land steward for each of the estates, so neither of us need take on too much to begin with. I'm not trained to it either, Louisa,' he reassured her, kneeling on the hearthrug in front of her to take her chilled hands in his and warm them. 'I'm the second son, remember? Nobody taught me to judge yields or breed livestock or price timber. I can ride well enough, but Marcus was the real horseman, and I'm more accustomed to a quarterdeck than an estate office. We'll learn it all together, Louisa, and do well enough, I dare say; I don't think there's much you couldn't do if you set your mind to it.'

'Then I *am* a managing female,' she said tragically, recalling her previous conversation with her brother.

'So long as you don't try managing me, you can exert your organising skills on my father's houses and estates with my blessing,' he told her, pulling her forwards so their gazes were level and she could see all the feeling he dared show in his eyes.

'Houses? Estates?' she questioned as he fought not to lose himself in the blue depths of her eyes. 'You mean there's more than one?' she added as if he'd confessed to some sort of family mania or ancient curse.

'One or more, what difference does it make?'

'I'm becoming more of a misalliance by the second for you, Hugh—whatever will your family say?'

'My sister will love you, my ancient second cousin and heir will apparently approve of any woman I marry who isn't a noble whore like the last one, and my father has no say in the matter if he wants me home playing the dutiful heir for the remainder of his life.'

'Oh, that's all right then,' she said forlornly and he couldn't stop himself from leaning forwards that extra inch to kiss her on her temptation of a mouth in order to stop her uncharacteristic attack of self-doubt.

'Idiot,' he chided as he ran a line of kisses along the lovely, giveaway fullness of her lower lip, then back to explore her upper one with just as much care and fascination. 'This gives so much away,' he told her on a groan and pulled back to fight the powerful urge to lay her down on Kit's hearth rug and take her again in broad daylight.

For one thing, her brother would surely kill

him for it this time, and for another she deserved more respect, even if she didn't seem to want it. Instead of giving in to the urge to ravish and pleasure and enjoy her as fast and urgently as his body and most of his instincts demanded, he ran his forefinger along the sensuous curve of her lips where his mouth had just travelled and let his need and frustration and tenderness for this wonder of a female show in his heavy-lidded gaze as he watched her react to his touch.

'Gives what away?' she muttered as if only half-interested in his answer, much more concerned with the feel of him exploring the very words on her lips.

'The real Louisa,' he murmured as he outlined her mouth again. The feel of it under the sensitive pad of his finger end was almost as seductive as the marvel of it softening into eagerness and passion under his kisses. 'You're not what you pretend, or even entirely what you think yourself to be, but no wonder you had to defend the vulnerability of this, the passion of it, the fierceness of your feelings,' he told her as he ranged that fingertip along her fine creamy skin and up over her high cheekbones to drift it over her half-closed eyelids, her smooth, narrow brow and down along her jaw-line and back to that so-fascinating mouth again.

'Kiss me, Hugh,' she demanded shakily against the finger she tried to catch in her mouth, even as he danced it away again and her eyes burned every bit as passionately, looked as vulnerable and fiercely wanting as they had in those wild dreams of his.

'I dare not,' he whispered, giving in to the temptation to stroke that one slight point of contact he did dare between them by exploring along one of her finely made earlobes and learning the intriguing curls and curves of it to so tenderly he felt her shiver with desire. 'Once I started to, I couldn't stop,' he confessed and sat back on his heels to meet her gaze, waiting for her fierce accusations and the bite of her temper for half-seducing her, then drawing back, leaving her unsatisfied, restless and needy with the passion that ran between them like some untapped force of nature.

'The day after tomorrow, we won't have to stop,' she whispered, looking him straight in the eye and letting him see that wait would be hard for her too.

'Seems more like years, doesn't it?' he murmured ruefully, something greater than all his scruples and self-doubts threatening the isolation he'd forced on his old self in order to survive, something that might have been his heart, if he still had one. He ached with the hugeness and threat of what promised between them and sprang to his feet in cowardly relief when Kit made a purposely noisy entrance to his own book-room, carrying the tea tray Louisa had demanded.

'I assume you waited for me before looking for clues to your enemy's identity?' he asked as if he thought they'd been yards apart ever since he left.

'What considerate folk we are,' Hugh said blandly.

'So what does it say that we don't know already?' his friend asked and laid the tea-tray on the table at Louisa's side, leaving her to pour a cup with a look that said she probably needed it.

Hugh read through the sparsely covered page once more and stared into space for a moment, thinking about Rory and other one-time friends and neighbours and how they might fit into those terrible days he'd done his best to forget.

'There's something I can't quite understand what happened. It's there at the back of my mind, but not quite there, if you see what I mean?' he finally said, waving the paper as if it might incite the elusive memory into life.

'Then why not let us read it while you try?' Louisa demanded, forgetting all about those resolutions to be a little less forthright in her eagerness.

'So what did I once see or hear or maybe even imagine?' he mused, but absent-mindedly handed over his notebook for her to examine while he tried to pin down that annoying wisp of something not quite right.

Scanning through Lord Rarebridge's sometimes random memories of the letter that had set him off, Louisa felt acutely disappointed and more than a little shocked by the terse malice of it, so she passed the book to Kit and drank her tea.

'No more than a line or two at a time,' Kit said. 'The man's cunning enough not to risk getting carried away and being identified.'

'Which argues he has a talent for intrigue, or that Rory might know his normal handwriting,' Hugh replied.

'Did his lordship remember how the original letters arrived?' Louisa asked, still marvelling that the man could take such vitriol as gospel, then set out to damn an old friend on their say so. 'He knew his victim, didn't he?' she suddenly realised. 'He knew Lord Rarebridge was a credulous, bored fool with a *tendresse* for your sister and your father's acres.'

'Which argues that he's one of the *ton*, don't you think? A man who knows Rory and used those letters to produce the result he wanted.'

'But why would he want you found and followed by one of the most ruthless gangs in London, Hugh?' Kit asked, frowning at the pocketbook in his hand as if it would reform its letters and tell him the answer if he stared at it long enough.

'Maybe their real orders didn't come from Rarebridge, but the man himself. You know as well as I do that if you find the right gang master and pay him enough gold, he'll arrange a murder and even give up one of his less-valued gang members to take the drop for it.'

'And Rarebridge obviously thought he was giving the orders, but he's not exactly a deep thinker, is he? If they had been paid to kill you, rather than merely track you down as that spineless lordling of yours thought, then your dim friend would have taken the blame for your murder when those hired bullies were caught,' Kit replied grimly.

'It could have been part of his scheme to rid himself of two obstacles at once,' Louisa said, shuddering at the horrific idea of Hugh lying dead on a murderer's say so. 'But why put such a plan into action in the first place, after three years of sitting on his hands and doing no worse than stir up the odd rumour against you?'

'Because my father is so ill and I'm the only heir he's got to the Priory and estates, as my sister doesn't seem to want them,' Hugh answered.

'There's probably more to it than that, Hugh, but the very idea of your presence in the area seems to have our murderer in a panic. He obviously prefers you in London or halfway across the world and safely estranged from your family, and beyond the pale of local society,' Kit said thoughtfully.

'So he probably lives near your precious Gracemont?' Louisa asked.

'Either that or he visits regularly enough not to easily stop doing so if I was living there once more.'

'We need a list of the local families and their friends and relations, so we can eliminate them from the list of suspects, then visit the ones that are left,' Louisa said brightly.

'Over my dead body,' Kit rapped out harshly and Hugh just glared as if she'd suggested going about the neighbourhood with no clothes on.

'We need to do more than that, even if I was prepared to let you make such a target of yourself,' Hugh eventually said gruffly. 'It will be obvious enough to this rogue, whoever he might be, what we're up to if we turn up at every house in the area as soon as I get home with my new bride.'

'Precisely, bride visits,' Louisa said smugly and sat back in her chair to wait for them to realise what a perfect scheme it was.

'Most of the households in the area will turn me away from their doors, new bride or not,' Hugh replied with a bitter smile she recognised as armour.

'They'll be sorry when the real villain is unmasked,' she said hotly.

'Maybe,' he replied with a shrug of would-be indifference.

'And he's intent on not letting Hugh go home in the first place,' Kit pointed out.

'So we have tonight and tomorrow to track him down and stop him.'

'Of course we have,' Hugh agreed sarcastically.

'Let's get on with it, then,' she said, all

those resolutions to become more tractable and sweetly feminine flying out of the window.

'It'll take a while to write that list you're demanding,' Hugh protested, but sat down at the library table and drew the blotter towards him even so. 'An inventory of my wife's local lovers is probably the best place to start,' he said impassively.

'You knew who they were?' she asked, shocked that the woman could openly humiliate him like that.

'The whole neighbourhood knew,' he said as if it didn't matter.

'I suppose servants will gossip,' she said, half to herself.

'No more than their so-called betters and, for some self-torturing reason I can't currently understand, I made it my business to know who they all were.'

Hugh had to mend his pen before the list was done. As it went down one column and then another, Louisa felt naïve and astonished and quietly furious that so many men could treat a gentleman like him, and a serving officer in Nelson's navy who risked his life time and again for their protection, with so little respect. Apparently even her early experiences

of life on the streets hadn't quite prepared her
for the politer betrayals of the *ton*.

'Finished?' Kit asked with a wry look that
probably went a lot further towards softening
this ordeal for Hugh than all the temper and
tears she was fighting on his behalf and she
silently acknowledged there were times when
men understood other men very much better
than women could.

'No,' Hugh said as he stared down at the list
as if he didn't quite know where it had come
from, 'there's one name that still eludes me.'

'Let's see how your list compares with
mine, then?' Kit said calmly and unlocked
his desk to take out another closely written
sheet. 'I made it up from the information your
father had been able to discover and that very
instructive visit to your second cousin, who
appears to know all the gossip in the West
Country.'

'The old rogue,' Hugh said with apparent
fondness, as he studied both lists then added
one or two names to each one that had been
overlooked. He looked mildly surprised as he
read over them and still he hesitated to hand
over the lists for their consideration. 'One of
her lovers used to come to Ariadne's room
after dark, masked and dressed from head to

toe in black, at least according to Dickon and his friends in the taproom. They had hours of raucous amusement speculating over the young nodcock's identity, once they thought I was too drunk to care what they talked about any more.'

'Dressed in black?' Louisa echoed hollowly, unable to believe what her ears were telling her, although it was vital to their search. 'Oh, surely not?' she said aloud so they stared at her as if wondering about her sanity. 'Don't you recall how I was dressed the night I came back into your life, Captain Darke?' she asked Hugh when she'd finally decided she wasn't running mad.

'You were all in black, and it might be best if I didn't recall the exact details. Are you suggesting *you* might have murdered my wife and my brother, my dear? Highly unlikely, considering you were still in the schoolroom at the time and are obviously not that way inclined,' he reminded her with a wolfish grin that reminded her how very masculine she preferred her lover to be.

'Louisa *is* my sister, Kenton,' Kit protested with a fierce frown, but she was too busy fitting two and two together to worry about his ruffled sensibilities.

'And where do you think I got it from?' she asked, overly patient at their uncharacteristic slow-wittedness.

'It wasn't a problem at the forefront of my mind at the time,' Hugh drawled and she spared a warm shiver of delighted awareness for the heat and memories in his heavy-lidded eyes.

'I did notice,' she said drily, 'but I stole the shirt and breeches and lost an equally black coat along the way. I balked at the mask in case anyone saw me, thought I was intent on stealing their silver and raised a hue and cry.'

'Where did you steal them from, then?' he asked, suddenly as sharply interested in that question as she could wish.

'Charlton Hawberry,' she said, still hardly able to believe what her mind was telling her. 'He had them locked in a very fine cedar chest in his dressing room.'

Chapter Fourteen

Recalling her boredom upon being shut in that poky little room with a narrow truckle bed and nothing to do but poke around in his ridiculous wardrobe for most of the day, Louisa decided Charlton Hawberry would receive no less than his due if she'd stumbled on his darkest secrets while she was in there. It was probably best not to remember just now how she'd later been forced to take part in a seedy masquerade when her uncle was brought up to see her with her own clothes half-ripped off and ensconced in the vulgar splendour of Charlton's bedchamber as if she'd been there all day, and night.

'It seemed the ideal dress for a night-time escape, so I just stole it and didn't give much

thought to why it was hidden away so ridiculously. I did wonder if he'd set up some sort of
latter-day Hell Fire Club with what he thought
fittingly satanic regalia, but I was more interested in getting away than examining his motives for possessing such an outfit in the first
place. Keeping it in such a fine box, with a
lock that gave me some trouble to pick, was a
mistake as far as I was concerned, since I was
so bored in his horrible dressing room that I
whiled away the tedious hours, once I'd done
my best to escape by conventional methods,
with learning how to open it.'

'I should have tracked him down and killed
him just for that,' Hugh said with a grim smile
that made him look more wolfish than ever.

'And I should have done a lot more than
kicking him in the… Well, I'll leave you to
work out where I kicked him.'

That surprised a bark of genuine laughter
out of him and broke the heavy tension in the
room for a moment, but the implications of
what she'd found in that locked box were too
stark to ignore, given the story they were finally putting together.

'He must know that you picked the lock and
stole his disguise by now,' Hugh said, as if that
was the most significant fact of all.

'Whatever he knows, or doesn't know, it was proof of what he'd done and I took it away,' she reproached herself bleakly.

'If you hadn't opened it, we would have taken a great deal longer to work out what he is, even if I'm very sure I never met a man called Charlton Hawberry at any of my neighbours' houses, and I would remember a name like that, even if I was as drunk as a lord at the time.'

'It has to be an alias,' Kit confirmed tersely. 'I was a fool not to realise he was flying under false colours when he disappeared so completely after Louisa's escape that it was almost as if he'd never been.'

'Which of course he hadn't, not that he was worth knowing in any guise,' she added disgustedly.

'So who on earth can he be?' Hugh asked, as if she ought to know.

'How do I know?' she said impatiently. 'I heard and saw nothing that would give us a clue to his real identity, either before or after he abducted me.'

'But you did see him and, however he tried to disguise himself, he couldn't alter his basic physique or the colour of his eyes,' Kit pointed out, looking to her for a description of her erstwhile suitor she was struggling to put together.

'He's just nondescript,' she said with a shrug. 'The first time he attended one of Aunt Poole's At Homes, I couldn't recall a single thing about him afterwards, for all Uncle William kept talking about him as if the Prince of Wales himself had chosen to honour his drawing room with his presence.'

'Having been handsomely paid to do so, no doubt,' Hugh observed.

'No doubt at all, but if Charlton is the murderer, it makes his motives far more sinister, don't you think?' she pointed out. 'I am your employer's sister, which put me at the very heart of the Stone & Shaw business. If he'd managed to wed me, he no doubt believed he'd be able to get you dismissed and further disgraced, so you would never dare return home.'

'Not so,' Kit said grimly. 'Marrying my sister by force would not endear him to me and Hugh's no mere employee, he's a shareholder and a friend.'

'Does Charlton know that, do you think? His main strength seems to be his ability to fade away from a place as if he'd never been there, but he's weak in every other way and I don't think he's very subtle either, or he would never have committed murder in the first place,' Louisa said.

'No, he's clearly a reactor and not a planner, since his schemes are never particularly good, but that makes him very dangerous indeed,' Kit warned.

'And his plan has gone very wrong, since Hugh's about to marry into the Alstone family and not him. So who knows about the marriage so far?' Louisa asked her brother.

'The vicar of St Margaret's, most of the clerics at Lambeth Palace, and the lawyers, of course,' he replied grimly.

'An open secret, then?' she said and met Hugh's eyes with a rueful smile.

'More or less,' he agreed with a distracted frown. 'And what a fine way to kill all his birds with one stone if there should be a tragic accident on the way home from the church, don't you think?'

'An accident where all three of us were killed—surely that would be almost impossible to engineer?'

'Perhaps,' Hugh agreed distractedly, 'but he'll make some sort of move. He'll have to, since he knows he'll hang anyway if he's caught. What's the man got to lose by attacking us when he's committed two murders already?'

'Everything, I should imagine,' Louisa said as she realised anew just how desperate and dangerous this so-called Charlton Hawberry must be.

'Yes, and why wear that mask in the first place, I wonder?' Hugh mused. 'The rest of the county seemed happy enough to take the garden stairs up to Ariadne's chamber once the rest of my father's household were asleep; indeed, I heard it was nicknamed the Backstairs to Heaven by some of the local wags.'

'Perhaps he's married?' she suggested, trying not to pity Hugh for that appalling betrayal when he didn't want her sympathy or anyone else's.

'As are half the worst rakes of the *ton*, but they don't go about their carousing and seducing dressed in such a theatrical fashion,' Kit pointed out.

'You would know far more about that subject than I,' Louisa replied sternly, 'but perhaps Hawberry has more to hide than most men.'

'Or more to lose, perhaps?' Hugh said as he tapped the list on the edge of the desk and looked very thoughtful indeed.

'So he's a man who likes illicit pleasures, but lacks the sort of natural arrogance to find the risk of being caught out and identified part of the fun. Somehow he had to care about his reputation, even when visiting a lady of...' Louisa let her voice trail off because she realised what she had been about to say of Hugh's dead wife and, even if she'd sickened him with her lovers and her lies, he must have loved her once upon a time, or why marry her in the first place when he could have had his pick of the débutantes?

'Dubious morals and tarnished reputation?' he finished for her. 'No need to wrap it up in clean linen, my dear, I've had three years to come to terms with what my wife was. Indeed, by the side of her horrible death and my brother's murder, her chosen way of life hardly seems very important any more.'

'Maybe not to you,' Kit said thoughtfully, 'but it obviously mattered very much to our mysterious Mr Hawberry.'

'So why should it mean so much for him to be seen, when it would have been a minor setback to any other man?' Louisa asked, shaking her head over the puzzle of who, or what, Charlton Hawberry really was.

'Because he would lose more than them if

he was found out,' Hugh said slowly. 'He must be in a position of moral authority to dread discovery so.'

'Either a law lord or a politician of some sort then, or perhaps even a cleric?' she offered eagerly.

'Which fits him best then, Lou?' her brother asked. 'You have actually met the man, you've been in his home and, even if it was only a temporary one where he had to be careful not to reveal his true self, everyone gives a little away through their possessions and the way they insist their household is conducted. How would you best describe your insect-worm?'

'Secretive, fussy, nondescript,' she managed as she racked her brains to something to say about the man, apart from the fact that even the thought of being in the same room with him made her flesh creep. 'He's very cold, with fishy eyes that make you feel as if there's nobody much behind them, but really I got the impression he's very intelligent, but not very clever with it, if you know what I mean?'

'I do, which is a conundrum in itself,' Hugh said, as if he was trying to fit such a man against any he might know.

'It's almost as if he doesn't feel in the way that other people feel. As if he has no idea other people have emotions and needs, because his own are so important that they blot out anyone and everyone in his way.'

'And there stands any cold-blooded murderer,' Kit said frustratedly and she sighed, impatient with herself for not being able to describe the man who must be the ruthless killer trying to get Hugh hung for his own crimes.

'Such a man would speed rapidly along his chosen path to glory for a while, but probably only get so far along it before he hit obstacles,' Hugh said as if thinking out loud. 'Chilly ruthlessness will get a man so far and no further, but to rise to the top requires a touch of greatness, which it sounds as if this Charlton Hawberry lacks.'

'That's him exactly,' Louisa agreed, finally allowing herself to hope they could do this, track the monster down and overcome him before he managed to hurt Hugh even more than he already had.

'So who is he?' he said, obviously running all his former neighbours through his head in an attempt to weed one out. 'All we know is he's ruthless and ambitious with an unprepossessing exterior and a purely physical need of beautiful women.'

'He didn't seem to need me very much, thank goodness,' she said and saw Kit exchange a wry look with Hugh over her head. 'I suppose you're silently informing each other that he prefers whores to ladies?'

'Well, virtuous ladies at any rate—he doesn't seem to have objected to making my wife the object of his desire,' Hugh observed cynically.

'And I do know some men like to hurt women for their own filthy gratification,' she said before they could sidestep that issue as well. 'I grew up in the stews, you know, and I'm not blind or entirely stupid.'

'Louisa's right, Hugh, even if I wish she didn't know anything of such dark dealings. What if the perverted fool went too far that night, your wife tried to fight him off, then your brother heard her fight for life?'

'But why kill them both if he was masked and disguised like that?'

'Because a man could hardly keep himself masked and pristine when a young and desperate woman was tearing at his hands and face in terror for her very life,' Kit said, preoccupied with reconstructing the past as dispassionately as he could since Hugh would probably never manage to, being so close to the victims of that terrible night. 'Your brother must have seen enough to recognise her attacker before he went to raise the alarm. He was probably intent on making sure everyone knew exactly what he'd seen, rather than wasting time stopping to fight with the louse when I suspect your wife was already dead. Maybe he was even looking for his brother—if he could sober you up long enough to listen— but the bastard shot to kill, so Marcus Kenton never told anyone what he'd seen.'

There was silence in the cosy room as they took in the full horror of what had probably happened that night. Louisa found herself pitying Hugh's late wife's terrible end, even if the woman had inflicted such pain and damage on the man she loved as Ariadne Kenton could never have loved him, and done what she had.

Oh, no. She *loved* Hugh Kenton!

What an idiot to think she was safe from that huge and frightening emotion, just because her mother had loved a man who wasn't fit to tie her shoelaces. The idea that she had chosen far better than her mother, even if she hadn't known until now that she was choosing her true love, struck her, but she was too busy coping with this latest disaster to fully appreciate it just now.

'Are you going to faint, Louisa?' Kit asked her so sharply her shock must be a bit too obvious on her face.

'Of course not—when did I ever do that?'

'Never, but there's always a first time, I suppose.'

'Not for me. Now, how are we going to track this killer down? It's all very well knowing what he's done; what we need now is proof of his identity.'

Hugh looked very thoughtful as he considered ways and means. 'We must force him into the open somehow, so I wonder how contrite Rarebridge is.'

'Extremely, I should imagine,' Kit agreed and Louisa wondered how men held whole conversations with barely a word of sense between them.

'An elegant evening reception for an old friend and neighbour he feels he has wronged in the past and his new wife should serve,' she said before they could come up with some scheme to exclude her and put themselves in acute danger.

'I doubt if he'll spring for that; his father keeps him very short and his house is full with his sister's vast tribe of children descending on him. Apparently she refused to leave them at home, but insisted on bringing them up for the only Season when she's not been either with child or giving birth since her marriage. Even I almost felt sorry for Rory, surrounded as he is with four young children and attendant nannies as well as that unfortunate husband of his sister's,' Hugh said.

'Why is he so unfortunate?' she asked.

'I don't really know, he just is,' Hugh replied with an inarticulate shrug. 'No way of describing him other than that, really.'

'If you don't think he will co-operate, I'll visit our cousin Lord Carnwood and prod his conscience instead,' Louisa said calmly, although the notion of bearding the family dragon in his den made her quail.

'No, Louisa, I received news today that our cousin's grandson and heir has died, so I expect the Earl is only in town at all to find out if he can disinherit me, since I am his heir presumptive now,' Kit said with a wry grimace that told them how little he actually wanted to inherit the earldom and all its attendant responsibilities.

'I'm very sorry for him then, despite the fact he should have helped Mama out when we were young, even if Papa was a hopeless case. His heir must have been little more than a boy.'

'Sixteen,' Kit agreed and she could see how hard the news had hit him.

'His poor parents,' she said with a shake of her head for the appalling grief they must be suffering.

'They were killed in an accident eight or nine years ago,' Hugh volunteered. 'I believe the boy has sisters, but they can't inherit an earldom and as the eldest of them ran off with some unsuitable rogue a twelvemonth ago it's probably as well.'

'Aye,' Kit agreed abstractedly and went back to staring at nothing in particular while he brooded on the unexpected turn his life had taken.

'Then I shall have to work on Lord Rarebridge's uneasy conscience instead,' Louisa announced and could have sworn she heard a silent moan of dread.

It had been an unexpectedly magical day, Louisa decided as she ascended the steps of Kinsham House just as the sun was setting and the birds in the trees in the gardens around the square were singing themselves to sleep, if the *ton* allowed them peace enough to do so. She let the whispering silk skirts of her wedding gown fall to skim her slender ankles and embroidered satin slippers, then turned to smile at her new husband. Despite their enemy still being at large, Hugh seemed as happy and relaxed as he had been all day and she had just married the man she loved, so even with the vague unease she would always feel until Charlton Hawberry was apprehended, she still felt like dancing for joy.

'You look like the perfect model for a newlywed gentleman,' she teased her husband of half a day, and who would have thought Louisa Alstone, as was, would ever lay claim to one of those?

'And I daren't even look at you, madam wife, in case I ruin my gentlemanly façade by falling on you like a ravening beast,' he muttered in her ear before turning to smile benignly as Lord Kinsham's butler wished them both very happy on behalf of his lordship's London staff.

Hugh thanked him sincerely, but his smile for Viscount Rarebridge, standing behind his father's butler to receive them inside the generous marble hall, held much less warmth. Louisa soon saw that Lord Kinsham's elegant saloon was crammed with curious guests, despite the scant notice they'd received, and blessed the curiosity of Hugh's former friends and neighbours as she reminded herself she wasn't here to rehabilitate him in their eyes; that would have to come later.

'Am I allowed to kiss the bride?' Rory asked jovially, then backed hastily away when he saw the warning in Hugh's suddenly feral gaze. 'Only asking, old fellow,' he excused himself mildly and Louisa sensed her husband putting the beast very carefully back in his cage and shivered with delighted anticipation of later tonight, when this charade was over and their wedding night could begin in earnest.

'My dear Mrs Kenton,' Lady Calliope Hibiscombe gushed as she stepped forwards to fill the silence her brother's question left. 'You are both very welcome, and may I congratulate you on your marriage?' Lord Rarebridge's sister asked and turned to raise her eyebrows at the butler in her role as hostess for the evening, so he could usher in the champagne the world was not supposed to know Kit had sent round earlier for his lordship and his guests to toast the bride and groom.

'Thank you, Lady Calliope, I am very happy to be married to such a wonderful husband and it is indeed kind of you and your brother to throw a lavish party for us at such very short notice,' Louisa managed in return and they smiled at each other, while Hugh's one-time friends and neighbours looked on as if at a play.

'I believe you know my brother, Mr Christopher Alstone?' she asked as she motioned Kit forwards to take his share of the attention.

'Indeed I do,' Lady Calliope said much more warmly as she welcomed the Earl of Carnwood's new heir and Louisa suspected she was calculating how to marry him off to her best advantage.

Deciding that, of the two, she preferred Lord Rarebridge's amiable vacuity to his sister's calculated insincerity, Louisa gave a sparkling smile to the assembled company and clung to Hugh's arm as if she never intended letting go.

She was introduced to a succession of guests and had to fight hard not to glare at each one and ask why they'd been such false friends to Hugh when he stood so much in need of them. He kept up a blandly smiling appearance at her side and seemed charmed to be reacquainted with them all and, if he could act so superbly in the face of their hypocrisy, she could stand at his side and pretend to be as naïve as the majority of the guests clearly thought she must be to have wed him in the first place.

'Such a shame that Sir Horace and Miss Kenton could not be here to share your joy, is it not?' one of the more openly curious ladies asked her once most of Hugh's attention had been engaged by her downtrodden husband.

'Indeed, when you consider how ill the poor gentleman is, no doubt you understand why we wed with such haste? I simply had to be at my husband's side over the next difficult months to provide as much comfort and support as can be had in such circumstances,' she said with modestly lowered eyes.

'It does you credit, my child, but what a shame you lack the guiding hand of a steady parent at such a time, for his situation could become very difficult indeed,' the lady said spitefully and if this was the sort of unspoken malice Hugh had to contend with, Louisa decided it really was no wonder he'd preferred the gutter, then the sea.

'You have observed my brother, I believe, ma'am?' Louisa asked sweetly.

'Oh, yes, of course,' the woman replied

with a sidelong glance at Kit that said she had observed and relished the sight of him, as a still-handsome married woman who felt free to attract such dangerous gentlemen must, once her husband had his heir and a spare as hers apparently did.

'If I need guidance through shark-infested waters, I shall be able to call on him for any help I need. Although I doubt I'll require it, considering my husband is such an expert on sharks.'

'Quite,' the lady said sourly and went off to inform her fellow scandalmongers that the bride was a harridan in the making, and probably deserved to marry a man with the shadow of murder lurking so persistently over his head that no true lady would agree to have him.

'Fighting dragons for me again, Louisa mine?' Hugh asked softly as he clinked his champagne glass against hers and smiled down at her in an intimate toast that momentarily excluded everyone else.

'I can't help it, Hugh,' she murmured in reply, 'they are so very brazen.'

'Which is why they became dragons in the first place,' he said gently and she was tempted to forget all about rooting out their villain to lure her new husband out of this room and find one a lot more private.

'Has anything jogged your memory?' she whispered as if exchanging sweet nothings with her bridegroom.

'Not until now,' he told her distractedly and she tried to shift round to see who he was looking at so intently, but he confounded her by moving to block her view.

'Now who's the dragon slayer?' she muttered crossly.

'I am,' he said unrepentantly and she could tell he'd just sent her brother some sort of signal because Kit suddenly materialised at their side. 'Did you see?' he asked brusquely.

'Before he slipped upstairs and no doubt developed a sick headache? I certainly did, but we can't scotch that particular snake tonight unless he slithers back into view, given his position in the household.'

'No, indeed, the height of bad manners,' Hugh agreed with a satirical look at the assembled company that said he had a very poor opinion of the polite world just at the moment.

'And deeply unfair on the man's unlucky family,' Kit confirmed and Louisa stamped her foot and glared at both of them.

'Talking about bad manners, neither of

yours would stand up to scrutiny tonight,' she said haughtily.

'Will you accept what I say and carry on with this charade as if all we have on our minds tonight is rehabilitating my reputation, love?' Hugh asked and Louisa felt her anger subside far too easily.

'Very well,' she agreed with a heavy sigh. 'Don't expect me to become a pattern card of wifely obedience though, will you?'

'Perish the thought,' he said with a smile that did strange things to her insides.

'I think we could all dance, don't you?' Lady Calliope was cleverly appealing to the older matrons who might disapprove. 'I know dear Hugh and his bride begged us not to throw an impromptu ball to celebrate their nuptials, but I see no harm in a few elegant measures between old friends.'

'Excellent notion, Cal,' Viscount Rarebridge agreed and a pair of superannuated ladies agreed to provide the music, so the butler supervised the rolling back of the fine Aubusson carpet and one of the ladies struck up a merry tune, then pronounced herself satisfied with both music and instrument.

'The bride and groom must begin the first dance,' Lady Calliope announced as Hugh and

Louisa walked on to the floor hand in hand and a ripple of applause and nervous laughter ran round the room.

Chapter Fifteen

'They really don't know what to make of us, do they?' Louisa asked as she and Hugh went through the formalities and waited for the other couples to take the floor in their wake.

'Not fish, nor flesh, nor good red herring are we, my Eloise?' he asked with a wry look that made her want to walk into his strong arms and stop there.

'I'm not, but you were their neighbour and playmate once upon a time. No doubt you set daughters' and sisters' hearts aflutter when you came home from the sea a hero of Trafalgar and all those other dreadful battles you were engaged in. They must have known you as a fine and honourable young gentleman, sure to go far on your chosen path to glory, but now they pretend they barely know you.'

'Not everyone is courageous as you,' he told her philosophically. 'We arranged this farce for our own purposes, so we can hardly complain if they're here to satisfy their rampant curiosity, rather than be reconciled with a rogue like me.'

'You're not a rogue,' she defended him against his own strictures as they began the measure and passed down the line of waiting ladies and gentlemen.

'Oh, come now, my dear, you know perfectly well that I am,' he said wickedly and gave her a blazing look before he solemnly bowed to the next lady in line and whisked her off to perform the figure with elegant aplomb.

'You're right,' she whispered as they passed each other in the dance.

'I know,' he murmured back and was off again with another fascinated lady.

'Just as well I'm an adventuress, then,' she told him at the next opportunity and gave her partner a fascinating smile before flitting off down the line with him.

'He just told me I'm a lucky dog,' Hugh muttered dourly next time they met.

'Well, you are,' she replied and smiled even more enchantingly at the next gentleman in line.

'All right, you can stop now. I'm more than jealous enough to punch the next man you smile at in the mouth, in the midst of the dance or not,' he informed her more than half-seriously as they settled back into their pairing for the weave to be taken over by the next pair.

'Well, that really would provide fodder for the gossips,' she said demurely and settled back into the blissful state of only seeing her new husband for the rest of the dance, then happily consented to move among the spectators at his side during the next one.

'Feeling better now?' she whispered as they drifted from one middle-aged couple to another.

'What do you think?' he demanded with a message in his silver-shot blue eyes that made her shiver with sensuous anticipation.

'How much longer do we have to stay, do you think?' she asked as they halted between acquaintances to look only at each other.

'It is our party,' he demurred.

'Then surely we should be able to leave it whenever we choose?'

'With your vengeful purposes still unsatisfied, my Louisa, are you sure you're feeling quite well?'

'I might not be,' she trailed suggestively. 'I could be overwrought and even a little bit overawed by the solemnity of the occasion, if you would like me to be.'

'Not when you're glowing like the happy dawn, my love. Have I told you that you look breathtakingly beautiful in that gown, with your hair so perfectly right for you and that sapphire set Kit gave you the same glorious shade as your eyes? I wish I'd thought of buying you something half as lovely, but I suspect I wouldn't have found anything to equal them in London.'

'He said they came from a very shady gem merchant he met on his travels, and he wouldn't tell me exactly where he acquired them. I can't help wondering if they were really intended for me when he bought them though, Hugh, for there was such a faraway look in his eyes when he gave them to me it was almost as if he was saying farewell to a dream.'

'Whereas I've got my dream here in my arms,' he told her so unexpectedly she really was almost overcome, if more by a surge of lust and love and anticipation of tonight than by the occasion.

'You say such lovely things to me,' she murmured, not caring that his father's neighbours and most of his former acquaintance was watching them, either openly or under cover of making conversation with each other.

'And you don't believe a word of them, do you?' he said as if her lack of faith in him jarred on his newfound contentment.

'I can't accustom myself to being anyone's dream, Hugh,' she said seriously.

'And no doubt I'm more like your nightmare than *your* dream,' he parried bitterly, as if he had to defend the sensitive man she now knew he was, behind all that to-the-devil-with-you air of his, from being trampled on once more.

'You are so much more than a dream to me, my love,' she finally declared, because she wouldn't see him hurt ever again if she could prevent it, even if she was the one doing the hurting. 'You're my hope, where I only had loneliness and isolation before I met you, and my warmth and laughter, when I expected to go alone to my grave. I want you rather urgently as well, which surprises me even if it doesn't seem to shock you. After all, I was perfectly content to be called the Ice Diamond before I encountered Captain Darke one fine day and began to melt on the spot. So you *are* the dream I never dared even dream before I met you, Hugh, and I still don't quite know what I did to deserve you, or that I ever did, in fact, and now I've got you I can't wait to be your wife in every sense of the word.'

'Oh Louisa mine, I love you so dearly I swear that I never even knew the meaning of the word until now,' he said on a long sigh of relief and acceptance that made her heart sing, 'but please let's go home and put it all into practice as soon as we can get out of here without insulting someone irretrievably, as they're probably going to be our neighbours all too soon,' he added and she looked up at him with love and laughter and complicity in her eyes and agreed without another word.

'I'll have my maid find your cloak and anything else your woman left here ready for your homeward journey, my dear,' Lady Calliope assured Louisa as she shepherded her into the ladies' withdrawing room and did her best to pretend she believed her glowing guest of honour was truly overcome by the heat and the strain of marrying a rake earlier today, in the teeth of all the evidence.

'Thank you, Lady Calliope,' she said meekly and subsided onto a conveniently placed chair to wait and dream of her own particular rogue in peace.

'Are you sure you wouldn't like another of the maids to attend you, as you seem to lack one of your own at the moment?'

'Quite sure, I thank you, it has been a lovely evening, your ladyship, but I should like a little quiet to recover my senses before we leave,' she said truthfully enough, for she wanted to sit and treasure the incredible fact that in a few minutes she would be going home with the man she loved and he loved her in return.

Lady Calliope nodded as if quite content to let the lie Louisa was in the least bit overcome stand, so she could get back to gossiping about her with her friends. Louisa hardly noticed her hostess go as she hugged such a wonderful revelation to her heart. It was such an unexpected delight that she'd somehow discovered her one real love, and he her, that she begrudged sharing it with a group of people who had failed to appreciate his wonderful qualities so appallingly in the past.

'At last, my dear, I thought I should never find the chance to get you to myself once more,' a voice that truly came out of her worst nightmares told her silkily, before she'd hardly even got started on dreaming about her husband and lover and deliciously anticipating the night to come.

She gasped and sprang to her feet at the sight of the man she knew as Charlton Hawberry, standing just inside the door opposite the one she and Lady Calliope had used, looking as if he'd had all his dreams come true as well tonight, and certain that she wouldn't like any of them.

'Nothing to say, oh-so-intrepid Miss Alstone?' he sneered.

'Mrs Kenton,' she corrected before she could stop the words on her tongue.

'Ah, yes, how satisfying it will be to take his second wife as well as his first one from him. I dare say the loss of the famous Ice Diamond in his marriage bed will break him and this time he really won't care if he lives or dies. What a good joke that the first Mrs Kenton took lovers with a little less thought than she changed her gowns and the second is as frigid as an icicle. I'm probably doing the man a favour by depriving him of a fine case of frostbite when he tries to bed you.'

This time she refused to rise to his sneers or his revolting words and just stared at him for a moment, then looked away as if from something repulsive. All the time she was trying to find a way to escape him. If she could just keep him boasting about his cleverness for long enough the maid would come in with her splendid new evening cloak, and surely she'd scream for help when she saw the lady she came to help being held at the point of this vile little man's pistol.

'You wouldn't dare shoot me here,' she challenged as she mentally searched the room for a weapon to defend herself with, because she'd never wanted to die less than she did tonight.

'I was thinking of something more subtle,' he said as he removed a white-silk stocking from his pocket that looked very similar to the ones she'd donned earlier, with a rush of joyous anticipation at the thought of Hugh taking them off again, very slowly and sensuously. 'Courtesy of my wife, you understand,' he informed her as if she would want to know whose stocking he wanted to strangle her with.

'You're Mr Hibiscombe?' she asked and suddenly knew she was right. No wonder he'd known exactly how to play on his brother-in-law's weaknesses, no great surprise that he'd hidden his guilt for so long with such powerful connections and a seat in the House of Commons to help him do so either.

'Yes,' he said flatly. 'I am *Mr* Hibiscombe and very shortly even your undeserving husband will be a baronet. My wife has a title, her idiot brother has a better one and my very noble father-in-law had to be blackmailed and bought to accept me as his son-in-law, but *I* do not have a title, madam, and I intend to get one very soon, although unfortunately you won't live to see it.'

'Why on earth would you want one?' she couldn't help but ask, picturing Kit's grim face when he told them he'd become heir to an earldom.

'You are a very stupid woman—of course I want to distinguish myself from my inferiors and take up my seat in the House of Lords at long last. Do you think being a mere Member of Parliament is enough for a man like me? Staying a mere mister will not do for any gentleman with ambition and drive and I've had enough of being no more than tolerated by my aristocratic relatives by marriage.'

'And you'll never receive a peerage of any sort if you're in Newgate awaiting hanging.

No, I quite see your dilemma now,' she said as blandly as she could.

She could see with hindsight why he could afford to attend her uncle and aunt's At Homes because they had no political bent and moved in very different circles to the ones he clearly aspired to. The vanity of the creature astonished her; perhaps if she encouraged him to trumpet his cleverness over the rest of the world, she might stand a chance of getting away from him unscathed after all.

'Why on earth did you kidnap me if you were already married?' she asked casually, as if his answer hardly mattered.

'I suppose there's no harm telling you,' he mused as if unable to resist the chance to preen at his own superiority. 'I had no interest in marrying the Ice Diamond—what could you bring me, especially once I learnt a little more about your colourful past? No, your disappearance was merely to ensure your oh-so-clever brother was occupied while I rid myself of the problem caused by Hugo Kenton's inconvenient reappearance.' With his back to the door he'd come in by, he hadn't seen it open a mere crack as the maid heard voices within and decided to find out if it was safe to enter without breaking up some unimaginable tête-à-tête.

'How extraordinary of you, Mr Hibiscombe, but I don't understand how the first Mrs Kenton fitted into your grand scheme of things?' She trailed the question in the hope the maid was quick on the uptake and would realise her mistress's husband was a murderer, so she could fetch help before he did it again.

'My wife is boring,' he said coldly and she wondered how Lady Calliope tolerated him on even a day-to-day basis, let alone taking him to her bed often enough to give rise to the brood of children Lord Rarebridge complained about at every opportunity. 'She would never have agreed to wed me if she wasn't,' he added with a shrug. 'The late Mrs Kenton was exciting and forbidden and I enjoyed cuckolding that idiot you just married without anyone knowing I was doing it. All the others were as lacking in subtlety as the woman herself and, eventually, I found out that she was quite incapable of discretion. She laughed at me and then she threatened me,' he added, astonishment in his reedy voice as if he was almost talking to himself and marvelling at the temerity of Ariadne Kenton for daring to mock him.

There was silence from outside the room and Louisa could only hope that the maid had either gone to get help, or was listening to the vain little peacock damn himself further. She had no intention of dying to oblige this cardboard monster, but it would be such a relief if she didn't have to fight him for her life, tonight of all nights.

'What did she threaten you with?' she managed to ask.

'Exposure,' he said with a prim shudder. 'She said she would go to my father-in-law the Earl and tell him what sort of man his precious daughter had married and then she would confront Calliope and make sure she knew as well, so nobody could keep it from her for the sake of her peace of mind.'

'I can see your problem,' she lied.

'It was very vexing; obviously government ministers have mistresses and expect their juniors to have them too, but such women should know their place and at least keep a still tongue in their heads. That strumpet Kenton married went about in the same circles as I, as if she was fit company for gentlemen; she even suggested she was quite happy to let him sue me for criminal conversation with her. She actually wanted to be divorced by the blundering idiot, she told me so.'

'Why?' she asked unoriginally, but she didn't think he would be marking her for varied conversation when all he cared about were his own words.

'Apparently she felt guilty about marrying him, but not about me or any of the unsuspecting fools she took as lovers afterwards. She told me she should never have wed him, which was quite true, of course; she should have sought employment in the nearest brothel, since she had such a natural talent for whoring.'

'It sounds more like a sickness to me,' she said, at last feeling compassion for the obviously very damaged woman Hugh had wed.

Hearing what had horrified this self-serving monster the most, she almost forgave Ariadne for the terrible damage she had inflicted on Hugh. Under all her vanity and frenetic flirting and that parade of lovers, the poor soul had obviously possessed something her murderer so signally lacked: a conscience.

'It was stupidity. I would never have had to kill her if she'd agreed to keep quiet as she promised to do before I agreed to bed her.'

'You'd never have had to kill her at all if you

had resisted the urge to betray your wife in the first place,' she pointed out rather rashly, but having recalled how this man was leading a campaign to cleanse the Haymarket of prostitutes and banish them to prison or houses of correction, she simply couldn't keep a still tongue in her head in the face of his hypocrisy.

'Why not seek pleasure in her bed when I had precious little in my own?'

'I suppose you dared not beat or half-strangle the daughter of such a powerful man for your own sick gratification?' she scorned and realised her mistake when an insane gleam of excitement lit his water-colour eyes.

'I see you truly are a child of the streets for all that much vaunted coldness, my dear,' he said with dawning excitement in his fishy gaze and Louisa fought the urge to retch at the very thought of all he wanted to do to her, before he inflicted the same grim death as he had on her predecessor to silence her and torture Hugh.

Fighting her fear and revulsion at what he'd done, and what he wanted to do, she backed a little further away and closed her hand on a pretty little French clock on one of the pier tables behind her.

'What about Hugh's brother?' she made her-

322 A Most Unladylike Adventure

self ask, in case the maid was still listening and this revolting little man actually did put a bullet in her, because that was what he'd have to do if he wanted to kill her. She wouldn't let herself be violated and cowed at the point of a gun.

'He always was an idiot—it's a family trait, you know? Service to your country and honour and duty and a lot of other nonsense. Apparently he wanted his precious brother to divorce that woman, too, so he'd been keeping a list of all her lovers to be used in court whenever he finally managed to persuade his father the woman was a blot on that precious honour of theirs and must be got rid of.'

'So you snuffed out two far-better people than you could ever be that night,' she told him recklessly.

'How dare you? How can you compare *me* to a whore and a fool?'

'Discreditably,' she told him fiercely and hefted the clock at him, but then had to hunch her shoulders in an instinctive move to protect herself from flying debris, as the little clock shattered in midair when he shot it to save his gun hand, and proved a far better shot as well as even more instinctively cunning than she'd credited.

'Did you think I only had the one?' he asked with a sneer, as he took the second of the pair from his coat pocket and sited it at her heart.

'I thought I could damage your gun hand so badly that it wouldn't matter,' she said just as coolly, but there wasn't the slightest chance it would work twice.

He waved the stocking at her as he moved towards her. 'You forget, my dear, it's important that Kenton's second wife go the same way as the first so there can be no doubt left in anyone's mind to his guilt.'

At last she saw the door behind him open wider and a huddle of shocked faces behind Hugh's agonised one as he focused on the deadly weapon so steadily targeted at her heart. Remembering their last conversation, she did her best to blank all expression from her face as she met Hibiscombe's dead eyes to keep his gaze solely focus on her—better to die herself than watch him kill Hugh, then have to live without him.

'Do you think these rooms are altogether soundproof?' she asked to try to keep his attention solely on her.

'Who cares? They're making enough noise at your nuptial dance to drown out cannon fire,' he said with a dismissive shrug. 'It will be your wake as well.'

'I think not, Fulton,' Lady Calliope declared as she opened the main door into the room and stepped into his line of fire before he could even react to her presence. 'And I care that you risk our children's future; I care that I made those poor children with a monster; and I care far more that they will have to live with the knowledge of what you've done for the rest of their lives.'

'Why?' he said blankly. 'I've got it all under control now, so nobody will ever find out. If you will just stand out of the way for a few seconds, my dear, I'll kill her and all will be well again. When it's done we can go back to the ballroom and announce that the bride has been killed and let everyone reach the obvious conclusion that her husband has killed again.'

'No, you won't. Even if I were as mad as you clearly are and agreed to your ridiculous scheme, do you think they're all going to keep quiet and go away, just because you tell them to?' Lady Calliope demanded as she waved rather theatrically at the group of spectators behind him.

By now there was such a gleam of insanity in the man's once-blank eyes that Louisa wondered if he might even shoot his wife and be done with it. Instead, he twisted round very suddenly and aimed at Hugh instead. He was actually in the act of pulling the trigger when Louisa's next weapon hit him on the shoulder.

In the shocked silence that followed Hugh inspected the tear on the sleeve of his once-immaculate wedding coat of darkest blue superfine and raised one eyebrow at his bride. 'Just as well there was nothing in it,' he said blandly as he eyed the shards of demure white pottery now scattered on the carpet.

'Well, there was nothing else handy that might have done the trick,' she explained coolly, as she eyed the broken remnants of the impromptu weapon she'd found in the pot cupboard nearby.

Complicity and laughter and such warm relief that neither of them dared explore it at present shone in his eyes as they met hers over the top of their enemy's head.

'Catch hold of him for me, will you, Rory, before he weasels out of here?' Hugh asked the Viscount, who was standing inside the door by which his sister had entered the room with his mouth open.

'He was going to shoot my sister,' Lord Rarebridge said as if they might not have noticed.

'And murder mine,' Kit said grimly as he seized one of Hibiscombe's arms very roughly and the Viscount grasped the other.

'Since he actually murdered my brother and Ariadne, I hope you're not planning to provide him with a purse full of guineas and a swift passage to the Americas so he can disappear?' Hugh warned before they bustled the loudly protesting Hibiscombe out of the room and into the Earl's library where they could hold him more easily, and privately, while they decided what was really to be done with him.

Chapter Sixteen

'You have my very sincere sympathy, Lady Calliope,' Hugh observed as he made a coolly composed bow to the visibly shaking woman, 'and my profound admiration for your courage,' he added and kissed her hand.

'I've been a fool,' she said with a sad shake of her head as she squeezed his hand and took a moment of comfort from a very old friend before she let it go.

Looking round for someone to support such a brave woman in her hour of need, Louisa shot the assembled spectators a look of contempt and tentatively offered Lady Calliope her own arm, since no other was forthcoming.

'I don't think so,' she argued. 'Nobody suspected what he truly was. Not one single person here tonight can put their hand on their heart and honestly declare they had even the shadow of a doubt about Mr Hibiscombe's actions or indeed his sanity until tonight,' she lied, because she had a very shrewd notion Hugh and her brother had begun to suspect both.

'He is a very plausible villain and I certainly never suspected him of anything more than being a sanctimonious young upstart,' one of the piano-playing ladies observed and stepped forwards to take Lady Calliope's other arm and her sister came out of the crowd to guard her flank.

'And whatever happens, you will always have the support of your family, my dear,' a gentleman Louisa vaguely recalled being introduced as a cousin of the Earl's stepped up to say as if he really meant it.

'Yes, indeed, it is quite obvious you knew nothing of what he was up to, now or in the past,' his wife said rather less sincerely, but she gave Louisa a nod that said, *This is my job*, as she ousted her from Lady Calliope's side, ready to escort her from the room and offer that support privately as well as in public.

'Will you see that all our guests go home

safely?' Lady Calliope asked rather helplessly, before leaving the room with her attendants.

So Louisa and Hugh went back into the saloon and offered vague explanations about a sudden family crisis and Mr Hibiscombe being taken 'really rather ill' that nobody truly believed, but found it impossible to argue with. At last even the most persistent gossip of them all gave up and ordered her carriage before she could find out what had really gone on tonight, and they listened to the wheels of her ancient town chariot rumble away across the square and exchanged a look of profound relief with the much-tried butler. Wrapping her thickly lined velvet cloak more closely round herself against the chill that was probably more in her head than on the surprisingly soft April breeze, Louisa turned to look up at her new husband, and reassure herself again that he was nearly as unhurt as she was by Hibiscombe's best efforts to kill them.

'We will find out what your brother and Rarebridge are planning to do with the rat and then go home, shall we, love? I don't know about you, but I think I've had more than enough excitement for one day,' Hugh said with a rueful smile.

'I thought he'd killed you,' she confessed

shakily and he ignored the presence of Lord Kinsham's staff to pull her into his arms and lead her inside, snuggled against the reassuring warmth of his side like the cherished new bride she was, rather than at the proscribed distance for a politely allied pair of aristocrats.

'And if not for that brave woman, he would have done his evil best to kill you in front of us all,' he said and tugged her into a quiet ante-room so they could embrace and soothe and marvel over each other in relative privacy for a few moments. 'Poor little Callie, and to think we all laughed when she wed that vermin and told ourselves he must possess hidden depths only she could see.'

'Yet they must have been happy enough to have produced the tribe of children your friend is always complaining about,' Louisa said as she marvelled at how little Lady Calliope could have known her repellent spouse to have embraced motherhood so enthusiastically.

'Looking back, I can see now that she only wed him in order to produce children and love them. She was brought up to think herself unlovable because she was the first-born and happened to be a girl child, instead of the heir everyone wanted. Isn't it astonishing how much harm we do our children with our expectations and faulty priorities?'

'Since all we were ever expected to do was stay alive at little cost to our father, I have no idea how you aristocrats bring up your progeny.'

'There you are, you see? You thought you were underprivileged, but how we poor downtrodden second sons and irrelevant daughters would have envied you such astonishing freedom from expectation,' he said with an expression of saintly resignation and hint at hardships borne so patiently that she hit the battered shoulder of his wedding coat and saw him wince.

'He did hurt you,' she said desperately, trying to rip the already-damaged cloth off his shoulders so she could examine him for damage, her heart racing and breath threatening to step up into panic as it seemed to her he was gallantly hiding some terrible injury he hadn't wanted to reveal in front of the curious.

'It's nothing, Louisa, just a graze and a slight bruise. I doubt there's even any blood on me for you to fuss over; if you undress me here and now to make sure, there will be no preventing me from doing the same to you. We don't need to get ourselves caught out in a scandalous liaison to add to the other eventful happenings this evening, love,' he protested and tugged the once-beautiful tailored garment back on to his shoulder as he gave her an exasperated look. 'And I really thought you Alstones were made of sterner stuff than this.'

'I'm not an Alstone any more though, am I? So how should I know how you Kenton/ Darkes go on? I'm new made, Hugh. Mrs Hugo Kenton apparently to be of Gracemont Priory has a lot of self-discovery to endure over the next few weeks and I think I would far rather have been Mrs Darke of the high seas.'

'You'll cope, Mrs Kenton, with everything else you've survived up to now; a surly father-in-law, a few hundred tenants and a crumbling old barn of a house in the middle of Somerset should pose you few enough problems.'

'Thank you, I feel so much better now,' she said ruefully.

'I would have found it far more demanding to be Captain Darke, who had to endure the terror of knowing his wife was aboard every time he saw an enemy sail on the horizon. You have no idea how terrified that would have made me for your safety, my darling, and what my father has inadvertently spared me by deciding to want his errant son home after all.'

'Shall you miss the life though, Hugh?' she said seriously, knowing that she would hate it if he was forever longing for a freedom that was now over.

'Not really, life at sea is nine-parts tedium to one-part frantic action much of the time and you really have no concept of how terrified I was every time we cleared for action and waited for the enemy to fight.'

'But you haven't been in the Navy these last three years,' she pointed out, still doubtful he wouldn't grow bored with her and rural contentment.

'And the occupation your brother and his best friend offered me was exactly what I needed at the time, but we're agreed that becoming a full partner in their enterprise will keep me out of mischief once I've got the Gracemont estates under control. Any longing I ever had for adventures on the high seas has long faded away, Louisa, and I would far rather be ashore with my beautiful bride and a growing band of nigh-ungovernable brats in our image.'

'Good, then perhaps it's high time we went

home and got on with making them, husband,' she reminded him demurely.

'No perhaps about it,' he assured her huskily, 'but first we must tie up one or two loose ends,' he added more soberly and her thoughts turned to the unfortunate woman upstairs and the hard life she must now face as sole parent to her own tribe of children.

'They can't gossip and snigger and pillory Lady Calliope as they did you, can they, Hugh? Like you, the worst she's guilty of is misjudgement about the person she married and she's paid heavily enough for that already. I don't think she's been at all happy with him, do you?'

'No, I think she made a mistake and lived with it as well as she knew how, but her family will stand by her now you've shamed them into it. There will still be gossip though, love—it's in the nature of dragons to gather and broadcast that as eagerly as they possibly can.'

'It must be very noisy as well as deeply unpleasant in their lairs, then.'

'Oh, deeply,' he said and ushered her out of their temporary sanctuary and along the wide corridor to knock on the library door without even trying to leave her behind, so at least he'd already begun to include his wife in his life, or decided there was no point in trying to exclude her.

'I'm so glad you've finally realised I'm not a die-away miss to be sheltered from the uncomfortable realities of life,' she said with a provocative sideways glance at him as they heard Kit's invitation to enter and opened the door.

'I may be an idiot, but even I know when I'm flogging a dead horse, and don't forget you're not a miss of any sort any more.'

'I know,' she said with great self-satisfaction and made him grin boyishly at the idea that she eagerly embraced marriage to him.

The reminder of all that was to come for them as man and wife was the antidote he probably needed for the sight of the repellent Hibiscombe, hunched over the Earl's desk, frantically scribbling. The Viscount was standing over him like the sternest of schoolmasters, looking as if he was about to correct his spelling and handwriting in no uncertain terms if he strayed from the straight and narrow lines he'd drawn up for him.

'We offered him a choice between a convenient shooting accident while he was cleaning those guns of his and writing a signed confession, then submitting to the madhouse, and d'you know what?' Rory asked incredulously. 'The little rat's plumped for the madhouse.'

'Dear, dear,' Louisa observed sympathetically, suddenly fighting what must be hysterical laughter at the flummoxed expression on his lordship's face. 'Some people really are totally outside the pale, are they not?' she added for good measure and felt Kit's glare at her facetiousness from across the room.

'You may trust us to deal with him from now on,' her brother informed her and Hugh sternly and directed the little rat in question to keep writing and not leave anything out.

'Yes,' his lordship replied simply to her question, with a fearsome frown that told them exactly what he thought of his brother-in-law. 'Alstone and I have sent for one of the magistrates from Bow Street, whom he assures me is discreet and not liable to broadcast the tale when we explain about my sister and the children. Then my man will go and fetch whichever lunatic doctor he recommends, so that we can have this vermin officially declared insane and remove him from poor Cal's life for ever. Sorry about such a hole-in-corner end to this miserable business, Kenton, but there's my sis-

ter and her brats to think of now, and a trial
wouldn't have brought anyone back, would it?'

With those rare words of wisdom from his
lordship echoing in her mind, Louisa meekly
allowed her new husband to guide her out of
the house and into the waiting carriage and
even managed not to mind very much when
the release of so many years of tension meant
that all they did that night was sleep in each
other's arms, even though it was their official
wedding night.

Chapter Seventeen

❦

'That's it, then, we're properly married and alone again at long last,' Hugo Kenton said to his bride the following evening as they finally ran up the steps of the elegant Palladian-style villa a few miles outside Brighton that he'd hired for the next week or two. 'And hopefully there's nobody else who will have the gall to try to keep me from my new wife and my clear marital duty to seduce her until she can't recall her own name, let alone those of our enemies and anyone else who might feel they have the right to interrupt our honeymoon.'

'I was beginning to wonder if I'd have to climb out of a window again to get you to myself,' Louisa replied.

'Perish the thought,' he said sternly.

'You don't have much faith in my abilities, do you?'

'I'm sure you could give the most furtive cracksman lessons, but I don't think my nerves would stand it.'

'Faint heart, but I promise not to climb anything more dangerous than those stairs yonder, so long as it isn't a dire emergency, and you wouldn't want me to sit about dithering if it was one of those, now would you?'

'Well, that's something, I suppose; all I have to do now is keep you away from burning buildings and marooned kittens and my hair might not have to go white overnight after all.'

'I think you'd look very distinguished, and you have to admit that if I hadn't done it in the first place we would never have met again.'

'That's something else I must learn to be thankful for then, I suppose,' he said with a lugubrious sigh and such warmth in his silver-blue eyes she wondered how she'd ever thought them cold, but she couldn't let the topic go, despite the temptation to just let that warmth wash over her and waft them both up stairs and into a dreamy night of kissing and caressing and an awful lot more.

'But the way we met for the second time,

the way I behaved that night and the next, meant that we had to get married, Hugh,' she said seriously, for it still rankled that in rescuing herself she'd trapped him.

'And are you regretting that already?' he asked gruffly.

'Of course not, but you must have mixed feelings about taking another wife.'

'You make me sound like a pasha who has far more than just the one wife about the place and just thought he might casually add another to his stock of them.'

'Don't get any ideas and don't change the subject. You know very well what I mean and you haven't exactly won yourself a prize in me.'

'By the time another day dawns, you won't have a single doubt left in your stubborn head as to how much I want you as my one-and-only wife, Louisa,' he threatened deliciously and she went breathless with anticipation as he took her light cloak and draped it carefully over a gilt chair, before pulling out another from the laden dining table and seating her with one or two apparently accidental touches that threatened to melt her from the inside out.

'Ooh, I shall look forward to that, then.'

'Not too much I hope, considering we have

our delayed wedding night to plough through somehow or another first,' he said and she laughed and felt the shocks and upsets of yesterday recede at last, leaving behind them the delicious tension of anticipating the longed-for night to come.

'I expect you'll find a way to get us through it,' she told him blandly.

'Plainly I'll have to, since bold and beautiful Eloise La Rochelle was only a figment of our heated imaginations.' He slanted her an untrustworthy smile and she pencilled 'ruthless pirate' back on to her internal picture of him and shivered with delighted anticipation.

'You could teach me how to become more like her,' she suggested.

'And have half the West Country beating a path to our door to try and wrest you from me? Not in a million years.'

'I meant in private,' she protested. 'And Eloise and her pirate captain never really got to know each other properly, did they?' she added wickedly. Seeing how his gaze went blank, then lit with fire at the idea, she filed it for later and allowed all her love and wanting back into her own gaze. 'I will never look at another man, Hugh,' she promised him solemnly at last. 'Why should I when I have you?'

He took her hand and played with her beautiful rings as if to remind himself of all the promise and promises between them, then he met her gaze and deliberately let his guard fall until she could see something of the hopeful young man he'd once been, before he raised those barriers to protect himself from a loss and grief and fury that must have felt nigh intolerable to him.

'If everything hadn't happened just as it did, I wouldn't have met you one dark and fateful night, Eloise-Louisa, and just think how boring my life would have been. Now I really hope you've finished eating, because I'm fast discovering love is a very poor preventive of amorous intent and other husbandly lapses of consideration.'

'I never wanted to fall in love,' she said with a reminiscent shrug for her once-guarded self.

'Do you think I ran round London dancing with glee when I found out why I couldn't get you out of my head day or night? You're one of the most beautiful creatures I ever laid eyes on, and I only have to feel you enter a room to want you mercilessly.'

'When I first met you I thought you were dark and dangerous and there was something in your eyes that promised me you could make me feel things I have never wanted to. No wonder I dreaded ever setting eyes on you again.'

'Aye, well, at least I can understand that much, having felt something very similar myself.'

'Then understand this, Hugh Darke, or Hugo Kenton or whoever you happen to be calling yourself just at the moment. I meant to seduce you that first night at Kit's house, when I found you so castaway and gruff and bearlike and completely, unimaginably desirable that I wanted you so badly that it hurt to draw back.'

Louisa saw him doing his best not to let his eyes cross at the very thought of her so rampantly predatory and filed away that idea for future reference as well.

'Why did you, then?' he asked hoarsely.

'What would you have done then if you woke up next morning to find me in your bed and remembered you'd just taken my virginity?'

'I'd have railed at you for giving it away so lightly, I expect.'

'You railed at me anyway,' she pointed out with a half-smile, half-frown for the drunken antics of unregenerate rakes.

'It was obligatory after the weeks I'd endured longing for you with almost every waking and sleeping thought. But since you want to know, if I'd woken to find you in my bed like that, I would have dragged you off to my lair and had my wicked way with you again and again for our very mutual pleasure, until Kit came back and found out what I'd done to his precious little sister and killed me. After that, I wouldn't have been able to do anything much.'

'Good point.'

'I like it, although I wouldn't have done if it had actually happened.'

'Now I'm confused, but to get back to that night, even though I was so tempted to be an ex-virgin and escape Uncle William and Charlton forever, I nobly resisted your stubbly kisses and sweaty embrace.'

'I remember that bit,' he grumbled.

'Are you sure?' she sniped, then reminded herself they were having a very serious conversation here and frowned at him severely.

'Even if I was dead I would remember that bit,' he confirmed as if it was engraved on his heart.

'I wish you'd stop harping on death. I want you alive, Hugo Kenton.'

'So you can have your wicked way with me?' he asked hopefully.

'So I can make you regret ever being born if you ever take up with the likes of Eloise La Rochelle again. But now we're on the subject of Eloise once again, I knew that I'd put myself in the most ridiculous situation with you by pretending to be her and I wanted you so badly it almost made my bones ache, yet I couldn't have you because if I did then you'd know I'd lied and wasn't Eloise at all. Then you were followed and I was so scared, Hugh. I was so terrified, so utterly afraid they'd succeed in capturing and killing you and that I'd lose you, that I didn't care about such a little thing as whether or not I was a virgin anymore, I just wanted to be as close to you as I could get.'

'So you cared about me a little bit, even then?'

'I cared about you so much it felt like a betrayal of every promise I had ever made myself not to follow in my mother's footsteps, not to love blindly and never to need a man so much I'd put up with anything he did or said to just so I could have the privilege of carrying on loving him.'

To her furious amazement, Hugh laughed at

this agonised confession and tugged her out of her chair with an impatient glance at the cold collation under their uninterested noses.

'You're no more capable of blind adoration than I am of wanting it in the first place, my own particular virago,' he informed her firmly. 'Do you imagine any fault I rejoice in will ever go unrecorded and ruthlessly reformed by my wife, because I can assure you that I don't,' he said as he towed her back into the hall and stopped in front of the fine pier table and the large gilt-framed mirror above it. 'Look at yourself, Louisa,' he urged, gently turning her face from his towards their reflected selves so she could examine her own face, or she could have if she hadn't been so busy devouring his with hungry eyes. 'No, really look at yourself; you have my full permission not to take your eyes off me once we've got this last ridiculous folly of yours out of the way, but concentrate for now.'

Reluctantly she obeyed him and stared at her own reflection, surprised at how different she looked under the spell of passion, but otherwise unimpressed. 'What am I supposed to be looking at?'

'Not what, but whom: this woman is Louisa Kenton, she is recklessly brave, ridiculously determined not to divulge to anyone how afraid she sometimes is of climbing out of windows and playing the female buccaneer, and she would throw herself to the lions if they showed signs of wanting to devour someone she loved instead of her. Her besotted husband knows her to be the most enchantingly lovely lady he ever laid eyes on, and he very shortly intends to lay more than his eyes on a whole lot more of her, by the way. He adores her quick wits and her bold tongue and even finds her short temper and pithy turns of phrase amusing most of the time.

'No doubt, in time and after a lot of brimstone-and-bluster temper tantrums of his own, he'll learn to control his fury at her unruly habit of running herself straight into any danger that happens along, hopefully before he's ground his teeth to stubs and bitten his nails to the quick. One thing he will never do, though, is expect her to follow any of his commands without at least an hour's debate about it, or encourage her to believe he'd like her better if she was a passive doormat of a woman he could swagger off and forget about while he was busy drinking or gambling or carousing himself into an early grave.'

He raised his hands to caress her shoulders

and the woman in the mirror now looked as if she'd been presented with the moon and stars as his gaze softened with what she knew was true love.

'I don't doubt your mother was a good woman, Louisa,' he carried on more gently. 'Or that she suffered a very great deal for indulging her youthful passion for a man who clearly didn't deserve her, but you are not your mother.'

'No, I'm not, am I?' she agreed as she finally believed it.

'And before you start another avenue of self-flagellation, you're nothing like your father either. Somehow they gave life to four remarkable people in you and your brothers and sister, so their ill-starred marriage clearly wasn't in vain. I would have out-waited and out-snarled and out-stamped your brother, even after he'd beaten me to a pulp for taking your maidenhead, if he'd opposed our marriage, Louisa. I'd even have taken the battering I undoubtedly deserved from your gigantic friend Ben Shaw's mighty fists when he came home, if that was what it took to marry you. In fact, I think I would have done anything to gain you as my wife, so look what a lionheart you've gained in me?'

'More of a chicken-heart that first night I'd have said at the time, if you'd only asked me,' she teased and stroked the side of his face, feeling a slight suggestion of beard under her appreciative fingers and bringing back sensual memories of that first night and a very stubbly Hugh Darke, and the wild woman who'd descended on him out of the night and would have fallen into his arms like the wanton she'd claimed to be, given even a smidgen more encouragement.

'Shrew,' he whispered as he shivered with desire and anticipation from that one exploring caress.

'Not a mouse, then?' she asked as his mouth seemed to come satisfyingly close, then disappointingly firm and evade hers as he seemed to despair of ever getting her upstairs under her own steam.

'Never a mouse, my love, more of a tigress,' he informed her just before he hefted her over his shoulder as easily as if she were a sack of feathers rather than a healthy young woman and started up the stairs while she was still startled about seeing the world from upside down.

'I'll certainly scratch your eyes out for you if you don't hurry up and put me down, you toad,' she protested furiously, but he carried on doggedly getting her where he wanted her by the fastest method possible. 'Insufferable, intolerable weasel that you are,' she raved at him, secretly wondering which of them would be the more breathless and lightheaded by the time he reached his destination, then he did and she found out.

'Isn't it lucky that some considerate person left the door to the master suite wide open for us, my dear?' he asked her as if they were taking a leisurely stroll about their luxurious temporary home. 'Otherwise I might have had to dump you into the nearest chair whilst I wrestled with the door and that would have quite ruined the mood, don't you think?'

'Dump me...' she spluttered before recovering a few of her wits. 'You uncouth beast.' She hit what part of him she could reach with her fist as he turned round with her still writhing about on his shoulder to survey their extravagantly furnished bedchamber with such leisurely appreciation she knew he was enjoying himself a little too much at her expense.

'Run out of creatures vile enough to compare me to, my sweet?' he asked smoothly and shifted her so her body draped itself very closely about his as he let her slide back on to her feet even though her skirts were rucked up against his breeches and she knew just how aroused he was after her explicitly informative journey back to solid ground.

'I'll think of something,' she assured him breathlessly, but he didn't give her the time.

Instead he took her mouth in a fiercely desperate kiss that told her volumes about his state of mind and body and any doubts she'd ever had that he wanted her to the edge of madness evaporated under the heat of that kiss. Every bit as eager, she opened her mouth wantonly under his. His tongue tangled with hers and she closed her eyes and just revelled in real, substantial Hugh under her exploring hands, where she'd had to make do with the most shocking dreams and frustrating memories for far too long.

Engulfed in her Hugo's warmth and strength and feeling as if she was surrounded by urgent, so very much-needed man, she ignored the vague discomfort of an elegant bedpost at her back as she used it to stretch further up against him than she could of her own accord as he backed her blindly towards whatever surface stopped them first. Oh, this was wonderful, so all engrossing that Aunt Poole and half the strictest hostesses of the *ton* might have been watching on a set of very odd chaperon's benches for all she knew or cared. She let out a very necessary breath and gasped in another while she had the chance and felt so many of her inhibitions and insecurities leave the room along with those imaginary dragons.

'I love you, Hugo,' she informed him, using the name she was only now adjusting to, as he realised just where he'd placed her and turned her about so his back was to the smoothly turned mahogany instead while he busied himself exploring her back through the ivory silk of her gown; then, while he happened to be round there, he undid each satin-covered button until he could get down to just exploring uncovered Louisa instead. 'I really and truly love you,' she added and all the surprise she felt about the startling reality of their love must have been obvious in her voice, because it made him laugh and she felt as well as heard it since they stood so close his voice echoed through her own narrower ribcage and had a delightful effect on her already hard-peaked nipples and very aroused breasts.

'Good,' he spared breath to tell her before he silenced them both by shucking her un-done gown off her shoulders and setting his mouth to one of those begging nipples before he could disentangle her arms from the puffy little apologies for sleeves a spring bride could afford to have on her going-away gown.

Trapped in a fine web of loving and absolute desire, Louisa felt her head go back as she arched to encourage her husband's possession and she gasped out something incomprehensible to both of them as words faded from her understanding of the world. Then she was lying dazed and not quite sure how she'd got there on the bed, with her gown a pool of neglected dusky-rose silk on the floor and she was vaguely conscious that Hugo was busy ripping off his own finery with eager abandon. Somehow she managed to force her suddenly heavy-lidded eyelids open so that she could appreciate the view; maybe the sight of them—all darkest of midnight blue, and dilated at actually being able to see the splendour of his golden-skinned torso, heavy with muscle and taut with wanting her—properly for the first time made him even more urgent. Lying like some wickedly sensual empress eyeing her lover, she let her kiss-swollen mouth open on an 'Oh?' of curiosity and just the slightest touch of awed apprehension as he tore off his boots, then struggled out of his breeches and finely clocked stockings in one fluid move and stood for a moment in all his naked glory.

It really surprised her that he was such a glorious sight, despite that magical interval in Kit and Ben's deeply shadowed warehouse. Thanks to him she knew exactly how a man made love to a woman, but he was so beautiful in his obviously extreme need of her. Not a word he'd appreciate if she said it out loud, of course, but he was all finely honed muscle and long, lean limbs, but her gaze centred on his manhood with eager fascination. A girl— and she realised she had been a girl until he made her his woman too many days ago now to recall—could speculate and wonder about what gentlemen were like under their clothes and even peer curiously at classical statues of apparently perfect young gods without their togas, but nothing could ever equal the fact of a naked man's raw desire for a woman he very clearly wanted very badly indeed. Or at least it couldn't equal her naked man's desire for her, as she had no interest whatsoever in seeing any others.

'You're obviously a very proud man in every sense of the world,' she managed to recover enough language to tell him huskily.

'Very proud of you, love,' he rumbled back, 'very desperate for you.'

'Then you'd best come closer,' she whispered, 'very much closer would be my best guess, as well as my pleasure.'

'So close we'll be one,' he half-promised and half-warned her as he smoothly surged on to the bed and the heated fact of his skin against hers sharpened every sense she had with anticipation.

'We already are,' she murmured and wondered at his rumble of male amusement, until he moved so he was resting half across her splayed body while still holding most of his weight on his impressively muscled arms.

'Just wait and see, or rather wait and feel, how very much better it can be with a decent bed under us and the whole night ahead of us,' he promised, then sank his head and a little of his weight towards her, so he could kiss her with what felt like all of him as well as just his wickedly knowing mouth.

Silenced for once, she loved the weight and strength of him and wriggled her legs against his to urge him closer, faster into this, their first sanctioned, married loving and she wondered that it could feel so wonderful and novel and right. Frustratingly he just used his supe-

rior strength to lift himself off her again for a
while to gently, almost soothingly brush kisses
across her brow, then her eyelids, then her
cheekbones as her eyes opened again almost
of their own accord when he worked his way
down those cheekbones to slip kisses along
the line of her jaw and back up to her mouth.
There he lingered, eyes open and full of all
he felt for her as they stared wonderingly at
each other. His gaze was molten silver, shot
with blue, his breath quick and shallow and
she could feel herself quivering with excitement and scorching desire. Maybe even Hugo
thought she was ready for more, because he
hiked up the gossamer chemise that was all
the boning and lining of her gown had needed
beneath it and set himself to learn the burning heated place at the centre of her again as
she parted her thighs eagerly to welcome his
touch. Their mesmerised gazes still held as he
tantalised and roused her, teaching her how
much he loved the dark, springy curls at her
secret centre, how he loved the soft wet folds
of her outer sex even more and how he absolutely adored her molten inner core.

Her hands were almost as busy, even if she
was still too shy to boldly set her hand to his
rampantly aroused member. Yet she learnt

how sleek and sensitive the corded muscles supporting his spine were as they flexed under her fascinated touch. He delved one of those wickedly exploring fingers of his further into her and she moaned a demand as that pulse of pure need tightened, then subsided around it only to burn again even more strongly. She gasped an incoherent protest and tried her best to pull him closer to her, kneading his tightly muscled buttocks with demanding fingers as she knew she had to have him inside her and love him in every sense of the word. Had to appease the hot, almost painful need to be full of the rigid, straining manhood he was denying them both until she was nearly weeping with frustration.

'Hugh,' she demanded reverting to the name of the man she had first fallen for, 'you in me. Must have you in me', and if he didn't spread her legs and take her soon she'd have to scissor her legs together and try to appease this grinding, magical need without him.

'Aye, it's high time we had each other again, my love,' he affirmed and raised her knees, then eased his emphatically aroused shaft into her at last and she sighed with blissful relief, so stretched and full of this wonder of a man, and her wide-eyed gaze sought his for confirmation that this was them, husband and wife, together on the road to somewhere wonderful at last. 'Let me come right into you again, my darling love,' he demanded and she relaxed her inner muscles, took the fact of him into herself in more than just the physical and trusted him absolutely.

She felt the freedom of this time, after he had gentled himself so much to take the fact of her virginity last time they'd loved, and that never-to-be-forgotten first time gave way to this equally important next time, now they truly loved and openly acknowledged it. Then he raised her knee a little higher, rocked back until he could angle her more receptively for one long, desperate thrust and she was his lover in every way there was once more. It didn't hurt this time and she gasped as he slid home into the very depths of her and burning need took over as Hugo withdrew from her so far that she let out a long moan of frustrated desire, then he thrust home again and sweet heat bloomed inside her like wildfire. The rhythm of his thrust and withdrawal taught her an even deeper delight in each other than she'd dared imagine before now and she eagerly moved to learn it.

His body set a glorious rhythm and his

mouth enforced it first on one tightly aroused breast, then the other until she was thrashing her head from side to side in desperate pleading as that great and relentless force they experienced before beat at them in unison and beckoned that sensual edge to all this blissful closeness she remembered falling over last time they loved so completely, even if neither of them had fully known at the time how powerful that love truly was. He increased their already-wild rhythm, plunged into her even more deeply as he gasped out a plea of his own, then took her mouth in a long, desperate kiss, his eyes wide open on hers this time as his tongue plunged in time with his mighty body and something so exquisite bloomed between them that she felt tears glaze her open eyes, as she gazed into his wildly silvered blue eyes and finally let go.

They span into ecstasy as she felt her body spasm with heat and light and fulfilment, pulse after pulse of absolute pleasure ripping through both of them as he convulsed in driven fulfilment inside her and she felt the hot surge of his seed release within her, even as the last ripples of her own unimaginable pleasure smoothed her into satiated bliss and complete freedom and lovely little pulses of their ecstasy occasionally rocked her as she drifted at least halfway back to earth.

'Love you,' she said as soon as she had enough breath.

'You certainly did,' he murmured huskily as he withdrew from her and rolled them over far enough so he could pull the covers over them and cocoon their cooling bodies in the warmth of their marriage bed.

'I'm so glad I love you, Hugo, my own Hugh,' she confided.

'Then I'm very glad that you do to,' he teased.

'Monster,' she told him with a sleepy, contented chuckle that couldn't be bothered with *faux* outrage just at the moment.

'And very happy to report that I still love you, even after having my wicked way with you once more.'

'It really was lovely and wicked as well, wasn't it?' she asked, still a little insecure about her own attractions, even though he'd just proved how irresistible he found her in the most unarguable fashion imaginable.

'Just as you are, my lovely, wicked wife,' he told her with a long, sweet kiss of confirmation and heat stirred and snapped deep inside her belly all over again for a moment, before subsiding to a contented thrum of satisfaction.

'How many times a night do husbands and wives get to do that, husband?' she asked sleepily as she nestled her wildly tangled, dark-chestnut curls against his naked shoulder and sighed with contentment.

'Wasn't that enough wonderment for one wedding night?'

'This is certainly a very memorable wedding, but does it matter to you that we didn't wait for tonight to love each other, Hugo?'

'No, I shall look back on that stack of coffee sacks and a musty old warehouse with fondness for the rest of my life, love. But I shall now have to buy this place after all, exactly as its current owner wants me to and probably at some ridiculous price, because he'll know how much it means to me as soon as I open my mouth to agree. Then at least we can come back here every year and remind ourselves how exquisitely we made love on our actual wedding night, then do it all over again,' he told her with a quick kiss to the top of those rebellious curls of hers.

'We have so much in front of us, Hugo,' she said a little too seriously for a woman who'd just made spectacular love in her husband's arms, and he secretly marvelled at his own self-restraint in not hammering into her with wild need as soon as his unruly body had rubbed against hers once more and longed to do so from that first desperately sweet kiss to the last.

'We have each other, love. Nobody else stands a chance against Captain Hugo Kenton and his warrior wife now we're finally united.'

'Least of all Captain Hugo Kenton,' she told him with a great yawn and settled into his arms with a sigh of utter happiness.

'He was a lost cause the instant you set eyes on him.'

'So how many weeks do you think we'll spend at Gracemont Priory before you have enough and we can go to sea together instead, Captain?'

'Not that again,' he said in disgust. 'I think I've created a monster,' he added as he recalled how it was his own fault if his wife now believed in herself enough to fight for the right to carry out every hare-brained scheme that came into her lovely head.

'No, just a wife,' she argued and butted her head against his shoulder in a gesture of affection he found more touching than any poem or sophisticated phrase his first wife and one or two other lovers had deployed to try to capture his until-now elusive heart.

'And I challenge any man in England to produce a more ruthless, scheming, intractable one than I've won myself, my Mrs Louisa-Eloise Alstone-Kenton.'

'But you love me anyway?' she asked eagerly.

'Oh, yes, until the day I die and beyond, my love,' he promised and luckily he was a man of his word.

* * * * *

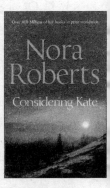